UNTIL NOTHING REMAINS

A GUN PLAY NOVEL: VOLUME 1

C.A. RUDOLPH

EMPOWERED PRESS

 Created with Vellum

"A GIFT IN SECRET BLINDS THEIR EYES. THEY KNOW NOT BECAUSE THEY WILL NOT UNDERSTAND. NONE SO BLIND AS THOSE THAT WILL NOT SEE. THEY HAVE BAFFLED THEIR OWN CONSCIENCES, AND SO THEY WALK ON IN DARKNESS."

MATTHEW HENRY

ONE

The morning had begun not unlike any other, preceding a day deprived of obliging plans ahead. My outdoor Adirondack chair felt as comfortable as it ever had, and my only preoccupation at the moment was deciding what warranted most of my attention: the frosty stein of *Hofbräuhaus* Weissbier perched on the table inches away from a plate of half-eaten Weisswurst, or the remarkable view of the snow-capped Watzmann in the distance.

Being perfectly honest, I'd never been able to avoid feeling captivated by the mountains here, not that I had ever put any real effort into doing so. They were breath-taking. I grew up in the Shenandoah Valley of Virginia, where the tallest peaks of the Appalachians extended to the four-thousand-foot range at maximum—mere foothills in contrast to the elevation and overall grandeur of the German and Austrian Alps.

Growing up in an area westwardly bounded by national forest and with a popular national park in prox-imity, much of my youth had been spent in the moun-tains: hiking, backpacking, and camping. The trails I'd traversed there had oftentimes been demanding, but not nearly so much as those I'd stumbled across in the *Old Continent*. Like most devoted hikers, I'd typically chosen paths that led to a payoff of some kind, such as a foamy, cascading waterfall in the middle of nowhere or a highly sought-after scenic overlook. The payoffs for the exertion put forth in the Alps? Much of the same, teamed with a slightly dissimilar, more delicious form of indulgence.

Within walking distance of our flat, one could choose from any number of trails and, minutes later, find oneself ascending a mountain to discover a local Biergarten waiting at the end of the journey. And, before hitching a ride on a gondola for the return trip, one could partake of the local fare in copious quantities, should one choose.

I'd performed this routine on sundry occasions in my time here. And, at least in my opinion, there was no experience in the world comparable to Bavarian beer-goaded insobriety after a day of high-intensity, sweaty mountaineering. In fact, I felt thirsty at the onset of thinking about it.

The air felt particularly dry today, as in next to zero humidity, and I could sense its unwavering chill on my skin, much as I had in the days before. Admittedly, I hadn't been prepared for climate nor culture when I'd first relocated to Germany, and regrettably, it was taking some time for my Virginian bones and American-born viewpoints to acclimate. Berchtesgaden was a lovely village in Bavaria, its inhabitants merry and vibrant, and there was a bounty of rich history here to accompany the picturesque landscapes. Though I'd never been exactly partial to it, it was Natalia's birthplace and I'd sworn to her long ago that we'd eventually move here, establish permanent residence, and hopefully retire here—if the cards were ever dealt in our favor.

The assignment we had scheduled next week had a substantial payout attached to it. Executed successfully and properly sanitized, it could easily put us on the verge of achieving our ultimate plans: retirement from this routine for the remainder of our lives, followed by an eternity inseparate of one another. It was something I'd deeply desired for more than a decade now, ever since we'd made the decision to follow our current career path.

After forking another slice of lukewarm Weisswurst into my mouth, I washed it down with a swig of beer while detecting the sound of the door being slid open behind me. A few seconds after, I felt the familiar squeeze of two hands on my shoulders through my down jacket's loft. I turned my head slightly to the right, and an arrangement of petite, scar-blemished knuckles came into view, those belonging to the one and only love of my life.

Natalia's appealing voice purred as only hers could. "*Guten Morgen*," she said, sending a smile my way through closed lips.

I smiled involuntarily back at her. Natalia's intonation always conveyed her Bavarian accent with such emphasis when we were here. It made sense, though. This was her home, and she found comfort in the familiarity of what surrounded her. When staying here, we'd always maintained a low profile and with no adversaries in sight for kilometers, she found it easy to relax and be herself, that is, as much as one could in our vocation. One can never be too conscientious, unless one foolishly favors one's own extinction.

I faced forward, feeling a gentle kiss on my frigid cheek. "Good morning, yourself. Did you sleep well?"

Natalia smiled at me as she glided past to the edge of our balcony. She folded her arms over her white fleece bathrobe, squeezed tightly and quivered. "*Scheiße, es ist kalt!*" she moaned, lamenting the ambient wintriness. "Springtime in the Alps. And you're just sitting there like it's not even bothering you."

"Well, it's really not."

"You're not even shivering." She turned to have a good look at the level of beer in my stein. "How long have you been out here?"

"It hasn't been long. I woke up early and went for a run. When I got back, I fried up some sausage and checked our schedule. Our agenda being open for the most part, I decided to relax a little. And…hydrate."

"Yeah…I noticed." Natalia looked over her shoulder again and sent me a playfully malicious glance. She gestured to my beer. "How did you elect to *pour* it?"

Detecting her overemphasis on the word *pour*, I didn't offer her an answer right off the bat. This had been an inside joke between us for years, and I knew her well enough to deduce what was coming.

My better half had resided in countries all over the globe while remaining a proud German, having been born and raised in the heart of Bavaria, not far from where we lived today. Her father had owned a bar, and she'd worked there alongside him as a fledgling wait-ress, outfitted in a miniature dirndl to serve food and drinks—mostly drinks.

There was a unique method in which certain beers were poured from a bottle here, one which I had proven to be rather inept at. The process involved positioning a tall beer glass overtop the bottle and flipping them gracefully upside down as one. The bottle was then lifted slowly out of the glass over a span of time while allowing the contents to transfer, resulting in a flawless pour with the perfect amount of *Schaum*, or head. If done correctly, it was excellence personified, and the brew's fortunate owner was able to enjoy the reward brought about by the efforts. That being said, if done even the slightest bit incorrectly, the pour would foam over in a matter of seconds—detonating with the force of an erupting volcano into a frothy, sticky mess. Here, in the heart of Bavaria, it was considered to be nothing short of an abomination to perform in such a way.

Long story short, I'd developed a particular notoriety for the latter version of the pour. And because of this, I always elected to pour my beer using the forever-rebuked Westerner method, applying a standard decant over a slightly tilted glass.

"I poured it the only way I know how," I said. "The American way, of course." I returned her glance with an enhanced copy of my own. "Thanks for bringing that up again."

Natalia giggled while her body shivered in response to the brisk air. "Sorry, I couldn't help myself. You're so adorable when you try to be German. It's cute and endearing…and oddly enough…even a little erotic, in an anomalous way."

"Erotic, huh?"

"Mm-hmm." She nodded and turned away shyly.

"In an...*anomalous* way?"

She sniggered inaudibly. "Yeah, Q. Anomalous. Like our life in general." Natalia turned and moved in closer to me while she ogled my plate. "You know... you're not eating a complete breakfast."

"How's that?"

She angled her head back and sniffed the air. "You can't smell that?"

"Smell what?"

"Q, we live overtop a bakery. Yet your plate is always so dreadfully devoid of starches."

I took a whiff, now able to smell the aroma she was referring to. It could only be one thing—fresh homemade pretzels. If offered a choice for her last meal prior to execution, there was little doubt in my mind she'd ask for them. "Pretzels, bread, and doughy foods are your vices, not mine. And this wheat beer gives me enough bloat as it is." I regarded her quivering, which seemed to be getting worse. "Are you getting sick? You look colder than usual this morning."

Natalia nodded, her delicate hair flopping in the breeze. "I feel fine. But you're right, I'm freezing... likely due to the lack of garment I'm wearing under this bathrobe."

I smiled inside, but I might have let it show on the

outside as well. "Your choice of morning attire intrigues me. Or should I say, the absence of it."

"You've never been one to complain, have you, Quinn?" She turned and inched closer with a smirk, sliding her palm over my shoulder and digging her fingernails along my jacket as she moved past. "Are you still planning on taking me shopping in *München* later today?"

"I haven't arranged any other plans for us, if that's what you're asking."

"Good," Natalia said. "There are a few things I want to pick up before we head to the States next week." She paused before continuing, her tone finding a more serious note. "We're still on, right? For the gun play?"

Natalia had always referred to our assignments as *gun play*, and I'd never really understood why. Like most of the other nuances that kept her mysterious and exceptional to me, I'd never delved deeper than the surface. Face value had always been sufficient for me whenever it came to her.

I nodded affirmation. "I haven't heard otherwise. But I'm guessing we won't know for certain until we get there. As usual."

"Yeah. I know how that works," Natalia said. "Okay, I've had enough of this wretched polar air. I'm going to take a shower or perhaps a steam bath. You can join if you like. There's an open invitation for you."

I turned in my chair in time to watch her flirtatiously shuffle her bathrobe-covered body back inside, turning her head only enough to eyeball me before she slid closed the glass door.

She stood inside for a moment, giving me plenty of time to act on my primal instincts, while providing me with a lascivious mental photograph of what lay underneath her robe. After a few minutes, she shuffled off into the shadows.

It was all I could do not to follow her. Natalia was a looker—her beauty incomparable to that of any woman I had ever crossed paths with. Her frame was a divine effigy, and admittedly, I'd been ostensibly addicted to her since the moment I'd fallen for her.

Ten years ago, I would have tackled her before her hand made contact with the door handle, and followed up by making ferocious love to her. That being then, and this being now, our marriage had reached a point where the spontaneity wasn't as prevalent as it had been. Intimacy and passion still existed, but it had taken on a new face, morphing into something more secure and symbiotic. While it's kept me warm and has made me the happiest I've ever been, it was still difficult to describe.

Though it sounded like a cliché in saying so, it remained true; I'd never met anyone like Natalia in my life before. My eyes had locked on to her, and I'd been drawn to her since day one. She was beautiful—stunning, actually, from the natural highlights in her thick, espresso brown hair, to her Mediterranean skin, which seemed to absorb sunlight, preserving an olive hue year-round. Her charm was unparalleled, and she possessed an enigmatic smile capable of conveying any emotion at her beckoning. She was intelligent as well as perceptive, and with an IQ somewhere in the one sixties, she was verifiably one of the smartest people I'd ever known.

Her beauty and aptitude aside, Natalia was just as lovely and bright as she was deadly. A killer by trade and by virtue, her predatorial instincts and near super-human resilience practically flowed through her blood. And in my opinion, both as her coconspirator and her husband, she was more lethal and effective than any assassin alive today of the same caliber.

The degrees of violence Natalia was capable of had even managed to astonish me at times. I'd seen her send a half-dozen expertly trained counterassassins to their graves, using nothing more than her index fingers and an incandescent smile. That was a slight exaggeration, of course. But in using it to reference the volume of effort she expended, it would be categorically accurate.

Natalia had never been completely forthcoming about the intimate details of her life prior to the two of us coming together, and I'd never pushed her to tell me about them. Still, she'd offer up tidbits every so often during times when she'd felt secure enough to share.

From the blanks randomly filled in over the years, I'd learned that her childhood wasn't all peaches and cream and sunshine and rainbows. It had begun here in Berchtesgaden, but hadn't remained that way. Some rather bad things had happened to her and her family, and consequently, she'd been removed from them.

She'd lived a normal life once. Her mother was a Belgian-born German transplant who had owned a flower shop here in town. Natalia's father had met her mother while stationed at the US Army Garrison in Garmisch during his final tour. He'd courted her, they had dated for a while and married not long after, then purchased a bar and a bed-and-breakfast somewhere not far from the *Dachgeschoss*, or top-level flat, in which we lived today. Natalia was brought into the world a year later, where she was raised in a jovial, nourishing, traditional Bavarian home for many of her childhood years.

Her parents both had successful businesses, but were horrible with managing their money. They had procured currency to pay off debts by borrowing more money elsewhere, accruing substantially more debt in the process, along with added interest. To top it off, Natalia's father had tumbled into a serious gambling liability with the Russian mob and ended up getting in way over his head…an appendage they kindly removed in trade for his insolence. Bratva hit men, being the hardcore pricks they tended to be, along with a partiality for never leaving behind witnesses, had carnally violated and murdered her mother as well, doing so in a rather ostentatious manner. From the way Natalia had explained it to me, I imagine it resembled something along the lines of Joan of Arc's execution.

As further means of recouping their losses, they'd removed Natalia from her home and took her in as an underling. They had never hurt her, though—never so much as laid a finger on her. She'd always been adamant about that detail. In fact, one of the Bratva *Avtoritets*, or bosses, a man named Koslovich, had taken quite a liking to her soon after her arrival, citing how much he enjoyed her spirit and admired what he'd referred to as her 'killer' instinct.

At his order, Natalia had been treated as a member of the family instead of the recompense for which she'd originally been appropriated. Koslovich had even assigned her a guardian—a Ukrainian mercenary previously employed by the KGB, and who'd had a previous level of involvement with the elite *Vympel* group of Spetsnaz.

Natalia only recalled his first name: Dmitry. And it was Dmitry who had trained her and taught her much of her tradecraft. She spoke of him infrequently at best, and when she chose to mention her memories about him, she did so only in fragments. I did know that in order to escape her bonds with the mafia, Dmitry had been one of several men Natalia had been forced to kill, and though she'd known it had been necessary, she'd never been proud of having to do so.

Natalia was my polar opposite in so many ways, both then and now. My early development into our trade had begun as a lowly E-3 sniper retained by MARSOC, the US Marine Corps Special Ops Command.

I've never been one to brag, but I was pretty damn good at my job. In fact, as things turned out, I wound up ranked among the best—having been christened with the call signs 'death adder' and 'overkill' in the course of my tours in the Helmand Province of Afghanistan, during the nonstop, much-acclaimed American war on terrorism. My fellow grunts labeled me a natural-born killer of men, but my skills, though considered by many to be elite and cream of the crop, had been disregarded—their spotlight shrouded by what had become my most profound character flaw.

While lying prone in my final firing position, I had a tendency to go above and beyond. Meaning, I didn't just delete the intended target as ordered. I'd been inclined instead to acquire and destroy everything and everyone, everywhere in the vicinity, and anything else that got in the way while I was at it. I'd been disinclined to show or offer remorse for my actions, my justification being that all targets terminated and made dead had, in fact, all been enemies and, as such, deserving of their fate.

My superiors had been less than inclined to agree with me.

I supposed one could surmise that I had a lot in common with manufactured goods. I was a product of my environment. I had been orphaned when I was young, and I'd been alone for much of my life, having to fight my own battles for as long as I cared to recount. No one, failing myself, had ever come to my defense. I didn't remember my real parents, and didn't care to recall the halfway houses or the countless foster families I'd been handed off to on temporary loan, either. As such, I'd never had a family to back me up or a place to call home, at least until I'd found Natalia. Living an isolated existence for the majority of my life, devoid of interactions and normalcy, served to coarsen my heart over time, and I'd been content to let it remain that way. I figured maybe I'd been lucky enough to be born without a conscience, and it wasn't until meeting my better half that I learned what a conscience even was.

My history of inequities and going full *overkill* had become the foundation for a court-martial and a guest appearance before a US Navy JAG Corps, followed by a less-than-honorable discharge from the Marines. My deeds hadn't gone unnoticed and, for reasons known only to them, served to cultivate my subsequent recruitment into the Special Operations Group of the Central Intelligence Agency, though I never quite fit in there. My fellow agents were all ex-military like I was, but were far too disciplined and polished. I felt like a sledgehammer tossed into a pile of pins, needles, and fine brushes. After several successful and a few unsuccessful wet operations, some of which had been particularly bloody, I was offered a chance at becoming a non-official cover operative, and I jumped in headfirst.

In that capacity, I traveled the world, making deals and securing assets, some of whom Natalia and I utilize to this day. I made a couple of friends and a good deal of enemies, argued with overzealous ambassadors, and got into several fistfights with a few pompous CIA chiefs of station. It was a role that taught me a lot about myself and what I was capable of, but it was also one doomed for failure, and had probably been from the word go.

A few years following my conscription, my access was delimited, and I was ultimately excommunicated. An official burn notice, signed by the director himself, sealed the deal, citing my overall lack of controllability as justification for the action. It hadn't been clear to me if I'd been deemed a legitimate enemy by the intelligence consortia, or if I'd simply been shit-canned, but I felt it best to part ways and distance myself from the agency.

Natalia's skills had been instilled in her by a man who'd been a tenured professional—an expert in foreign intelligence, espionage, and clandestine assassination with impunity. She'd been accepted, molded, and hardened by one of the most elite trained killers in the world to become one of the same. Yet she'd always been able to exercise levels of scrutiny and fairness that I'd never cared to. Natalia was calculating, deliberate, and all business, but would never allow the killing of innocents. In fact, she hadn't once hesitated to call off an operation when it meant eliminating a target she believed didn't need killing or didn't deserve to be killed.

I'd always been equipped to move forward as planned—ready, willing, and able to do whatever was needed to achieve the objective, regardless of the outcome. But my wife was wired differently. Natalia had told me on several occasions, if we had followed through to the consummation of some of our more questionable ops, she wouldn't have been able to live with herself.

Sometimes, I wished I knew what she meant by that, but maybe I wasn't meant to. Maybe that was why we were together, or at least, one of the reasons we found each other. Because we offset each other and helped one another find a semblance of balance. Who knew? I was convinced that she and I both lucked out. We were made for one another, and we were made to do the things we do. And now, we just did them together as a team—as husband and wife.

In a few hours, my bride and I would be boarding a train en route to Munich for a weekend of diversion before we hitched a flight to the US to tend to our latest business venture. I didn't mind the work—I never had, but I'd be grateful when there was enough money in the bank and we wouldn't have to do this anymore. I wanted to see Natalia's smile free of the façade she'd obscured it with for so long. I wanted to see it become genuine and unfabricated someday. I thought she'd earned the right to be happy and live an ordinary life far away from the death we triggered off whenever we got the call, especially after all she'd been through.

And it was reassuring knowing when that time came, neither of us would have to live that life alone.

TWO

Olympia shopping mall, Munich, Germany
Friday, 21 March, 1335 CET
Nihayat al'ayam minus 6 days, 10 hours, 25
minutes

The train ride to Munich involved a quick swap in Salzburg, Austria, and was scheduled to last just a little over three hours. I remembered Natalia telling me before that the trip was usually much shorter, but typically took more time the closer it got to the weekends.

While the wife spent much of her time preoccupying herself with geopolitical concerns, such as her country's overpopulation and how it served to affect ride times, I remained enthralled with the majestic views outside my window, unable to concentrate on much of anything else. It couldn't be helped. The ecological scenery in Bavaria is nothing short of extraordinary, even from this lowly train passenger's point of view.

The trip's duration wasn't a bother to me, though Natalia was right, the cars were jam-packed today, as in up to the elbows with fares. With an acute eye and a sharp tenor denoting her frustration, she explained that at one time, a train ride in her country hadn't been unlike any conventional airliner flight. Tickets were purchased in advance, purchasers reserved, and were therefore assigned seating. Standing passengers had never been permitted, for safety's sake.

While that might have been the case in the past, today it appeared those rules had been tossed aside. The seats had all been taken, forcing groups of travelers to stand uncomfortably in the walkways and utilize the train car's grab rails as their only means of support. At the speed we were travelling, somewhere around three hundred kilometers an hour, equivalent to one hundred eighty six miles per hour imperial, I didn't envy them.

To add to that, the multitude of faces wasn't made up of a preponderance of the train's standard occupants. At least, insofar as I could discern. Many of the passengers seemed as though they didn't belong on board the train…or within the country, for that matter. They acted unfriendly to those standing anywhere close to them, and gave off the impression they were either unable or unwilling to blend in. To me, they appeared as outsiders or unwelcome foreign guests, though not exactly tourists. And by the looks plastered on the faces of adjoining natives, it was easy to tell I wasn't the only one making that determination.

The outsider types had brownish complexions and wore well-used, mismatched clothing: the types often-times seen at swap meets or found in thrift stores. The language they spoke wasn't the usual mixture of Bavarian German and broken English I had grown accustomed to hearing since living here. Most notably, they were brash, uncivilized and lacked manners, some-thing seldom experienced on high-speed Intercity Express trains, even when riding in second class.

On the final hour of our trip, and several minutes into a daydream of watching the landscape roll and cascade past the window, a man slid by me aggres-sively, lifted the armrest and plopped himself into the narrow space between Natalia and me. At first, I thought he had lost his balance and taken a fall, but the frenzied expression mounting on his face told me otherwise.

He appeared of Middle Eastern or North African descent and had a set of jet-black eyes, which were nearly as dark and glossy as the curly, greasy hair on his head. While eyeballing me, he rubbed his stubbly beard and smiled tauntingly, as if begging me to say some-thing to him about his impulsiveness. And I would have, had I not seen Natalia's confident, restful smile, along with the slightest rotation of her head. She was signaling me to remain put.

The man squirmed and wriggled and, while pushing me farther away, closed what little gap had existed between himself and Natalia. Seconds after, his impetuosity crossed the border into flat-out disrespect. With a shit-eating grin on his face, he placed his left hand on my wife's right leg and squeezed it. Then he slid it forward ever so slowly to the edge of her knee.

He turned his head fully away from me and whispered something to her. Natalia's only response was to cast a stare straight ahead and continue smiling as though nothing were amiss. As his lips came within one precarious inch of her ear, he turned his body toward her, taking hold of her leg with his right hand so he could slide his left hand backward.

My blood went from lukewarm to a boil in a matter of seconds, and as the notion hit me to separate this invading insect's thorax from his abdomen, I felt something poke my neck. I turned to look and see what it was, finding myself locking eyes with a second man, one possessing an almost identical complexion as Natalia's visitor, along with the same jet-black eyes and similarly slimy hair. He slowly parted his lips and shot a grin my way, displaying a set of deteriorated teeth, then pushed whatever he had in his hand into my neck with more force.

I adjusted my posture enough to take a peek at what he was using to imperil me. It was one of those el cheapo, spring-assisted knives any Joe Schmoe could order off the internet in kit form and put together himself. They were junk, the edges only good for about one or two uses, but nonetheless, couldn't be discounted. Even the tawdriest blades this close to a jugular vein or carotid artery were plenty lethal. All it would take would be the slightest flick of his flaccid thumb for the blade to spring out of the handle. Then, game over.

I nodded my recognition to him, then turned away to mind his partner's hand while it caressed Natalia's leg. She hadn't made so much as a move and was still bidding me to hold back, meaning she had already decided on a course of action and was awaiting a suitable moment to execute.

This country was her home territory. We lived here now, and it was therefore preferable that we not perform as we would if accosted anywhere else in the world in the same manner. I understood that, but watching this uncultured mongrel touch her the way he was wasn't exactly making it easy to accept.

At the point my wife's molester whispered something else into her ear, this time with added volume to the point most others in proximity could hear, Natalia placed her right hand onto his left, stopping him before he made it to within an inch of the crease in her thigh.

He responded immediately, lurching away at first. But, feeling the gentleness of her touch, his posture relaxed, and he sat back again, allowing her to rub his hand. Poor sucker. If he only knew how many times the hand holding his own had killed. Most men had never made it this close to mortality in their lives without actually dying.

That was when I heard it, and I had no doubt I wasn't the only one. A sudden, unmistakable, stomach-churning *SNAP*. Natalia had latched on to his pinky finger with her index and ring fingers and pulled back on it—all the way to the point where his fingernail contacted the skin of his forearm.

When the man cried out from the pain of a single hyperextended, broken and dislocated finger, Natalia silenced him with a hand over his mouth. She'd even arranged herself closer to him and pretended to kiss him to cause the situation to appear relatively normal to onlookers. She curled her fingers against his cheek and toyed with him with her nails while he writhed in pain, then let loose of his pinky, only to take hold of the rest of his fingers. She said something to him in his language, then constricted her grip with every bit of strength she possessed.

I cringed at the sound of crunching and snapping phalanges.

The man yelped aloud in agony, but Natalia only

pushed into his mouth with more firmness, both muffling his cries and preventing his escape.

The one with the knife at my neck had finally caught on to what was happening to his friend. I could feel him stiffen up, readying himself to strike, and that left me with less than a second to make a move.

I whipped my right arm in a backward circular motion overtop of his, disarming him and sending his toy knife skipping across the train car's epoxy-coated steel floor. Then I went for the only location on a man's body proven to produce immediate, staggeringly effective results. It wasn't my most preferred way of dispatching a male adversary, but I'd become agitated after watching his colleague fondle my wife's leg, and very much desired for this impromptu encounter to end straightaway. The sound that followed was nearly in tune with the one Natalia's accoster's fingers had made when she'd crushed them.

Standing as I allowed my attacker's limp body to fall into my seat, I snapped the seatbelt in place over him just as Natalia made a motion for us to relocate. The threat eliminated, and with no onlookers having yet been aroused, I followed her to the rear of the train, where we switched cars before the crowd caught on to our misgivings.

Upon finding a spot to stand amidst another group of grinning, nodding, happy-go-lucky German passengers, I asked, "What was that all about?"

Natalia's pleasant grin flatlined. While looking at nothing and no one in particular, she shrugged her shoulders gracefully. "Nothing."

"Nothing?"

She hesitated before responding, placing a finger over her simpering lips as a reminder for me to mind the level of my voice. "Just a despicable pair of miscreants who've no business being in my country."

After working our way through several shops with names I couldn't pronounce if I tried, Natalia led the way through the mall's exit and on to *Hanauer Straße*. We took a left-hand turn and began our search for the café she'd given glorious reviews of, regarding their lunch menu. While she chatted away about things like fresh homemade breads, pastries, and *Butterkäse*, my mind wandered in pure, unadulterated interest of what varieties of beer they might serve.

If Bavaria had become a friend to me for any reason of my choosing, it had undeniably been the beer. The choices were endless—from medium-bodied pilsners and yeasty, sometimes fruity Hefeweizens to traditional lagers, Dunkels, and bocks. This place was heaven on earth for any beer lover, making it damn close to Valhalla for me.

When Natalia pointed to a painted wooden sign that hung over a café just ahead, all I noticed were the unmistakably identifiable brewery logos just below it for Hofbräu, Hacker-Pschorr, and Franziskaner, among others.

"Is this the place?" I asked, very much hoping that it was.

Natalia nodded enthusiastically. "I haven't been here in years. So much has changed, though...I hope they still have the same menu."

"Well, even if they don't, it looks like they serve some great beer."

She shot her eyes at me playfully. "You're incorrigible."

"Don't expect that to change anytime soon."

"Oh, I don't. I expect it will get worse."

I pushed the door inward and followed Natalia into the café, where we were immediately greeted by a very young, very blonde hostess by the name of Ingrid, whose smile, though gleaming and unpretentious, was missing a few teeth.

"*Willkommen! Tisch für zwei?*" she graciously asked.

Natalia nodded her head and spoke to Ingrid in her native dialect for a moment while our light-blue-dirndl-garbed hostess seated us at a quaint table in the corner. I went to take the seat that faced outward toward the entrance—but so did Natalia. I smiled and yielded to her this time, though. This was her territory, and if anything off-kilter was afoot, her eye would be much keener than mine. Her understanding of the language and culture here also gave her the edge. Advantages aside though, I always hated sitting with my back to the entrance.

When I took my seat and noticed the mirror on the wall in the back of the café offered a perfect reproduction of what was behind me, I felt consoled. It offered almost as much solace as the feeling of the suppressed Glock 19 on my lower vertebrae when I leaned into my solid-backed chair.

Ingrid handed us each a thin menu printed on hemp paper before bidding us a few more toothy-grinned declarations and strolling off. I opened the menu and, of course, everything inside was written in German, and there weren't any helpful photographic illustrations to go along.

My dismay must've been evident because Natalia picked up on it right on the spot. "Do you require assistance?" she asked, a look of mild concern coupled with a sheepish grin displayed on her face.

"I might need you to order for me," I replied. "Everything in here looks like hieroglyphics."

Natalia tilted her head. "Maybe you should take the plunge and learn some German. You do have a semiper-manent residence here, after all."

"Or maybe you could just translate for me and save us both the frustration."

Natalia sat up and reached for my menu. After a

quick glance to verify mine was an identical copy of hers, she said, "A lot of these older-style cafés don't have visual cues in their menus like the commercial Biergartens you're used to. What are you in the mood for?"

I thought for a moment. What *was* I in the mood for? Most times I was a sucker for the basics—sausage and beer, but I'd already had that for breakfast. "Suggest something. Something different than what I usually go for."

She sent along that smile again, then sat back in her chair, taking the menu with her. "You're feeling markedly ballsy today. You sure you're up for it?"

"Hit me with your best shot. I trust you."

Natalia shook her head as her smile dissipated. After a moment, she pointed her index finger at the page and said, "*Schmalznudel.*"

"What the hell is Schmalz…noodle?"

She giggled quietly. "It's a pastry. Kind of like a cross between a donut and a croissant, but deep-fried. Tastes like a funnel cake. You'll love it."

"So, a pastry, then. For lunch…"

"Quinn, please. You eat brats and drink Weissbier for breakfast nearly every day when we're not working."

I shrugged indifferently. "What's your point?"

Natalia only stared at me crossly.

"Okay, apparently there's nothing wrong with

eating pastries for lunch in Germany. But will it make me fat?"

"Babe, you're in your early forties now," she mused. "Everything you eat and drink makes you fat."

There was a lot of truth to that statement and she knew it. I knew it, too, I just didn't like it. In fact, I hated it. And she knew that, too.

"Fine. Order me a Schmalz...whatever, then," I said.

"It's *Schmalznudel*. Say it with me."

We spent the next minute going over the proper articulation of the word. I tried my best but gave up soon after, the specific emphasis on each syllable having gotten the best of me. The entire German language seemed overemphasized to me, along with being loud, somewhat obnoxious, and unnecessarily boisterous. I wound up mocking her attempts at tutelage until she sent me a clear indication to discontinue.

When Ingrid came back to take our orders, Natalia kept her there and entertained a short conversation with her. At times during their dialogue, Ingrid's eyes got wide and she pointed to her face, her mouth, and to her teeth. Natalia responded with looks of disbelief and, occasionally, looks of disdain. After the conversation concluded, Ingrid took our menus, bid us a farewell of mixed German and English, and skipped off.

"What was that about?" I asked, watching her bounce away.

Natalia shook her head and scowled. "Mostly small talk. But I wanted to know what happened to her teeth."

My reply, carrying a tone of mild disinterest, followed. "Okay…"

"She was attacked," Natalia said flatly, her expression hardening.

"What are you talking about?"

"She said a group of migrants did it."

"Like the ones on the train?"

Natalia nodded slightly. "She was walking home after work and they surrounded her on the street near her flat. When she wouldn't give them what they wanted, they took turns beating her up. One of them punched her in the face a few times…knocked one of her teeth out and jarred another loose. It was irreparably damaged, and a dentist had to remove it."

"Jesus," I said. "What did they want? Money? Or something else?"

Natalia closed her eyes and shook her head. "Hell no. They're animals. And animals only want one thing," she muttered, turning her head away. "She's lucky she wasn't raped. Usually, those attacks are way worse than what she endured. I'm surprised they even bothered to solicit her before they jumped her."

"What the fuck?" I said somewhat louder than I'd intended.

I had never been fond of hearing about things such as this—women falling prey to vicious organisms with one fascination occupying their feeble, puerile minds. The stronger taking advantage of the weaker for no aim other than the fact it could was a concept of nature I had always found intolerable. It utterly infuriated me. And Ingrid's predicament was no different.

"It's the way things are around here now, apparently," Natalia lamented. "Attacks like that have become commonplace and almost an acceptable behavior, if you can fathom it. There are reports of women being attacked and sexually assaulted and even disappearing almost every day in Munich. The attackers are almost always identified as migrant males of Middle Eastern descent. Rapes, assaults, stabbings, all have become rampant, and *die Polizei* are beleaguered by it and seem powerless to do anything. Ingrid says incidents such as these are happening in cities all over the country—and all over the EU now, for that matter."

"Why the hell can't the police do anything about it?" I asked.

Natalia's smile had traveled miles away. "Because this is Europe. And bureaucratic bullshit rules here above and beyond a citizen's right to defend his or herself. It's due in part to hidden agendas, globalist politics and far too much political correctness. Our progressive leaders have been allowing these things to ensue for years. It became our responsibility to provide asylum to the refugees—those poor people fleeing the civil wars and atrocities committed by ISIS." She paused. "Despite what you saw on the news, not all the citizens living here were altogether for it—but our votes were rendered null and void, and the EU began forcing refractory countries to welcome refugees or face consequences. Parliament sold it to the German people as a humanitarian effort, initially. It's the new Europe, after all—the inception of two consecutive World Wars occurred here. It's the reason we renounced the use of force and disarmed our citizens and moved to solve all our conflicts through diplomacy and pacification. A lot of good that did us."

My eyes locked with hers as I took it all in. "A lot of good that ever did anyone."

Natalia smirked grimly before continuing. "The depiction was they were all Syrian refugees in need of aid—families of husbands, wives, and their children. But what came were largely single men—young, strong, virile men with no families to speak of. Some appeared Syrian, but others looked Somalian or even Nigerian. Some of them had cell phones and wallets filled with euros, and some were even wearing designer clothing. You'd think since the war in Syria is being perpetrated by Islamists, the majority of refugees would be Christians or Jews. But they're not. They're Muslim, many of them radical. And it's not difficult to distinguish because they pester whites, Christians, and Jews, and they berate and attack women, like Ingrid.

"Our government welcomes them here and allows

them to live on our welfare system. They're given money and respectable places to live, and free rein because of their theoretical plight, so we're told, but when they get here, all they do is start trouble. They refuse to work and they're completely incapable of integrating into our society...but they never had any intention of doing so, anyway." She paused and rubbed her nose. "When I was a kid, I remember my dad throwing a fit over the Turkish moving into Germany by the thousands. He called it a politically sanctioned unarmed invasion of Europe. Now, looking back, I'm almost certain he was right."

I shook my head, taking all of what my wife was telling me into consideration. "I know what you're saying is true...but it doesn't make any sense. The *why* doesn't make sense. I just don't get it."

"That makes two of us, Q," Natalia said while running her fingers through the glossy layers of her hair. "The people here are being played for fools, being told to just suck it up and deal with the situation as it stands. If you don't want to be attacked, better to just stay home."

"Easier said than done," I said. "How is anyone supposed to live their lives like that? Waking up every day constantly in fear?" My curiosity was now fully engaged with this whole mess of a situation. "The *why* is still confounding me. There has to be an endgame—a purpose for allowing this to happen."

Natalia shrugged. "Endgame?" She hesitated. "I can't imagine it's for anything other than the eventual takeover of Europe. We appear weak to them now and therefore vulnerable and easily attainable. And as I've heard you put it before, we pissed in their Cheerios…a long time ago. Islam isn't just a religion, it's an ideology. Its original basis was to explicitly pursue political and societal dominance over every living individual on the planet. It's about submission and a primitive social hierarchy, and the elimination of human rights. Women must submit to men, men and women Muslims submit to Allah, and non-Muslims must submit to Islamic rule. We were told the refugees were being allowed into developed European nations to escape the atrocities of sharia law—beatings, stonings, amputations, beheadings and such. Most of the cruelties affected women, yet the vast majority of refugees have always been men. I don't know. I've never had the time to fully study the Quran. Maybe I should now." She paused. "I know it's a big world and there are many different sects of Islam, some being much more peaceful than others. But I have yet to see any modernists stand up to their fundamentalist relatives."

"So…rapes and attacks on women?" I asked while motioning to Ingrid, who had her back turned to us. "Is that how they intend to achieve their primary objective?"

Natalia shook her head impassively. "I think their

primary objective is genocide, in one form or another, and that could include breeding us into extinction. Rape, especially when accepted as normal behavior and gone unpunished, is an efficient way to accomplish that."

"That's some sick shit. Europe certainly has changed since the glory days."

"The glory days?"

"Yeah. Like the Berlin Wall, and so on."

She smiled softly at me. "How much do you know about European history?"

I didn't answer her. She already knew how uninformed I was.

"It hasn't always been like this," Natalia continued. "But it has gotten a lot worse over the years. We natives have become a minority in our own country. People like Ingrid are afraid to leave their homes at night for fear of what might happen to them, all in the name of solidarity and compassion. Islamophobia has even become a prosecutable crime now. It's such bullshit." She fidgeted a moment as her eyes narrowed. Her shoulders drooped, and her stare became distant. "If you don't mind, Q, I don't want to talk about it anymore, okay? It's just too much right now. We have a lot to consider and get done in the days coming, and I don't want my mind clouded by this."

I held up my hands and capitulated. "Then we won't talk about it anymore."

It had been a while since I'd seen her this caught up or saddened about something, but Germany was Natalia's native soil, and seeing it in this condition had to be disheartening for her. I imagined she'd already begun constructing ideas on viable solutions—no doubt the type that ended with a lot of dead bodies strewn about. The gears of perdition inside Natalia's mind never stopped grinding.

Now, I'd never eaten a *Schmalznudel* before, and after having one, I wondered why it had taken me so long to take the plunge. It was fantastic. It tasted just like a funnel cake—or at least something very similar to one. And the Hacker-Pschorr Weissbier I'd washed it down with was delicious, even though it had been served at room temperature, something that was customary here and I still hadn't gotten used to.

After we finished lunch, Natalia and I grabbed our shopping bags and headed back outside and onto the sidewalk paralleling *Hanauer Straße.* We passed a half-dozen shops before something she didn't care for very much came into view. I followed her eyes, and when I saw what she was seeing, I understood immediately, especially after our most recent verbal exchange.

Burkas. Lots of them. And from the look on Natalia's face, it was lucky for those wearing them that the street traffic separated us.

Natalia shook her head with repugnance. "I swear to God, Q. It's taking every bit of self-restraint I have left to keep from walking over there and eviscerating them where they stand."

"Hey…easy there. We don't know for certain they're jihadists," I said. "They could be carrying anything under those drapes…and I don't mean explosive suicide vests, either. It could be books or groceries—"

"I don't care if it's AKs, Type 81s, and full battle rattle underneath," Natalia said, cutting me off. "They'd be carcasses before they knew what hit them."

What she was saying was true. She knew it, and so did I. Natalia wasn't generally this insufferable, but the maelstrom of problems affecting her home was really bugging her.

I started imagining her approach and actions in my mind, based on prior performances I'd been witness to. Like a small game of personal trivia, I tried to guess what she would do first, who she'd pick as her initial target, and what her choice of weapon would be —if any.

Natalia was a master of both Systema Spetsnaz and Krav Maga, and what her hands alone were capable of was usually more than enough to incapacitate a foe. Come to think of it, I didn't remember ever seeing her lose a fight before.

"Can we get out of here?" she asked, turning away and letting out a tremendously drawn-out sigh. "Please? Before I lose my cool?"

"Of course we can," I replied. "But just so we're clear, if I hear one *allahu akbar*, I won't be walking over there…I'll be running. And you'll have a footrace on your hands."

Natalia looked to me agreeably. "Challenge accepted."

THREE

DULLES INTERNATIONAL AIRPORT
MONDAY, MARCH 24, 7:30 A.M. EDT
NIHAYAT AL'AYAM MINUS 3 DAYS, 16 HOURS, 30
MINUTES

True statement: I've never been a foremost fan of commercial flights, especially international commercial flights that spend an inordinate amount of time overtop hundreds of nautical miles of freezing, salty, ruthless ocean. Crash into a mountain or onto the hard, unforgiving earth and death comes instantly, whether in the form of a heart attack, blunt-force trauma, or suffocation, as the impending inferno sucks all the oxygen from your lungs like a superheated Dyson. The end comes, and you feel nothing.

I've always laid claim that crashing into the ocean

would serve to provide an entirely dissimilar set of horrors. The diligent pilot would hero up and try to save everyone, because that's what he's supposed to do. He'd attempt to land the bird as mellifluously as possible, and the plane would, in turn, glide and hop along the ocean for some distance before coming to a stop—intact, for the most part. There'd be no fire present to burn us alive and even if there were, it wouldn't be a conflagration, since it's physically impossible for flames to exist where water is present.

So there we'd be. Afloat in the middle of a vast ocean, cruising around like a piece of driftwood, with no rescue in sight or in range, confined to a flimsy sarcophagus of plastic, titanium and other materials lacking buoyancy.

If we somehow made it out of the plane, considering two hundred other people would also be endeavoring to do the very same thing—all while fighting for their lives in a panic, I envision an ending similar to the one in the movie *Titanic*. Natalia would be atop some floating section of airliner and I'd be the unlucky swimmer, immersed in seawater, developing frostbite and hypothermia at a rapid pace. I'd slowly lose my mind while uttering the most absurd things, transform into a human ice cube and sink a mile down to the ocean floor shortly thereafter. Pleasant dreams.

After making our way uneventfully through baggage check and pushing through the thick lines of disgruntled passengers at customs, we ended up outside the main terminal, where a car should've been waiting for us, but wasn't. We stood there in the dry, frigid, winter air of the mid-Atlantic, both of us not saying a word, and we remained that way for several minutes until my wife couldn't take it anymore.

"Fucking Americans," Natalia said indignantly, the humidity in her breath condensing in the air. "If you're not overcomplicating the simplest things, you're making a mess of them."

I shrugged and dropped my duffel to the ground beside our other luggage. "He said he'd be here. I've never known him to be late before."

"There's a first time for everything," Natalia stated. "This isn't good, Q. We have a highly specific itinerary, and it's imperative we adhere to it. This is a big job for us."

"It's a *huge* job for us," I said. "And you don't have to lecture me about it. I'm just as invested as you."

Natalia sighed, turning to face me. "I'm sorry. I know he's your friend. There's just so many details riding on this, and we've allowed him so much in terms of leeway. I hope we can trust him."

"He's more than a friend. And I trust him as much as I trust you."

As Natalia pouted and folded her arms over her chest, a freshly washed black Volkswagen Touareg with fully tinted windows pulled up in a flash in front of us.

No sooner did it come to a tire-screeching halt, managing to snag the attention of two Metro Washington Airports Authority police officers behind us, the passenger door opened to expose the pristine, vacant, leather insides of the SUV.

Jonathon Rockland, an old friend from my agency days, ducked his head low and waved to me as the new-vehicle scent tugged at my nose. "Sorry I'm late. Traffic was a bitch. All of Northern Virginia has transformed into the commuting scene from *Office Space*."

While Natalia continued to stew, I decided it best not to offer a reply. I didn't want to give off the indication that I was making light of the situation—even though I didn't think it was anything worth getting distraught over.

Jonathon popped the rear hatch and I packed the luggage in. Natalia helped herself inside to the rear seat, and I stepped into the passenger compartment. Once inside with the door closed, my nose detected something pungent enough to overpower the new-car scent. One glance back at my wife told me she could smell it too.

"I probably should've had you guys take the metro in," Jon said while wiping his nose and thumbing his thin yet well-shaped beard. "Traffic around here is…I don't know," he chuckled and added, "it's fucking impossible."

I watched him for a moment while he fretted more

than what was usual for him. His attire was wrinkled and in complete disarray, almost as if he'd slept in it. His eyes were glassy and sunken in, and his movements, though deliberate, were delayed.

"Jon?" I asked.

"Yeah?"

"Are you drunk?"

He turned to me, offering a look of both indifference and denial. His eyebrows lowered. "Um…I'm sorry. Did you just ask if I was…drunk?"

I nodded. "That's what I asked you."

He nodded once and turned away. "I see," he muttered, thumbing his beard and sending a glance out his window. "It's nice to see you, too."

"Are you going to answer my question?"

He chuckled, then mumbled softly to himself nearly repeating my words. "Heh…am I going to answer his question…"

"Well? Are you?"

Jon cocked his head, casually nodded once and then slowly nodded again. "Yep," he said. "Pretty much."

"Pretty much…what?"

"I'm pretty much drunk."

"Jesus Christ!" Natalia bellowed from the back seat. "Are you fucking kidding me right now? It's not even eight in the morning!"

"All things being equal, I never paid too much attention to the time of day with regard to drinking,"

Jon said, followed by a semi-maniacal, overenthusiastic chuckle, one that had become one of his signature traits. "By the way, it's nice to finally meet the missus. I'm Jon Roc—"

"Go fuck yourself," Natalia growled. "But before you do so, kindly pull the vehicle over and let us the hell out."

"Whoa…whoa…whoa!" Jon cried, his hand motioning palm down in the air as if trying to fan a small fire. "Calm down there, little lady. Everything here is under control. We are on schedule and on point. The weather is looking great, and we're about to catch us some big fish in the next couple of days. There's nothing to be upset about or worry over, I assure you."

My mind raced with astonishment. I couldn't believe Jon was drunk. I was blown away that he'd just called Natalia 'little lady'. If she was irritated with him for being late, and irate over finding out he was intoxicated, there was little doubt in my mind that she'd now crossed the boundary of outrage. And that, by and large, wasn't a good thing for anyone in proximity with her.

I turned around to take in the view of Natalia's impending wrath and make every attempt at de-escalation; and hopefully, save Jonathon's life in the process. I presumed—well, hoped that she wouldn't choose to kill him while he was driving, but I wasn't entirely sure. "Natalia, please calm down," I pled with a hand held up in protest. I turned back to Jon. "And, dude, you have some serious explaining to do. We have a very long, grueling set of days ahead of us. Why in the hell are you drunk right now?"

After a pause, Jonathon tilted his head and shrugged. "Why in the hell not? Anymore, I tend to stay this way."

"Drunk, you mean?"

"Yes, drunk, I mean."

"Okay, have you turned into some sort of alcoholic now or something?"

He chuckled. "I've always been 'some sort of alcoholic or something', Quinn. It just so happens that as of late, I've become pretty damn good at it."

"And that means what, exactly?"

"Well, it means…hardly anyone even notices."

"I noticed as soon as I got in the car with you," I argued.

"Consider my husband's impression echoed from the 'little lady' in the back seat," Natalia quipped.

Jonathon chuckled slightly and followed it with a frivolous grin, which exposed his full set of perfectly white teeth. "Okay, well, I guess the two of you are the exceptions, then. Everything's relative."

Natalia cursed under her breath in her native language. "Quinn, seriously? I know this person is your friend, but you can't possibly take him in earnest right now. We can't move forward like this."

I waited a moment to see if Jonathon planned on

offering yet another impromptu ill-witted response, and used the time to gauge his driving. He was just pulling into the morning commuter traffic on the eastbound lane of the Dulles Toll Road. Scooting past car after car, he merged across four lanes and into the HOV lane with grace. If he was drunk, which I was more than certain he was, both by the smell and by his own admission, I couldn't tell by his driving.

"Did something happen?" I finally asked. "Something bad…that made you want to drink like this?"

"By something bad, could you mean life?" Jon asked almost rhetorically. "Because if that's what you mean, then the answer's hell yes."

"What are you talking about?"

"Life happens every day, Quinn. It happens to everyone, but it hates me. It loathes me. Life makes me drink like this."

"You're not kidding…"

"You're goddamn right I'm not kidding!" Jon said with a forceful tone and an even more forceful nod as his face hardened.

Natalia's indignant voice from the back seat responded, "Far be it from me to judge, but I believe you are what most proud, masculine Americans refer to as a 'grown-ass man', and life is what you make of it. You've obviously made a conscious decision to turn yours into a twenty-four-hour-a-day stupor."

"Life is a lie," Jonathon stated. "It's a big piece of

shit sold to us as something amazing…but in the end, it's just one big fucking lie. It's invention…and propaganda…falsehoods…and an endless highway of bullshit." He reached over my lap to the glove box and opened it to expose a half-empty plastic bottle of Aristocrat vodka. Pulling it out, he twisted the top off and took an exceedingly large swig from it, then wiped his mouth on the back of his hand and handed the bottle to me. "It's also pain," he added. "A lot of pain. And this numbs the pain. And if I drink enough of it, it even takes it away."

I looked down at the bottle, fully expecting him to take it back into custody and finish it off after that tirade. "Do you want me to drive?"

"No, thanks, buddy. I'm okay," he replied firmly, his face beginning to soften. "Think what you want, but I got this."

"Thinking what I want is irrelevant. We didn't come here for a social gathering or an intervention."

"Meaning…"

"Meaning I—*we* need assurances, Jon," I said. "And so far, I'm not getting the warm-and-fuzzies from you today."

Jon smiled and gestured his head back at Natalia. "That's okay. I don't think she is, either," he said, then turned to me and slapped my leg, a solemn look befalling him. His voice dropped to just above a whisper. "Everything is already set up. It's handled. It's solid, just as on point as anything I've worked on for you before. I would never let my brother down. The same goes for my brother's wife."

I reached forward and set the bottle of vodka back into the glove box. When I heard him utter the word *brother*, I was tempted for a second to take a drink and maybe talk things through with him. The profile of a Glock pistol nestled between some papers and the Volkswagen's owner's manual brought me back to the here and now.

"That's for you, by the way," Jon said, pointing his index finger at the nine-millimeter handgun. "I imagine they didn't let you bring yours with you on the flight."

I took hold of the weapon, performed a press-check, and released the magazine into my opposite hand to verify the reflections of all fifteen hollow-point rounds through the witness holes. "Yeah. The TSA is kind of funny about that." It was a fourth-generation Glock 19, the exact weapon I normally carried, less the custom barrel, raised sights, and suppressor. "So where are we headed first?"

"The Mayflower Hotel," Jon said proudly. "I took the liberty of reserving both presidential suites, so we'll have the whole club level to ourselves. The rooms are amazing, and I have a feeling you guys will enjoy them. They even have a terrace."

"Sounds expensive," Natalia hissed, the sarcasm dripping from her lips. "How considerate of you."

"Nothing but the best for my friends," Jon said, not detecting her tone.

"I wasn't aware this op had a carte blanche budget," Natalia snapped back. "Why the commercial flight, then?"

Jon inhaled, sucking air through his teeth. "I never gave it much thought, just figured any method to get you here was as good as any. I'm sorry, were the seats not comfortable?"

"The seats were fine. But a private flight wouldn't have necessitated passports and a voyage through customs."

"You're right. And like I said, I'm sorry," Jon relented, then continued. "So, after we get settled, we'll have a few hours to kill. We can wine and dine and take in the town for a while if you like. Our man is sched-uled to meet us at the DC Improv at twenty hundred hours sharp."

"The DC Improv?" Natalia probed.

"Yeah. It's an improvisational comedy clu—"

"I know what it is," Natalia broke in. She was on a roll now. "I'm curious as to why you thought a location like that would be suitable for a meeting of this magnitude."

Jon shrugged and looked over to me, as if wanting me to answer for him.

Regrettably, I had nothing to offer. "It's a legitimate question," I said.

Jon smiled, his teeth gleaming. "Indeed it is. The answer's pretty simple, actually," he uttered. "Because…it's fucking funny!"

While Jon laughed maniacally at his attempt at a comedic punch line, I couldn't help but chuckle along with him.

Natalia wasn't amused.

When Jon saw her face in the rearview mirror, he knew instantly that she didn't get the joke. "I'm kidding…I'm kidding, sorry," Jon said, his laughter slowly losing tempo. "Actually, it's where he wanted to meet."

I rotated around upon hearing Natalia let out a brief sigh coupled with a faint giggle. But, no sooner did I get her into my peripheral did her scowl return. I knew I heard it, though. Maybe she was starting to come around…but I doubted it.

"So we'll ice break and enjoy a couple of drinks in the main hall before we move into the private lounge, which will be cordoned off for us," Jon continued. "I have a crew working security there tonight, so we won't be bothered. We'll discuss particulars and concerns—if you have any."

"As long as the money is *where* it needs to be *when* it needs to be, there shouldn't be any issues," I said.

"The same goes for our safety net," Natalia said, "assuming one exists."

"It's in play," Jon assured her. "I have fallback positions and safe houses set up in multiple locations around the city, and various outs established for you both. This isn't my first rodeo."

"Nor mine," Natalia countered. "And I'm sure I don't have to disclose what's at stake if we're screwed over, even to the slightest degree."

Jon leaned over and shot me a glance. Whispering, he said, "Your wife is a hottie, bro. No doubt about it. But she's…really intense."

"Yeah, I know."

He hesitated. "Kind of fiery, too."

"You have no idea."

Jon nodded. "Or maybe I do. I know a threat when I hear one. Listen…I am *not* going to screw you guys over. You do know that, right?"

I nodded. "I do. But I'm not the one you need to convince. Still, irrespective of that, I'd take her warning at face value, or greater."

"Are you saying she's gonna kill me?" He chuckled over his undertone, acting as though he couldn't care less. "Because I don't have time for that shit tonight. Actually, I might have a date later."

I nodded slightly. "If that were her intention, she'd have the advantage. And, not to mention, a motive."

Jon pulled away, nodded and looked up into his rearview mirror at Natalia's reflection. "Understood."

FOUR

DC Improv Comedy Club, 1140 Connecticut Ave NW, Washington, DC
Monday, March 24, 6:55 p.m. EDT
Nihayat al'ayam minus 77 hours, 5 minutes

While we waited for our meeting to kick off at the comedy club, Natalia and I found entertainment at the Sauf Haus Bier Hall just up the street. Our headliner was an immature, rather presumptuous, German-born American uproot bartender who wore his lederhosen a bit too tightly. We thought it would be a good idea to take the edge off before dealing with business, so we shared a tall glass mug of Paulaner Hefeweizen, which to me, tasted almost as good as it had when I'd enjoyed a liter of it at the *Paulanergarten* in Munich several years ago.

We each also ordered one of the pub's warmed German-style pretzels, a menu item that Natalia said tasted only slightly better than *Kuh Scheiße*, or cow shit. I'd never sampled cow shit before, and pretzels weren't one of my go-to cuisines. Still, I had been forced to agree with her nonetheless. It was general knowledge that food items concocted to resemble authentic German fare in the States were rarely able to compare.

We'd taken Jonathon along with us, but lost track of him several minutes post-arrival. A relatively attractive brunette in heels and pink-framed spectacles caught his eye after his third or fourth straight-up Ketel One martini. Initially, I'd gone looking for him, but soon thought better of it, deciding it best to allocate my attention to the small segment of free time I had with my wife before going kinetic yet again. I knew him well enough, despite the new venture of intemperance he'd been subscribing to, that he wouldn't let me down. At least, not intentionally. Trying to get Natalia to understand that foundation, however, was a battle not even worth fighting.

While we walked down the chewing-gum-ridden concrete staircase to the basement-level location the Improv called home, Natalia reached for my hand and I took hers into mine willfully. At first, it almost felt like we were on a date, something she and I hadn't done in a number of years.

At that moment, the black formal dress she was wearing took me back to an earlier time and to a better, more exciting place; and I found myself unable to take my eyes off her. I could even feel my heart fluttering a bit. We were the same two people then, much as we were today, sans the novelty of a new connection. I remembered how we used to try so hard to impress each other. I'd always been articulate and well-spoken, but being around her had been daunting for me at first, and oftentimes, I'd stumbled over words. There were even times when I'd forgotten I'd even possessed a vocabulary. I'd wanted to win her over so badly then, the harder I tried, the more I failed. I'd only succeeded when I'd stopped trying so damned hard to figure out the ebb and flow and just allowed the waves to carry me in.

"You know, we never do this," I said.

Natalia turned to me, her expression almost beaming. "We never do what?"

"This," I said, adding a body gesture I hoped was more descriptive than my words.

Natalia smiled and moved closer to me as we approached the tinted glass entrance door. "I know what you're saying. Does it bother you?"

"Yeah, sometimes it does. We're always together though, no matter what we're doing. We just never take any quality time for ourselves."

"Away from the work thing?"

"Yeah."

Natalia smiled. "Q, did you ever consider that maybe we've just redefined our relationship over the years in substitute?"

Good question. Maybe we had. I didn't know for certain, but I didn't chance a response. I didn't want it to sound like an admission, and I knew it would.

Natalia stopped me before I reached for the door handle, and pulled both of my hands close to her. "After this job, you and I are done, Q," she said softly, yet decisively. "After this...I promise you, it will only be us. It will only be *about* us. And we can spend the rest of our lives doing whatever we want...away from this life."

"I know," I said, still unable to take my eyes off her. She looked incredible in that dress, but I imagined it looked even better lying in a mound at her ankles. "I just got caught up in the moment."

Natalia leaned in and kissed me. When she pulled away, her eyes narrowed, and she set her jaw in place. "There'll be plenty of time for us, but we have to get this done first. So let's focus. I need your A game."

"I'm your MVP. You always have my A game."

"I know," she said. "But we cannot afford to trifle with this one. This is serious, and we need to be prepared for anything—call or fold."

I nodded in recognition. That damn Paulaner was

hitting me more than I expected. "I just hope the hell Jon shows up," I said lightheartedly.

Natalia rolled her eyes. "Don't even get me started."

Upon walking inside and into the dimly lit vestibule, a young, vibrant female employee with caked-on makeup strode directly up to us and introduced herself while toying with her teased-up sandy blond hair. "Good evening, and welcome to the DC Improv," she said in a voice that bordered on screeching. "My name's Brigette, but please call me Bridge, like Brooklyn Bridge. I'll be taking care of you tonight." She waved a translucent black plastic clipboard within inches of her face. "Can I have your names, please?"

I peeked over at Natalia and caught her eyes, which would've been near bulging in surprise if she hadn't perfected her impassivity over the expanse of her career.

Remembering that our passports and IDs had made the two of us members of the Donovan family during this trip, I smiled and responded in kind. "Donovan. I'm Joel. This is my wife, Kate."

Natalia extended her hand outward semi-courteously to Brigette. "Kathrine."

Brigette shook Natalia's—I mean Kathrine's hand with a huge smile. After finding our names on her roster, she said, "Well, it's a pleasure to meet you both. Now, let me show you to your seats and we can get this party started! The two of you are on our VIP list this evening, so we have some complimentary swag for you. It's a full house tonight, but it's going to be great fun for everyone, so sit back and enjoy, okay? And make sure to let me know if there's anything I can do for you."

"Marvelous," the wife responded, in an almost perfect emulation of our hostess's supremely effervescent voice.

I had to admit, the mockery was well warranted. Where the hell were we? Disneyland?

We followed Brigette from the vestibule around a corner and into an equally dimly illuminated main showroom, complete with a rather miniscule stage in the front of the house. The areas near the stage were already borderline overcrowded with folks, but the area to which we were being led was adequately spacious. I assumed it to be the VIP area Brigette had alluded to.

Our hostess motioned to a round high-top table in the corner with four chairs propped against it. "And here we are," she announced, arranging the chairs. "Is there anything I can get the two of you to start you off? We've got appetizers, entrees, and a full bar of top-shelf—"

"Water," Natalia declared. "Just water, thank you."

Brigette cocked her head, looking dejected. "Are you sure? We have some great drink specials tonight, and happy hour is extended for our beloved VIPs."

"Yes, Bridge, I'm sure. Water, please," Natalia reiterated.

"Okay, water it is," Brigette said unhappily with a sigh. "And for you, Mr. Donovan?"

"I'll have a cup of coffee."

Another unhappy look. "Coffee?"

"Yes. Water and coffee, Brigette," Natalia said, a note of impatience in her voice. "Nothing else. Off with you."

Brigette hung her head. "Cream and sugar?"

I nodded and offered her a smile just before she shuffled away, almost in a sprint. The wife and I then took our seats, picking spots that would put both our backs to the wall.

Natalia sighed. "Why the hell does every girl in the world feel the need to so obnoxiously flirt with you?"

"She wasn't flirting."

"Oh, really?"

"Yeah...she's just young...and vivacious."

"She needs to learn how to properly do her makeup. And she's not vivacious."

"Okay. What is she, then?"

Natalia shot her eyes at me, her eyebrows elevated. "A whore." A pause before she continued. "What would you have done if she'd been a sparrow...sent specifically to seduce and extract information from you?"

I did my best to ignore the remarks while taking note of them. With regard to our present dialog, her response was predictable, but even Natalia recognized that for one, Brigette was far from being my type, and two, I had never been the easiest person to break. I had the scars to prove it.

Several minutes passed. Brigette never returned, but she did send a male subordinate over to deliver our drinks. I dumped a couple of packets of sugar into my coffee and disregarded the creamer, leaving it black. Surprisingly enough, it didn't taste too awful. Venues such as these were inclined to take more notice of beverages they stood to profit the most from, and coffee wasn't one of them.

More time passed. It was now ten minutes after eight, and the show had already started, and still no Jonathon. I was beginning to get worried, but Natalia had surpassed that notion long ago and was primed and ready to freak out. Just as she was ready to head out the door and pull me along with her, we both caught sight of two figures approaching from around the corner. One of them was Jon. The other, who lagged just behind, was a tall, dark-skinned man in a beige, double-breasted, well-pressed business suit. He was wearing a kufi cap and had a thick black beard, far from what could be considered unkempt.

I tapped Natalia on her thigh. "Two contacts dead ahead. Here we go."

Natalia didn't respond. She lifted her water glass to her mouth delicately and took a small sip from it, her eyes never leaving the unfamiliar face as it closed the distance. There was no doubt in my mind she had her other hand, the one I couldn't see, on a blade of some kind. She was coiled like a serpent in its element, equipped and ready to strike.

When Jon reached our table, he offered his companion a chair. I stood immediately and made my way between him and the other man.

Jon put his mouth close to my ear to overcome the ambient noise. "This is Ammar." He put his mouth to the other man's ear while gesturing to me, whispering something to him I couldn't discern.

After a moment, the tall Middle Eastern man held out a hand and tendered a closed-mouth smile. "It is an honor to finally meet you," he said, an Arabic inflection coating his words. "My name is Ammar. Ammar Yamin."

I took his hand into mine and we shook while taking turns evaluating each other. "Pleasure," I said, though I couldn't tell if he could hear me or not. I held a hand across the table in Natalia's direction. "My wife…"

"Yes…yes. I know full well who you are, madam," Ammar said, and reached over the table to offer his hand while rotating his body away from me.

Natalia produced her signature smile, warming the space and accepting his hand. I breathed an internal sigh of relief. She was back, utterly relaxed and fully in control once more. Was she really drinking water?

During a break in the laughter and clapping around us, Natalia said, "*Masa'a al khayr*," with distinct attention to the intonation of her Arabic. "*As salam aleykum.*"

Our visitor's smile became grand upon hearing his native language being spoken. He thawed quickly, as did his reply. "*Wa aleykum as salam.*"

After we all took our seats, a few moments passed while the four of us shared glances and approachable smiles amidst the crowd noise. Soon, however, the looks on our faces morphed into something much more sobering even the comedians on stage couldn't interrupt, dissuade, or discontinue in spite of their antics.

Brigette managed to surface again to bring Jon a beverage of clear, chilled liquid in a rocks glass with no ice—which I assumed to be vodka. She went to offer Ammar a drink and was instantly shot down, though he did thank her for her time. Ammar was either playing the part of a devout Muslim or was in full conscience with his faith and, as such, didn't partake of or consume intoxicants. This just wasn't going to be a good night in the VIP section for young Bridge.

After draining his drink in short order, Jon leaned over to Ammar and whispered something to him, to which Ammar responded with an acknowledging, yet fleeting nod.

Jon then turned to me and beckoned fervently. "Slight venue alteration." He thumbed his beard and casually rose to his feet while his eyes darted around nervously.

With Jon leading the way through a shadowy corridor, the rest of us followed him into the area designated as the private lounge. We passed a half-dozen sentries along the way, all of them operatives: paras, mercs, and the like. They couldn't have had a decade of military or tactical experience in total, combined between them. And if they were attempting to blend in, they weren't trying very hard. I sneered at each of them as colorfully as possible when I passed. If they stood out, I wanted them to know it.

Upon entry into the lounge, which was vastly more subdued than our previous location, we found our seats at a large round mahogany table centered in a red-carpeted room. Upon taking his seat, Ammar pulled out a bulky dark-brown cigar and ignited it. He pulled a tablet PC from the internal pocket of his jacket, placed it in the middle of the table, tapped the screen with his index finger, and watched it come to life.

He smiled from the corner of his mouth and took a long puff off his cigar before pointing his finger informally at Natalia and then at me. "I must begin by saying that I am slightly overwhelmed sitting here." Ammar's English was broken but well pronounced, and had an Arabic drawl coating it. "I am, as you say, starstruck."

I chuckled, twisting my coffee mug around nonchalantly with my fingers. "That's flattering. But we're not celebrities, Mr. Yamin."

"You shouldn't be so modest. After all, I'm convening with two of the most highly prized assassins in all of the world. It is a great honor for me." A pause. "And please, call me Ammar."

Natalia smiled, but didn't say anything. She sat as comfortably as she always had in situations such as these. Her legs were crossed, her fingers interlaced, and her hands were nestled in her lap. Her resilient, feminine posture was damn near faultless. *La Femme Nikita*, eat your heart out.

Ammar continued, his finger now withdrawn, his eyes wide and fixated on my wife. "You are the one with the nickname Stiletto, are you not?"

Natalia nodded her answer but didn't modify her posture, nor did she offer any change to her relaxed expression.

"I am told the Russians call you *tikhaya smert*, or silent death," he said. "Is that true?"

Natalia's poker face was strong tonight. She didn't waver. "I've been called a lot of things," she purred.

Ammar nodded and puffed his cigar. "Then it is true," he said with a crooked smile, then turned to face me. "And you. You are the one known by many as Azrael. The angel of death."

"While I'm not certain, I've been told the word translates to 'whom God helps' in Hebrew."

Ammar nodded passively and spoke with animated hands. "To the men fighting for their countries in the war-ravaged regions of the Middle East, places in which, I am certain you are familiar, you *are* the angel of death. Just so you know." A pause. "Your reputation precedes you, Mr. Azrael."

I nodded in return. "Consider me mindful…as well as diminutively flattered, once again."

"Very well," he said, and took another puff of his cigar, then pointed to the table. "Everything you need is there. Please take a few moments to study what I have brought for you to see."

I reached for the tablet before anyone else even made the attempt. I tapped the only folder icon I saw on the screen, and after a quick animation, it opened to reveal an assortment of files—both images and documents. One of the photos had been titled 'primary'. I tapped it, and a photo of a man of Arabic descent appearing in his mid-fifties with a white beard came into view on the screen.

"That is Khaleel el-Sattar," Ammar said, then hesitated. "He is your primary target. In other photos, you will find his wife, Saheera, as well as his daughter, Maisara, and his son, Haashid."

"Children weren't part of the deal," Jon inserted, his hand held up in a halting gesture.

Ammar nodded. "I know this, and my benefactors are not asking for them to be. Our only requirement for fulfillment of the contract is the primary target be terminated. How you choose to satisfy that task is entirely at your discretion."

I finished perusing the images in the folder and passed the tablet to Natalia. I'd never forget those faces, just like hundreds of others before them. Among my many gifts, or curses, I'd been bestowed with a vividly eidetic memory. A sniper by trade, it was both an advantageous and convenient attribute.

I motioned to the tablet and roused Ammar's attention. "Who is Khaleel?"

Ammar didn't respond immediately. He rolled his cigar around inside the glass ashtray, making a conical sculpture out of the ashes clinging to the tip. "Khaleel el-Sattar is an imam, the most recent to be christened a sheikh, a title of great honor to which no Muslim has been designated since Osama bin Laden," he explained. "He is currently one of the uppermost ranking leaders of the Islamic State of Iraq and al-Sham, or, as you Westerners commonly refer to it, ISIS. He is a true Islamic fundamentalist, regarded by many of his followers as a prophet. But perhaps most importantly, Khaleel is a direct descendent of the Quraysh…predestined to become the next caliph."

Jonathon shook his head in refusal and held up a finger. He almost chuckled. "You're lying, bro," he said casually. "There hasn't been a legitimate caliphate declared anywhere on the planet for more than a century. Tell us a new story."

"I am afraid...that you are misinformed, my friend," Ammar said, turning his attention to Jon. "Or perhaps oblivious, much like the preponderance of the intelligence community. I understand it is easy to turn a blind eye, but that is exactly how Islam has been able to multiply, propagate, and overtake lands as easily as it has over the years." A pause. "There are thousands of enclaves throughout the world—even now in your own country, where Islamic law has become the rule of the land and non-Muslims and white men such as yourselves are forbidden. Most, if not all, of these provinces are now radicalized. Those which are not are destined for this and soon will be. All but few have pledged *baya'a*.

"There are jihadist training camps in hundreds of locations throughout your country, and the threat of jihad has been waiting quietly by your doorstep for decades. The assertion of an American caliphate is close at hand. All of what I am telling you is verifiably accurate, yet no one in America seems the least bit troubled by it." Ammar smirked. "Too many pressing items to worry about on reality television, I am guessing."

Jon looked rattled. He'd brought his empty glass along with him, and I guessed it possible that he now needed a refill.

In the interim, I quizzed, "What exactly is a prominent ISIS operative like el-Sattar doing in the United States? There's no denying the country is one big surveillance state. It's been on a twenty-four-hour-a-day terror-alert standby since 9/11. Doesn't that seem odd to you? Or at the very least, imprudent?"

Ammar looked puzzled. "Forgive me, Mr. Azrael, but I was under the impression you performed your obligations in exchange only for financial compensation. I was not aware you required further detail, or motivation, for that matter."

"We don't. But occasionally, supplementary details can be comforting. Especially for a job this…significant."

Ammar lowered his head reverently at a slight angle before returning his stare. "As you wish," he said. "He is in the country to convene with regional jihadist leaders. It is a confidential meeting, one that occurs only once every five years. Before leaving Iraq, he arranged for temporary Kuwaiti visas for himself and his family under the assumed name al-Kamel. We imagine he brought along his wife and children to aid his cover, and we also believe he will use them as human shields if any attempt is to be made on his life."

"Great." Jonathon spoke up cynically, snapping his fingers at a passing waiter to order a new drink. "Kids and machine guns. That's always awesome."

Ammar tilted his head. "I never said he was a man of honor."

"False credentials, willingness to use his own family as walking bullet-catchers or not, he's taking quite a chance being here," I said.

"Khaleel is a true believer, Mr. Azrael. As such, and like all other radical Islamists, he is unafraid of martyrdom, and not frightened by much else."

"So by terminating el-Sattar, we'd be cutting the head off the serpent. Is that it?"

"Khaleel is the one man with full control of all Islamic State sleeper cells within US borders," Ammar said. "So in a word, yes. You would be eliminating the one man with the ability to order them out of hibernation. You'd be given another chance to once again serve your country, Mr. Azrael."

I chortled. "You speak those words as if you think I somehow give a shit."

Ammar held up a hand. "I do not understand. Have I insulted you?"

"No—not insulted. Underestimated. If you assumed my patriotism would serve as some master key to disengage my resolve and close this deal, you'd be considerably mistaken." I paused and stirred in my seat while Ammar's face hardened. I could tell he wasn't pleased with my response as he sized me up with his eyes over the table.

I waited a long while before continuing, allowing him to agitate. "So why use us? el-Sattar is obviously a national security threat to nations all over the globe.

To me, this seems more suited for a military or sanctioned overt operation. Why use private assassins to off him?"

Ammar took a long drag from his cigar, the tension in his face showing. "Because doing so in the open would produce…unpleasant implications, Mr. Azrael. el-Sattar's security is an army of men. Their skills are substantial, not easy to overcome or penetrate. Imagine a man…one with eyes in the back of his head. And imagine the legion of security that surrounds him, all having the same. Getting to him necessitates a level of stealth not many in military are capable of. You and your wife are renowned for being the best at this manner of infiltration. This is essential, because his death cannot and must not be misconstrued as being politically motivated. My benefactors want him dead, but they do not wish to start a war."

"So I take it he'll be rather difficult to find?" I asked.

Ammar reached for the tablet and tapped the screen a few times, then returned it to the table. I looked down to see the screen had become a topographical map of the area. A blinking icon of a bull's-eye not far away also caught my eye.

Natalia and I leaned in to get a closer look while Ammar explained further. Jonathon didn't move, his attention locked only on the drink in his hand. I assumed that to mean he'd seen this tech before and had

UNTIL NOTHING REMAINS 73

probably been tracking el-Sattar himself for some time before this arrangement had been set up.

"Khaleel was implanted with a nanotechnology transponder many years ago while under dental anesthesia," Ammar said. "The device transmits encrypted data on a spread of frequencies difficult to detect, and even has its own countermeasures. Very few are aware it even exists, and as you can see, it is still very much operational."

I picked up the tablet and used my thumb and index finger to zoom in on the blinking icon. It had been a while, but I recognized the compound by its location off Chain Bridge Road, just above the Potomac River.

I switched to the bird's-eye satellite view to verify, then suddenly felt confused. "Are you certain this is accurate? Your device shows him at the Saudi embassy in McLean."

Jon set his drink down and turned, astonished. "The...fuck? The one near Langley?"

"That's the only one I know of."

"Well, what the hell is he doing there, Ammar?" Jon asked.

"Gentlemen, please," Ammar said, not hesitating to respond. "I am afraid I do not possess all of the answers you desire me to have. But what I do have for you is a contract...for the termination of Khaleel el-Sattar in exchange for the sum of twenty million dollars, half of which will be deposited into an account of your choosing following an amicable conclusion of this meeting."

This was starting to *not* make sense. And if it wasn't making sense to me, I knew Natalia had long ago established it as bullshit. If everything Ammar said was true, el-Sattar was a well-known and identifiable enemy—a threat to populations, governments, and entire nations. Why, then, was he here? And why was he at the Saudi Arabian embassy instead of a mega-mosque or some ISIS training camp in backwoods rural Virginia, or a sharia-ruled no-go zone in Dearborn? The Saudis, for all intents and purposes, were our allies. If Ammar wasn't lying, that meant the Saudis were colluding with el-Sattar, and that meant involvement with ISIS.

What a mind-fuck this was becoming. And we hadn't even shot or stabbed anyone yet.

I turned my head to gauge Natalia's expression and could tell she was having second thoughts about this op. At one point, she reached for the tablet and studied the screen for an instant, though still said nothing. She sat motionless in her chair, in her smoldering black dress, still owning a perfect poker face.

Ammar began to get restless after about a minute and a half of uncomfortable silence. "I am sorry, but I feel as though we are running out of time," he said. "Are the terms I have presented acceptable to you, or should I have another team consider our proposal?"

"Another team?" Jon quizzed.

"Yes, of course," Ammar said. "We have arranged for several fallback options. Obviously, we prefer to use the best available to us. That is why I agreed to this meeting. But I do not have all night." He tapped his cigar, sat back in his chair, and folded his arms over his chest, then produced a look of perturbation as if he were counting the seconds away.

Natalia, even now, wouldn't look at me. She was obviously still busy churning over the good and the bad in her mind, and I wasn't about to answer for us. I'd always left the final decision up to her. If it were up to me, the verdict would've always been an emphatic yes.

Just when I thought she'd gone completely catatonic, she uncrossed her legs and leaned charmingly forward onto the table, her elegance immediately catching our Middle Eastern acquaintance's attention. "Are there any other pertinent details that you might like to provide us, Ammar? Anything that might aid the efficiency of the operation?"

"I am sorry, Mrs. Stiletto," Ammar said with a smirk. "I have given you all I have to offer. There is, of course, a list of motives for his execution, but those are confidential items that my benefactors have ordered me not to discuss under any circumstance."

Natalia smiled and leaned forward slightly in her seat. "Even benefactors have benefactors," she said. "And without money, the world stops turning. Doesn't it, Ammar? My guess is some conglomerate stands to gain a lot of wherewithal from this."

Ammar smiled and shrugged. "Perhaps you are correct, Mrs. Stiletto. Even still, I am not at liberty to discuss."

"You don't have to," Natalia said. "We accept your terms."

Ammar smiled broadly. "I am very pleased to hear that."

Jon looked back at me and I nodded the go-ahead to him. He pulled out a small piece of paper that had our numbers written on it in graphite, placed it on the table, and slid it over to Ammar with a single finger. Ammar palmed it and, after a few seconds, pulled out a cell phone and made a call.

A few minutes passed while Ammar spoke unintelligibly in Arabic to whomever was on the other side of the call. When the call was completed, he placed his phone on the table and gave me a quizzical look. "Would you like to verify?"

I reached into my pocket for the burner I'd brought along and presented it for him to see. "I hope you don't take this as an insult."

Ammar smiled and tapped the screen on his phone, ending the call.

When I heard ringing commence on the burner, I lifted the phone to my ear and waited. It picked up on the fourth ring.

"*EFG Zürich. Passcode, please,*" a female voice with a Swiss-German accent on the other end said.

"Gun play."

"*Very well,*" she said. "*Please authenticate. Zulu. Gunpowder. Lightning.*"

"Foxtrot. Hollow point. Hurricane."

"*Authentication confirmed. Good morning, Mr. Barrett. My name is Lara. How can I be of service?*"

"Confirmation on most recent transfer."

A moment went by while the sound of fingers tapping a keyboard came over the phone's speaker. She returned soon after and confirmed Ammar's deposit was intact and safe. The deal had been made. I thanked Lara, terminated the call, and shut off the phone directly after. "Everything checks out," I announced, making a mental note to burn the phone when we left.

Ammar nodded. "It is settled, then. Upon proven completion of your task, the remaining balance will be wired to the identical account, unless you specify otherwise. Now, you have had questions for me and I have only one question for you." He paused and leaned forward, his eyes on me. "How soon can we expect to hear from you?"

I shrugged, which deferred his gaze to Natalia.

"Within seventy-two hours," she said resolutely.

Ammar looked surprised. He waited for Natalia to backpedal a moment. "You're serious?"

Natalia displayed a look of pure unadulterated

certainty. "As a heart attack. So long as the target remains in-country and doesn't suddenly disappear from the radar, in less than three days he'll be deleted, and the contract will be fulfilled on our end. And then you and your benefactors need only concern yourselves with the one final contractual obligation."

Ammar nodded. "It will be done."

FIVE

Winchester, Virginia
Wednesday, March 26, 2:30 p.m. EDT
Nihayat al'ayam minus 33 hours, 30 minutes

The sun's dazzling glare off the freshly waxed clearcoat on his girlfriend's pristine cherry red Mustang GT caught Chris's eye instantly when he exited the school. Jessi's parents had bought it for her a couple of weeks ago as a pregraduation gift, even though she and Chris were still both juniors and had the remainder of the year in addition to a full senior year before that event was scheduled to transpire. He guessed, as with most things her parents did to spoil and appease her, they had gotten it for her out of guilt for all the time they spent away, due to their demanding careers and near-Hollywoodesque social lives.

Chris adjusted the weight of his backpack and ran his fingers through his bangs, which were thick and especially wavy today, exactly as Jessi preferred them to be. It had been her suggestion for Chris to have his hair styled this way: heavy in the front and trimmed short and layered in the back, a common fashion often seen on the crowns of lead singers in popular boy bands.

Chris strolled to the car and watched as the passenger-side window rolled down, exposing the sprightly, unblemished, smiling face of his teenage lover, draped on either side by velvety layers of well-kept strawberry-blond hair. He was surprised to see her holding a cigarette. "Jess, you've only had this car for, like, two weeks," he said, reaching for the door handle and taking a seat inside. "And you're already smoking in it?"

Jessi shrugged and took a puff while watching him enter the car. "Smoke, vape, blaze…whatevs. It's my car, isn't it?"

Chris carefully slid his backpack into the gap beside his seat and pushed it into the back seat. "That's not the point I was trying to make. Don't you want to enjoy that new-car scent a little longer?"

Jessi giggled, thin wafts of smoke escaping her nostrils. "I've been smoking since I was twelve. It's not like I could smell it, anyway. Nothing tastes or smells the way it should when you're a career smoker like me, Chris."

"I guess you're right." Chris sighed and buckled his seatbelt. "Thanks for the ride again, by the way. One of these days, I'll repay the favor."

Jessi shifted the car into drive and placed a hand on Chris's thigh, leaning over to kiss him on the cheek. "Baby, it's no problem, I don't mind. Some of us just got it like that. Besides, I didn't just decide to go out with you because of a car or where you lived."

Chris snorted. "Okay, that was original."

"What do you mean by that?"

"Nothing…it just sounded like a line from the *Karate Kid*," Chris said jokingly.

"What?"

"What you just said. It's something that blonde girl —his girlfriend—says in the movie."

"What movie?"

"Never mind." Chris waved her off, hesitating. "I just don't want you to think I'm using you."

Jessi flicked her cigarette carelessly out the window, then rolled it up a few inches as she pulled out of the parking lot, chirping a tire. "Chris, you worry too much about too many things. You need to just live your life and let the chips fall where they may. You don't know the future, none of us do. So why give a shit?"

"Heh…you really want to know why I give a shit?"

"Yeah, seriously. Why do you?"

Chris shrugged. "Probably because the future is important to me, Jess. It's just always been drilled into my head like that. My dad's always pushing me to be ready and think about the future in some way. And I don't mean deciding on college and career stuff, either."

"Well, I think all that's fucking pointless," said Jessi snidely. "I mean, come on, we could all be dead tomorrow because of some crazy catastrophe. Aliens could attack us, or that super volcano caldera thing could explode and kill us all. Or some rampant pandemic could happen that wipes us all out in the blink of an eye. It's so much easier just to live life day-to-day and say to hell with it. Screw the future." She paused, glancing over at him. "It's okay if you don't feel the same, babe. It's not like I'm going to think less of you or anything."

Jessi hung a right on Apple Pie Ridge Road, turned a corner, and pulled to a stop at the intersection with US Route 522. After the light turned green, she hung a left and took an immediate right onto state Route 37, a four-lane freeway that ran along the western outskirts of their hometown.

"Where are we going?" Chris asked. "It's quicker to get to my house the other way or even through town."

Jessi smiled broadly. "Duh, I *know* that. We're not going to your house yet. We're taking a little detour."

Chris turned to her. "What sort of detour?" he asked, his eyes showing apprehension.

"Relax," Jessi said reassuringly. She lifted her phone to eye level and glanced at the screen. "I was texting my cousin Barbie yesterday about our concert plans, and she wants to see the car. So I want to stop over there for a few before I take you home. Is that okay with you?"

"I guess. Wait…what concert?"

Jessi mocked him under her breath. "The huge rave thing tomorrow night at Jiffy Lube pavilion…everybody's going." She peered over at him. "You should go with us."

"With who? Everybody?"

"No! With Barbie and me."

Chris sighed. He began to wonder what his parents would think of those plans. As much fun as he knew it would be, he knew they'd never go for it. Even at the age of seventeen, he hadn't been allowed much in terms of freedom away from home.

His dad wasn't so much the problem. It was his mother, the despot, who'd always been the one to put her foot down. Had it been an afterschool extracurricular project, organized sporting event, or church gathering, she might've offered her go-ahead to this one. But a rave with hundreds of teenage miscreants in attendance? Never in his wildest dreams. "I take it your parents don't mind you going."

"You assume correctly," said Jessi. "You should know by now, my parental units don't give a shit, Chris." She paused to light up another cigarette. "We've been planning this for a month now, and we've got everything we need for a small tailgating party too…I just hope it all fits in the car. I didn't exactly pick this one because of its trunk space. We have food, coolers, a mini grill, cornhole boards, you name it."

"Beer…"

Jessi giggled. "Well, yeah. Can't leave home without the party."

As they drove past the ball fields, Chris considered his options, what few of them there were. "I have practice tomorrow."

"Skip it."

"Sure. Skip it. No problem," Chris jested. "But what about school on Friday?"

Jessi shrugged. "We could just as easily skip school, too. But…I don't think we'll need to."

"Why's that?"

"Because they're already talking about canceling school on Friday."

"Really? For what?"

"Jesus, Chris. You really need to read a newspaper sometime," Jessi sounded off. "It's because of those anti-gun protests. My dad emailed me about them. He said he's heard rumors there could be upwards of several thousand people coming into town. It'll be a nightmare, just like the last time it happened. They'll be marching and holding up signs everywhere and blocking the roads…traffic is going to be screwed. Anyway, Dad said the school board sent out a notice yesterday that they were considering closing schools on Friday in advance—kind of like they do when the weather's too hot or too cold, or when there's an inch of snow on the ground."

"Now that you mention it, I heard my parents talking about it at dinner the other night," Chris said. "I guess I didn't think it was going to be that serious."

"Gun control *is* serious, Chris. People are way pissed now—that's why they're protesting. Guns kill, like, a million people every day, and something has to be done about it before we're all dead."

Chris chuckled and shook his head slightly in amusement. "Jessi, that's preposterous. If a million people died every day, the country's population would be decimated in a little over a year."

Jessi huffed. "Look, I don't want to argue. I know we don't agree on the topic. So let's just not talk about it, okay? Let's get back on the concert train and figure out our plans for the weekend."

Chris's brows elevated. "The concert *does* sound like a lot of fun."

"It's going to be a ridiculous amount of fun. And you should go with us, for real." Jessi rubbed Chris's leg. "I could make it worth your while, you know. We could spend some…quality time. I know how you enjoy that sort of thing."

"How are we supposed to have any alone time with your cousin around?"

"Oh, Chris, stop it. You leave the details up to yours truly. I promise you, baby, I have it covered. The only thing you have to do is say the word that you're going. I might even let you ride shotgun."

Chris leaned over and planted a wet kiss on Jessi's florally perfumed cheek. "If I do come along, my ass is going to be in a sling. So if I make it happen, I'm going to do a lot more than just be right passenger in this beast."

Jessi smirked. "Okay, fine. Fine, *Casanova*. I'll *allow* you to drive. For a few miles or so. On the highway. *Maybe*."

With the Mustang's radio blaring the latest pop music from satellite radio's top-forty channel, it left little room for conversation along the way to Barbie's house. Jessi hung a right at the Opequon exit, turning onto Cedar Creek Grade, and made a left-hand turn on to Jones Road about a mile after. They passed by the Stonebrook subdivision, which for a time, several decades ago, had been one of the more prominent places to live in the county, complete with its own golf course, Olympic-sized swimming pool, and racquetball club. Houses located within were in the upper-middle-class range, very similar in size and property value to that of Chris's family's home.

Chris glanced over at Jessi, who was busily lip-synching to the song currently playing. There was little doubt in his mind that he had lucked out having her as his high school girlfriend. She was probably one of the top five most beautiful girls in his school, and quite possibly in the county, for all he knew. He'd occasionally heard others in his class refer to Jessi as a *dime-piece*, which to members of his generation meant a female whose beauty, even without makeup, ranked a perfect ten. He could only imagine what this cousin of hers might look like, especially with a name like Barbie. She no doubt had been given the name aptly and, therefore, had to have thick flowing blond hair, steel blue eyes, luscious pink lips, an ivory smile, and abundant breasts to go along with the package.

Chris chuckled to himself as his young mind raced through the possibilities, unanchored by inhibitions. Jessi hung a right onto Brookneil Drive and into the ornate rural subdivision, which sat adjacent to Stonebrook.

"Your cousin lives here?" Chris asked while reaching for the volume knob and turning the music down a few clicks. "Is everybody in your family rich?"

Jessi grinned at him, exhaling smoke from her cigarette. "Not everybody. Uncle Ian owns a civil engineering business. He's loaded, but he works his ass off for it, just like my dad does."

Chris squinted. "Yeah, but your dad is a doctor."

"What's that supposed to mean?"

Chris shrugged. "Nothing. It's just the two careers aren't even the slightest bit similar, that's all."

Jessi flicked her half-finished cigarette out the window. "My dad works just as hard as anybody else, Chris. He works so many hours, I hardly ever see him anymore. So do me a favor, okay? Just shut up about it."

Chris held up a hand and apologized as they pulled into the driveway at Barbie's house. The home was much larger than Chris had imagined. It was two stories with a four-car detached garage and a U-shaped drive-way. It looked at least twice as large as his own home. A veranda protruded from what he assumed to be the master bedroom suite overtop the covered cathedral front porch.

"Okay, I don't see her car anywhere. Let's see if this hooker is home yet," Jessi said, holding her hand down on the horn.

After Jessi had honked a handful of times, Chris pulled her hand from the steering wheel. "Okay, that's enough. I'm sure if she's here, she's heard you by now."

Jessi yanked her hand away. "Barbie's bedroom is

in the basement," she said, opening the door and exiting the car. "So maybe not."

"Oh." Chris stepped out of the car slowly and watched as Jessi hopped merrily to the front door and began tapping repetitively on the doorbell button. Before long, the front door opened and a young brunette similar in height to Jessi stepped out.

While she and Jessi embraced, Chris studied her from afar, realizing how wrong his hypothesis regarding her appearance had been. *She doesn't look like any Barbie I've ever seen*, he thought to himself.

Indeed, she didn't. Barbie was slender and muscular, and her skin was radiant and well tanned, perhaps artificially so, considering the winter months were only now coming to an end. Her hair wasn't blond by any means. In fact, it possessed such a darkened hue it almost appeared black, depending on the angle of view. It even had an anomalous sheen to it, which seemed to mirror the sun's rays at times. One thing was for certain, the girl was just as much a perfect ten as Jessi was.

Jessi called to him. "Chris, stop standing there with your tongue hanging out like some *darby*. Get the hell over here and meet my cousin."

Chris waved and nodded, then trotted over, catching a hangdog smile from the brunette. He held out his hand to her. "You must be Barbie. I'm Chris."

Barbie snatched his hand in a surprisingly rigid

grip. She smiled expectantly. "Nice to meet y—wait…
you're Chris Young, aren't you?"

"Yeah, that's me."

"Chris Young…the track star? The state champion
pole-vaulter?"

Chris cocked his head semi-bashfully. He could feel
his cheeks warming. "Yeah, I've won a few times. But I
don't like to brag about it."

Barbie chuckled timidly. "I never imagined you'd
be so modest! If I had as many trophies and ribbons as
you, I'd brag about it." She squeezed his hand before
letting go. "I've seen you in action. You got skills,
Chris. And your team trounces us at almost every meet.
It really is nice to finally meet you…in a noncompeti-
tive venue, that is."

Chris smiled awkwardly. "You too. So…you
compete?"

Barbie's smile faded, and she sent him a cross look.
"Are you saying you don't remember me?"

Chris racked his brain, doing his best to recall her
face. "I'm not trying to sound insulting, but I can't say
I've ever seen you before."

Barbie's lips tightened. "Oh, I see. Too busy
winning first place and being interviewed by reporters
to notice the little people."

"No, it's not that. Seriously. It's just that—"

Barbie offered a reassuring smile. "Chris, it's cool.
I'm fucking with you. And to answer your question,

yes, I compete. I'm a sprinter, but I also do shot put and long jump."

"Okay, that's cool. So, you're varsity?"

The brunette nodded. "Yeah—just nowhere near as good as you are. But I'm working on it. In the gym, hard-core…six days a week." Barbie tapped on the muscles of her upper thighs, the texture of which could easily be distinguished through the thin, almost sheer material of her leggings.

Chris's eyes couldn't help but be drawn to the natural athletic curvature of the teenager's legs. Six days a week in the gym? Evidently, he needed to up his game.

Jessi snapped her fingers. "Okay, enough of that shit," she said, drawing out her syllables. "I don't know anything about pole vaulting or shot putting or running or whatever, so can we change the subject?"

Chris and Barbie smiled clumsily at Jessi, both attempting to shield their mild fascination with one another.

Barbie motioned to the red Mustang in her driveway. "Is that the new ride? Damn, Jess. That thing looks like a freaking jet."

Jessi smiled broadly. "Yeah, that's it. And trust me, it moves like a jet."

As the trio made their way to the car, Barbie glanced at Chris. "What say you, Chris? Is it as fast as my cousin claims?"

Chris nodded. "Oh yeah. It definitely flies."

Barbie tapped on her smartphone screen, and the far-right door on the detached garage to their right opened, exposing the rear end of a pearl white Mercedes-Benz E-Class. "Think it could take that?"

Chris's jaw fell open at the sight of the German-engineered automobile. "Is that yours?"

"Mm-hmm. You like it?"

"I love it," Chris said, forgetting himself for a moment. He moved awkwardly away to stand closer to Jessi after noticing the suspicious look she was giving him. "Both of you have sexy cars, but I'm not sure the Benz could take a five-liter V8. I think Jessi has you beat by about a hundred horses."

"How do you like that shit, slutbag?" Jessi pondered playfully.

"Jeez! Listen to you! Pull those Hanky Pankys out of your crack," Barbie said with a semi-content smile. "I was just asking."

"No need," Jessi replied, eyeballing Chris and strutting away. "I'm not wearing any."

SIX

While filing his fingers through his whiskers, Adam Young gazed down upon the pristine well-oiled receiver of the Armalite AR-10 he'd purchased for a dollar amount just short of an arm and a leg. He toyed with the rifle's components while it lay dormant in its case and tried hard not to think about how much money he'd spent, knowing all the while that his wife was going to give him hell the moment she found out. And she most definitely would find out.

Chuck Keeler, the owner of CK3 Guns, Adam's preferred FFL dealer, stood across from him on the other side of a display case. He set Adam's paperwork down and handed him a pen, then pulled open a desk drawer, reaching inside for a crinkled pouch of flavored chewing tobacco. "Everything checks out, as usual. You know the drill," he said. "At least, you should by now."

"Thanks, Chuck. It's good to know I haven't been charged with any new crimes recently."

Chuck looked the firearm over. "It's a solid weapon. Has real reach-out-and-touch-someone potential. What's the occasion this time? Wife's birthday?"

Adam smirked and shook his head, but didn't say anything. An AR-10 for Elisabeth's birthday? No way in hell. That would go over worse than a fart in church. Maybe a new stethoscope or something from one of her Scentsy or Pampered Chef catalogs.

Chuck crossed his arms. "You know…far be it from me to complain or anything, but it seems as though you've been on, well, a spree, as of late."

"A spree?"

"You know what I mean," Chuck said, placing a wad of tobacco in his mouth. "I wouldn't say anything at all if I wasn't trying to look out for you."

"Okay, well, I guess I appreciate you doing that. Not sure why, though."

"The ATF has been known to flag purchasers who go over a certain threshold, though they fail to inform us exactly what that threshold is." Chuck paused. "How many have you bought so far this year?"

"This is the first one this year."

"First one from my shop, you mean."

"No, first one this year."

Chuck laughed. "Every weekend, I play Texas Hold'em, Adam. I know a lie when I see one. You can't bullshit a bullshitter."

"You should work harder on learning my tells," Adam said, grinning. "I've had to save several months for this baby. Consequently, I haven't had the money to buy as many as I would've liked."

"Well, if it's quality versus quantity you're going for, you chose the right one this time around. You need anything else while you're here? Maybe an optic? I've got some really nice match-grade ammo for it."

Adam shook his head. "I bought so many rounds last year, Homeland Security started making daily passes by my driveway," he joked. "I appreciate it, but I think I'm in good shape."

"Good shape, huh? Don't go getting too complacent on me. You can never have too much ammo. That's been my philosophy since…well, since forever." A pause. "So…are you headin' down to the rally Friday evening?"

"What rally?"

Chuck cleared his throat, coughing over a mouthful of spare saliva. "Are you kidding? The Second Amendment rally. The big one everyone's been talking about? It's been all over the paper lately. Being the devoted gun purchaser you are, I assumed you knew about it, is all."

"Oh, I knew about it," Adam said. "But I'm also aware of the counterprotest that's being ushered in alongside it, just like the last one. And I have no intention of going anywhere near that mess."

Chuck harrumphed. "Why not?"

"Better things to do with my time, I suppose."

"Ah, the diplomatic approach," Chuck said. "Shame. That's the same apathy common to many of our fellow constituents, unfortunately. It's what's allowed this country to fall into dire straits."

"I'm no diplomat, Chuck. And I'm far from being apathetic. I just prefer to be in control of my situation… and choose my battles."

"Adam, a right not exercised regularly is a right lost. If we don't start fighting back and showing them we give a damn, they're gonna rip the Constitution right out from underneath us like some old rug. This rally and others like it are our opportunity to have our voices heard in public. I guess I figured you different. You might want to consider getting with the program before it's too late."

Adam smirked. "Chuck, in a lot of ways, it's already too late."

"How's that?"

Adam paused, taking in a deep breath. "Do you remember back when everyone was in an uproar about the renewal of the Patriot Act? While legislators criticized its unconstitutionality, three fellow GOPers quoted George W. Bush as saying the Constitution was 'just a goddamned piece of paper'. Whether he did or didn't, that same attitude is shared by nearly every politician in office today, for the most part. They couldn't care less about our rights, and their voting practices confirm it. There've been laws, codes, and orders enacted on all levels since the Constitution's inception that've nullified it six ways to Sunday. No rally or protest is going to change anything, and nothing ever will, short of a revolution."

Chuck took a step back and fell into his seat, and it squeaked under his weight. "I see. I suppose it doesn't bother you one bit that they're planning on bussing in those counterprotesters and staging them downtown like some army? Sort of like they do in the big city every time one of our boys in blue has to shoot somebody's kid in the ghetto. They're going to turn our little hamlet into a damn war zone if we don't do something to stop it."

"Um, Chuck?"

"What?"

"Who are *they*?"

"They?"

"Yes, they. This elusive *they* I keep hearing about. The ones responsible for bussing in all the counterprotesters."

Chuck huffed. "Well, whoever's got the means to fund it all, I'd imagine. All of those people are paid to riot and counterprotest, you know. They even advertise it in the job listings on Craigslist and pay better money than you probably make. It's Soros and his gestapo crew, Rockefeller or another one of them billionaire globalist buddies of theirs. Mark my words, though, it'll probably be a few thousand of them. Black Lives Matter, Antifa, left-wing militants and the like. They've already been posting threats on Facebook about what they're planning, and our beloved Confederate Cemetery is one of their prime targets."

Chuck went on and on, but Adam was absorbed with his environment. He glanced over his shoulder, then his other shoulder. Chuck used to sell firearms out of his home but had done so much business in recent years, he'd been forced to open his own commercial storefront. The store was eerily quiet today, and to Adam, it seemed a bit abnormal. From what he could recall in his past dozen or so visits, the place had been bursting with customers, almost to the point of exceeding the building's occupancy rating as set by the local fire code.

This day and age, it seemed like a day couldn't go by without some breaking news report of a school shooting, someone being shot at the hands of another, or a law enforcement officer using his weapon or even being shot and killed in the line of duty. Almost immediately after and before all the facts could be discovered and made available to the public, the news media would home in on the story, focusing only on gun violence. They'd exaggerate, embellish, and stretch the truths, ignore whatever evidence existed, and do whatever they could to send the entire country into mass hysteria. While the crime itself and the perpetrator were treated with relative indifference, the inanimate objects, firearms themselves, were victimized, as were the law-abiding citizens who owned them, soon after in the timeline.

Discussions concerning revocation of gun rights and repealing the Second Amendment were incessantly brought up as the panacea to the never-ending onslaught of gun violence in the country. In turn, citizens, plagued and pulled on by mainstream media bias, felt obliged to choose one side of the fence or the other concerning the legality, as well as the morality, of owning firearms.

Adam had seen it time and time again. Mainstream media was a mechanism of propaganda, fully operational now, and everything they had to say concerning the nation's alleged problems had been said before. It was a broken record on repeat and had become predictable to him. He'd stopped watching television news long ago, opting to retrieve information about world events from alternative sources, both online and via the airwaves. Most news found on television was bogus anyhow. It was mostly commentary, political opinions by so-called experts, and disinformation—most of which had only one purpose: to rile up, drive a wedge between, and subjugate a misinformed populace.

Each time a violent act was committed using a firearm, the resultant media uptake was to victimize firearms and their owners, as if both were somehow to blame. Our forefathers' decision to allow citizens of the Republic uninhibited ownership of military-style weapons to regulate their own government was thereby put into question, and the wave continued into shore. As such, a panic of sorts would begin. Those worried or those who felt threatened that their rights were being infringed upon, or were close to being taken from them, would, in turn, buy more guns and more ammunition.

Adam had been no different. He knew he owned what many might consider to be a private arsenal. He even owned guns his wife didn't know about, and had hidden them in multiple places in and around his home and even in remote locations, should his right to own them become annulled.

There had been a rash of firearm and active-shooter incidents already this year, and anti-gun protests were on the rise and were starting to spread like wildfire. They began by hitting every major city in the country, and they were now branching out into the smaller, rural, more conservative communities, like Adam's hometown.

Adam knew full well what was going on. He'd seen the writing on the wall long ago. Not one single government in the history of the world hadn't been guilty of tyranny in some form or another. Not one government in the history of the world had been innocent of stealing, lying, or even democide—the murder of its own people, including his own. But there wasn't much he could do about it, and instead, long ago, Adam had made the choice to focus only on what directly affected him and his family in their own backyard. They'd always blended in. Never did anything flashy and never went out of their way to be outspoken in public, and especially on social media. Adam had always chosen to be like *the gray man*, following the mantra of fitting in and not standing out, and he'd managed to coax his family into doing so along with him. Or so he'd thought.

Their home was as modest as the vehicles they drove. He had been the quintessential prepper for years, though he'd never purchased large quantities of supplies at any single time so as not to catch unwanted attention. His preparedness moves had always been done incrementally. He knew if the shit were to ever hit the fan, anyone looking his way would be none the wiser unless they found some way to read his mind. Technology hadn't yet reached a point where it was able to do so. At least, he hoped. If the *thought police* of George Orwell's *1984* existed today, Adam would be screwed.

Taking notice that Chuck had finished his tirade, Adam took one last look at his newly acquired AR before securing the case. "On second thought, Chuck, I think I will take some ammunition today." He pulled out his wallet and set a credit card down on top of the case.

Chuck nodded, smiled, and sent a wad of tobacco juice into an empty plastic water bottle. "There you go. That's a start. How much are you looking for?"

"Five hundred for now. Enough to sight this in and some extra if you got them."

"Of course I got them," Chuck quipped. "Got a lot more where they came from, too. So if you need more, you know who to call."

Chuck efforted himself from his chair and walked away, returning moments later with a green fifty-caliber ammo can. He used both hands to hoist it onto the display case, then ran Adam's credit card through his machine. "Is there anything else I can interest you in today?"

Adam shook his head, chuckling. "No, thank you, Chuck. I think I've done enough damage. Once Elisabeth sees this, she'll be on the phone with our marriage counselor again. I don't want to push my luck any more than I already have."

Chuck nodded. "Yeah. I know how the saying goes,

'happy wife, happy life' and all that. I learned that long ago. Lord knows, I gotta go above and beyond on a daily basis just to keep Sheila happy."

Finishing the transaction, Adam handed the signed receipt back to Chuck and took his card, placing it in his wallet. "Glad to know you've got it all figured out. How many times *have* you been married, Chuck?"

Chuck huffed, pressing his lips together. "Sheila is wife number six for me. Very kind of you to ask."

Adam nodded and smiled coyly. He shook Chuck's hand, bid him farewell, and walked excitedly out the door to the parking lot, new prizes in his grasp. When he opened the rear door on his Jeep, a familiar set of chestnut brown eyes stared back crossly at him.

"More toys?" his wife, Elisabeth, asked, her body half-turned in the passenger seat.

Adam only nodded.

"You took forever in there. I was about to come in and tell you to hurry the heck up, but gun stores make me so nervous."

"I know they do, Liz."

"You know we have to pick up the girls by three thirty."

"I know that, too."

"Okay, that's good. Sorry…not trying to be a pest. I know how much you hate it when I nag." She paused. "So how much was it?"

Adam let out a sigh and climbed into the driver's

seat, instinctively reaching for the keys, only to realize he'd left the engine running to keep the heat on for his wife. "If I tell you, will you promise not to divorce me?"

"I suppose."

"Can I get that in writing?"

"Nope."

Adam chuckled. "Then I'm not going to tell you."

Elisabeth punched him playfully in the shoulder and then snapped her seatbelt on while Adam piloted their Jeep from the parking lot and onto Valley Avenue.

"Another gun to play with," Elisabeth chided nearly under her breath. "You only have two hands. I'll never understand why you feel you need so many guns."

Adam ignored the remark.

Elisabeth continued snidely. "I suppose it's…okay, in a way. And it doesn't bother me, so long as you're spending *your* money on it and it's not money we need for bills or groceries or things the kids need. All men, yourself included, need hobbies and…toys to play with. It's just one more to add to your toybox."

Adam glanced over at his wife in time to see her roll her eyes. "I know I probably sound like a broken record by now, but I don't consider guns to be toys at all. If anything, I consider them tools, and each one has a specific task assigned to it, including the one I just purchased."

"The only task they fulfill as far as I can see is

creating more work for me. That, and keeping you occupied when you're not working, watching sports or spending what tiny bit of time you have left over with your wife and children."

"Liz—"

"Maybe I should let you spend some time in the ER with me and clean out a few gunshot wounds. You could see what those things are doing to people in the real world."

Adam didn't say anything, only gripped the steering wheel with more exertion.

"Sorry, I guess I probably shouldn't have said that."

"It's okay."

"Well, I mean, it's your hobby and it's perfectly human to have hobbies," Elisabeth said. "In fact, it's healthy. I read an article last week about it in *Marie Claire*...or maybe it was *Cosmo*. Whatever. I just know it's healthy, especially in a marriage. I really enjoy getting together with the girls for book club each week, and I've recently become a big fan of sewing, thanks to that really nice Singer you got me for Christmas. The cooking classes I started are well on their way to transforming your loving wife into somewhat of a sous chef."

"Liz..."

"All I'm saying is...it doesn't bother me that you like to play with your guns. Just...so long as you keep them locked up and away from me and the kids."

Adam sighed. He knew there was no use in trying to explain his feelings about guns to his wife. He'd been raised around them, mercilessly educated about them, and had used them in some form or fashion all throughout his life, and Elisabeth hadn't. He'd tried many times over the years to introduce them to her on his level and allow her to get accustomed to them, but it had never caught on. Her career as an emergency room trauma nurse had only made it all the more difficult.

She'd made up her mind long ago that guns were dangerous, and Adam felt lucky he'd even managed to convince her to carry something as impractical as pepper spray for self-defense purposes. He'd even bought her a Kershaw assisted-open folding knife once, explaining to her the assortment of things she could use it for, and even reinforcing all the reasons why it was not only practical but judicious to carry one. He recalled seeing it sitting atop her dresser this morning in the same place it had been for weeks, collecting dust.

After a fifteen-minute drive across town, Adam pulled into the parking lot of Green Mill Elementary School. He aligned his Jeep where a long line of vehicles had gathered for student pickup. As the line crawled on, students moved one or two at a time from the safety of the building to their designated vehicles through a line of watchful educational staff standing on either side.

Before long, it was Adam and Elisabeth's turn, and

seconds after they pulled forward to a stop, two girls, each with blond hair and blue eyes, one only inches taller than the other, came running over to the Jeep and jumped merrily into the back seat.

"Seatbelts, please, girls," Elisabeth said sternly.

"Yes, ma'am," the girls said almost in unison.

Lander, the youngest of the two, immediately buckled herself into her booster seat. Claire, who tended to be more rebellious, jumped forward to give her father a hug before heeding her mother's request.

"Hi, Daddy! I missed you so much today," Claire said, her thick hair flopping into Adam's face.

"Hey. I missed you too, kiddo. Did you have a good day at school?"

"Um, it was okay," Claire said, falling back into her seat.

"I missed you too, Daddy," Lander called, not wanting to feel left out. "Did you miss me?"

Adam nodded. "Of course I did, sweetheart. Did you have a good day too?"

Lander shook her head and pouted. "No."

"No?"

Adam's youngest puckered her lips. "No. I hate first grade. And I hate my class. And I hate my teacher too."

"Lander, watch the language, please," Elisabeth said.

"I'm sorry, Mommy. I can't help it. I just hate school."

"*Hate* isn't a nice word," her mother said. "It's not nice to hate. And I want you to be a nice young lady who says nice things. Please put on a happy face and say it another way."

Lander nodded, but didn't respond. Her glowering persisted.

"*Hate* isn't a bad word, Mommy." Claire spoke up. "Mr. Marker told our class the other day. He said it was always better to say how we feel."

Elisabeth scowled. "Claire, it doesn't matter to me what Mr. Marker told you. It isn't a word I want to hear come out of your sister's mouth, or yours. Understood?"

"Yes, but—"

"Claire…"

Claire sat back and folded her arms over her chest. She looked dejected at first, but the expression soon vanished. "Daddy? Is *hate* really a bad word?"

Adam turned his head to see that his wife was giving him the stink eye. The two had never agreed on what was the proper way to discipline their children. Elisabeth had always played the role of disciplinarian, and Adam just wanted to be a good dad. Their differences had put them at odds with one another on countless occasions.

"Personally, Claire, I don't think it is," Adam replied to his daughter, then paused to watch his wife's eyes narrow and her face turn a shade of red.

The girls gauged their mother's expression from the back seat. Sensing the tension between their parents, both started to giggle.

"But if your mother thinks it is, we should all respect that. And we should respect her opinion."

Both Claire and Lander nodded their agreement.

Elisabeth threw herself back into her seat and sighed. "I swear. You do that just to make them like you more than they like me. It really ticks me off."

"I don't do it to sidestep you, I do it because they're my little girls," Adam countered. "And they're not going to be little forever. They'll be Violet's age before we know it. I'm their daddy and it's my job to make them laugh and keep them happy."

Elisabeth sneered. "What about keeping *me* happy? Isn't that your job too?"

"Sure it is. It's just a little more…complex."

"Complex?"

"Yeah," Adam said, hesitating. "What made you happy the day before typically stops working the day after. It's one of those jobs that takes a lifetime to get right."

Elisabeth's eyes narrowed. "Oh, really?"

Adam nodded, sending a timid smile his wife's way. "Yeah, but I'm willing to go the distance."

They proceeded from the school parking lot onto Channing Drive and, after a half mile, made several turns along a few tar-and-chip-paved county roads on the short journey that would lead them to their driveway and to home.

Upon pulling forward to their gate, Adam let out a disheartened sigh when he pushed a button on his remote and nothing happened.

Elisabeth shook her head disgustedly. "Looks like it's broken," she said. "Again."

"Thanks, Liz. I can see that," Adam said. He exited and stepped lively to the gate, forcing it ajar and giving it a frustrated kick afterward.

Once home, the family gathered their things and made their way to the front door. Elisabeth opened the door and allowed Claire and Lander to run inside with their backpacks and lunchboxes while firmly reminding them to remove their shoes and put their belongings away in the proper locations.

Adam marched proudly inside, his new rifle safely in his grasp. He was about to take it down to the basement, uncase it, and prepare it for its initial voyage, but a scrawny teenage girl with purple hair and earbuds blaring music into her ears collided with him along the way.

"Shit. Sorry, Dad," she muttered, pulling one of the buds from an ear. "I didn't see you."

"Maybe if you'd been looking…"

She shrugged, pulling her shirttail down to modestly cover herself in her black leggings. "Yeah, maybe. Hey, is that *another* gun?" She leaned in playfully and kissed

Adam's cheek. "How was your day? Good? Were you off work?"

"Your mom and I both were. So it was pretty good, thanks for asking," Adam replied, ignoring the gun question. "How was yours?"

Violet shrugged. "I wasn't off. So it sucked."

"Very sorry to hear that."

She shrugged again, toying with the white, unsharpened pencil she was using to hold a portion of her hair in a bun. "It's okay. I'm used to it. Characteristic life of an adolescent wannabee goth nerdy chick."

"What was that?"

"Nothing." Violet returned the earbud to her ear and started to walk off, but her father stopped her.

"Hey, hold up. Did your brother make it home?" Adam asked, looking past his oldest daughter into the hallway.

Violet shook her head, producing a look of indifference. "He wasn't on the bus."

"That's not what I asked."

"Fill in the blanks, Dad," Violet said, grinning. "Nice Armalite, by the way."

Before Adam could reply again, Elisabeth strolled up to him in a huff while their rather unconventional daughter glided away and into the kitchen.

"I'd say hello to you, Violet, but you wouldn't be able to hear me with all that trash screaming in your ears!" Elisabeth sighed, folded her arms, and looked to Adam. "Guess what? Your son isn't home yet."

"I know. Violet just informed me." Adam exhaled, setting the rifle case down and leaning it against the wall. "Wait...*my* son?"

"Christopher is *your* son," Elisabeth said. "And he only acts this way because *you* allow it."

"Liz, come on. Give me a break. Have you tried texting him?"

"Why? He never answers my texts."

"I take it that's a no?" Adam slid his phone from his pocket. "What makes you think he'll answer mine?"

"Adam, enough," Elisabeth grumbled. "We've been giving him too much freedom, and this is happening far too often. Here it is, nearing four o'clock already. He doesn't have practice, and there's no meet scheduled today. So if he's not home yet, you can bet where he's at—or who he's with, anyway. He's with that...that *girl*."

"Yes, Liz. I know."

Claire, who by now had edged herself around the corner with Lander in tow, began to chant, "Christopher has a giiirlfriend...Christopher has a giiirlfriend. Chris is gonna be in trouuuble...Chris is gonna be in trouuuble." After a moment, Lander joined in, echoing the hymn.

"Girls!" their mother growled. "I thought I told you both to take your shoes off!"

The two sisters sprinted away, disappearing into their rooms in a cloud of uncontrollable laughter.

Elisabeth sighed in despair. "Well? Are you going to do something?"

"About the girls not taking off their shoes?"

"No! About Chris!"

Adam nodded, thumbing at his phone while trying hard not to grin. "I am doing something. I'm texting him, telling him to come home as soon as possible."

Adam's wife nearly stomped her foot on the floor. "Really? That's it?"

"What else would you have me do, Liz? Go driving around looking for him? Report him as a missing person?"

Elisabeth gritted her teeth. "Spare the rod, spoil the child, Adam."

"He's not a child, Liz."

"And he's no adult, either."

"Yet. He's seventeen," Adam said. "And he needs to start learning what it's like to be responsible for his decisions."

"Fine. Whatever," Elisabeth spat, turning her back and walking off. "I'm done dealing with today. I'm going to get a glass of merlot and read for a while in the bathtub. Handle everything your way. You always do."

Adam finished his text and sent it, then reached for the gun case and headed for the basement. "I can't win."

SEVEN

Chris walked out of the school and across the parking lot, taking a seat in Jessi's Mustang and repeating the steps he'd taken in previous days when she'd provided him with a ride. Instead of immediately moving in to kiss her cheek after tossing his backpack and other things into the back seat, he hesitated while staring down contemplatively at the illuminated screen of his smartphone.

It was just after two thirty in the afternoon on a Thursday, and normally, he would be headed off in the direction of his team's locker room to dress and get warmed up for practice. About midway through the day,

Chris had all but solidified his decision to go to the concert with Jessi and her cousin Barbie. He'd packed an extra bag before leaving home this morning, containing a change of clothes and other items he might need in case he decided to go along.

Track practice would offer him a short reprieve, which would last several hours. Chris knew he would be expected home not long after, either via the activity bus or by catching a ride with one of his teammates. His phone was quiet now and would remain that way until a couple of hours after dark. But it wouldn't take long for that to change, and for his phone to start blowing up with messages and calls.

Chris pressed the power button and held it down long enough for three choices to be displayed on the phone's touchscreen: emergency mode, restart, and shut down.

Jessi pressed on the brake pedal, pulling to a stop at a red light in time to see Chris choose the latter of the three. "Well, well, well. Wonders never cease." She sent him a sly grin. "I guess I'm not taking you home now, am I?"

Chris tilted toward her to kiss Jessi on the cheek, but she turned at the last second so the kiss would land on her lips. "I guess not," he said, sliding his powered-down phone into his backpack. "I'm all yours for the next day or so." He laughed slightly. "Maybe longer if my parents kick me out of the house tomorrow."

Jessi reached for his hand. "Oh, babe, if that happens, trust me, I won't let you be homeless. You'll have a place to stay."

Chris shuddered a bit at the thought of playing house with her. "Are you serious?"

The light turned green and Jessi pressed the accelerator enough to chirp both rear tires. "Of course I'm serious. We're practically adults, anyway—might as well start getting ready for it."

Chris squeezed her hand and rubbed her knuckles with his thumb. "I like your attitude. I think I might keep you around for a while."

"You will if you know what's good for you."

Jessi took the entrance ramp to Route 37 and drove several miles exceeding the speed limit and hastily blowing by other vehicles, some as if they were standing still. They followed the same route they had taken the day prior and, within ten minutes, pulled into the driveway in front of Barbie's house.

Chris pointed at a freshly washed oversized 4x4 pickup truck that was sitting so close to the front porch canopy, it appeared halfway underneath. "Whose truck is that? Your uncle's?"

Jessi squinted and shook her head. "No. All his trucks are diesels and have magnetic contractor signs on them. I think that's Robbie's truck."

"Robbie?"

"Yeah," Jessi replied. "Barbie's boyfriend."

Chris looked at her sideways. "I didn't know Barbie had a boyfriend."

Jessi returned his stare. "Well, you only just met her yesterday. How could you know?" She paused, looking a bit wound up. "What difference does it make, anyway?"

Chris shrugged. "It doesn't. You just made it sound like it was going to be the three of us. I didn't know we'd be doing a double-date thing."

Jessi went to light a cigarette. "Chris, quit it. You're being weird. This isn't a double date, and I never said it was just going to be us three. You misinterpreted."

"No, I didn't misinterpret anything. You miscommunicated—by not mentioning Barbie's boyfriend would be coming along. And it would've been nice to have known that little tidbit way back at the beginning."

"What do you mean, 'way back at the beginning'?"

"Back when I didn't know if I was going or not."

Jessi blew out a puff of smoke, looking exasperated. "Oh, I see. If I went with my cousin and *her* boyfriend, it's not cool, but if she goes with me and *my* boyfriend, all's well with the world."

Chris was growing frustrated. He waved her off. "You know what? Just forget it. Forget I said anything. The bottom line is, if I would've known he was going all along, I wouldn't have hesitated to make my decision to go."

Jessi flicked a few minute particles of ash out her

window. She reached for Chris's chin. "Babe, it's okay. I'm sorry...I'm just really glad you're going. I hate being the third wheel. And I know how much you hate pissing your parents off." She leaned over to him and nibbled on his ear. "This means a lot to me. I promise you, no matter how bad it gets, I'll make it all better."

Several minutes after they'd made up, Chris and Jessi got out of the car and walked to the house. Deciding to forgo ringing the doorbell this time around, Jessi impulsively waltzed inside, motioning for Chris to follow. The couple slid into the foyer in time to hear Barbie's voice calling from her bedroom downstairs, though they couldn't discern what she was saying.

In an oversized kitchen with marble flooring, directly ahead and to their left, stood a tall, muscular man with a high and tight haircut and metal-framed glasses. Both the hair on his head and the stubble on his face and chin had patches of gray mixed in with darker shades. He appeared much older than his present company.

Jessi approached him without delay. "Hey, Robbie," she said, "what's up?" She pointed behind her. "This is my boyfriend, Chris."

The tall man remained expressionless and turned his head gradually to regard the recent arrivals. After a delay, he nodded to Chris, then sent a rather chilling stare to Jessi. "You're not supposed to smoke in here," he said with a gruff voice.

Jessi glanced down at her cigarette. "Oh shit, you're right. I totally forgot. I didn't even think about it."

"That was stupid, walking in here with a lit cigarette," Robbie said. "If Barbie's parents smell smoke in their house, they'll burn her at the stake."

Jessi took one last puff while turning and making a run for the door. Managing to hold it in, she opened the door and exhaled, then flicked the cigarette outside into the driveway. "Yeah, I know and I'm sorry. It's totally my fault." She waved her hand at the smoke that had made its way inside before closing the door.

Robbie stood unmoving, still as a porcelain figurine. "If they decide to crucify her, that'll be your fault too."

Jessi looked dumbfounded at the remark. "What? Crucify her?"

"You heard me. And you need to pick up that fag end you flicked outside before you leave too. No evidence."

"Fag end?"

"The cigarette butt!" Robbie scolded.

"Okay! Jesus!" Jessi said, completely taken aback at the tone he was using to get his point across. "I will."

Sensing the tension, and thus feeling a need to defend her, Chris moved in, positioning himself between the tall man with graying hair and his girlfriend. "Look, dude, my girl said she was sorry. So chillax. This is her aunt and uncle's house. There's no reason to be a dick."

Robbie's cold stare found its way to Chris. "I wasn't aware I was being a dick," he muttered, then yelled, "Yo, Barbie! Your friends are up here waiting on you! Let's go, already!"

Barbie's voice bellowed from the basement. "I know that, and I already told you I was coming! I'll be there in a minute!" Her voice, though highly subdued as heard echoing through the walls, hallways, and doors of the home, sounded provoked.

Chris turned away. He reached for Jessi and spoke into her ear. "I think we should go back outside and wait. I don't know what this geezer's problem is, but I don't like it."

Jessi hesitated, then nodded, fluttering her lashes. "Okay, babe. Sure, that's fine." She then hollered to Barbie, notifying her of their plan.

Chris escorted Jessi out the front door, securing it behind him. He pulled on her hand until they had gotten far enough away from the house that he was certain their conversation couldn't be overheard. "Okay, level with me. Who in the hell is that guy?"

Jessi's eyes searched low while she attempted to find the cigarette she'd flicked out moments ago. "I told you already. He's Barbie's boyfriend."

"Yeah, obviously. But how old is he?"

Jessi smiled when she came across her Marlboro. "I

don't know, like twenty-five or twenty-six, maybe. Why?"

"Holy shit," Chris reacted. "I guess that explains all the gray hair. He's almost a decade older than we are. Why is she with him?"

"Why do you care?"

"I don't care...I'm just curious."

Jessi shrugged with disinterest. "Barbie's always liked older guys." She placed the cigarette between her lips, relit it, and took a drag. "She's tried dating younger before, but it just never worked out."

Chris stammered a bit in disbelief. "He seems...I don't know, weird. That shitsleeve attitude of his...I can't place it. What does he do for a living? Is he a cop or something?"

Jessi shrugged, taking another drag. "I don't think so. I think Barbie told me he was a mechanic."

Chris snickered. "That makes sense, taking into consideration his personality, or lack thereof."

"Stop it, Chris," said Jessi, smacking him on the shoulder. "Don't be mean. I don't want you around them if you can't be nice."

"You don't have to worry about me. I can be nice. I actually possess a personality—along with a witty sense of humor. I don't think that dude has either."

"You just met him today and my cousin yesterday. Give them a chance, okay? For me?"

The door opened, and Barbie stepped out with her

much taller boyfriend towering over her in tow. She was wearing a full backpack, had a duffel bag hanging from her shoulder, and was struggling to carry a Yeti cooler while Robbie's hands remained astoundingly free.

Jessi ran to her aid and immediately took hold of the cooler. "Jesus, what the hell's in this? It weighs a ton."

Barbie began rubbing the hand she'd been using to grasp the cooler's carry handle. "What do you think? That's where I keep the party. Nice and cold."

Even using two hands to hoist the Yeti, Jessi fought to carry it. She set it on the ground, her eyes falling upon Robbie. "Why aren't you helping to carry anything?"

With a stone-cold expression, he slowly turned to eyeball her. "It's not my shit."

"That's nice," Jessi quipped. "That's real nice—real gentlemanly of you. Very chivalrous." She turned and called to Chris, who came to her aid in an instant.

"Thanks for the help, guys," Barbie said graciously.

"It's not a problem," Chris said, grunting initially at the weight of the cooler. "I guess now would be the best time to ask...whose car are we taking?"

Jesse and Barbie both went to speak until they were interrupted by Robbie. "Barbie and I will be riding in my truck," he said commandingly. "You two will need to take your car. We'll go separate in case we want to leave at different times."

Chris looked to Barbie for signs of approval but didn't get any. He then turned his attention to his girl-friend, who only stood silent and blank-faced. "That's probably for the best, anyway. We wouldn't want to intrude on what I imagine would be quite the delightful conversation between you two on the way there." Chris hoisted the cooler into the back of Robbie's truck and turned away, reaching for Jessi's hand. "Let's go. I'm sure Mr. Perfect knows the way."

EIGHT

JIFFY LUBE LIVE PAVILION. BRISTOW, VIRGINIA
THURSDAY, MARCH 27, 6:35 P.M. EDT
NIHAYAT AL'AYAM MINUS 5 HOURS, 25 MINUTES

While holding three other beanbags in his left hand, Chris tossed a fourth underhanded at the cornhole board across the way. The bag smacked the board and slipped across its slick surface, landing on the gravelly pavement a few feet behind Jessi.

"Nice bag," Jessi said. She grinned and twisted at the waist so she could verify the canvas bag's final resting place.

"Thanks," replied Chris, tossing another and getting an almost identical result. "Shit. Did you grease these up before you left?"

Jessi laughed. "No, they're just brand new. The

'rents bought them a few months ago before one of their black-tie throw-downs. I don't think anyone's actually ever played with them."

"That's obvious." Chris finished his turn without scoring, and scanned the parking lot while Jessi prepared for her turn. He gestured to Robbie's truck parked beside her Mustang. "Those two sure have been gone a long time. Think they're coming back?"

"I don't know."

"I wonder where they went that's keeping them away so long?" Chris deliberated.

"Probably inside. To get good spots for us, I'd imagine," Jessi said, tossing her first bag and getting it in the hole effortlessly. "Why do you care so much?"

"I don't know…I guess I just assumed we'd be doing this tailgating-party thing together," Chris said, shrugging. "Nice shot, by the way."

Jessi smiled at him and sank another hole in one. "Thanks."

"You know, the game is typically more fun with two teams of two."

"You're not wrong," she said, sinking another.

Chris looked dumbfounded. "Really? Are you, like, a professional cornhole player or something?"

Jessi's final shot landed on the board, but didn't drop through. "Clearly not. But I'll admit, it's hard concentrating with you babbling about Barbie and Robbie again."

"I didn't think I was babbling at all. I was only wondering where they were."

"Wondering, babbling, whatevs. Why do you care so much about their whereabouts?" Jessi asked. She knelt and picked up Chris's stray beanbags from the ground. "I swear, it's like you're obsessed with them. Or maybe it's just her."

Chris looked stunned. "What? Don't be ridiculous."

"Am I? Am I being ridiculous, Chris? Because I don't think I am. It's pretty damn obvious you like her."

"Jessi! Really? Of course I like her. She seems... like a cool person. And she's your cousin, so why wouldn't I?"

"No...I mean you *like* her. Like you're completely attracted to her." Jessi folded her arms over her chest. "It's not the least bit surprising. This isn't the first time Barbie has done this to me."

"It's not the first time she's done what to you?"

"I don't want to talk about it. It doesn't matter—I saw the way you looked at her. She was flaunting herself, and you were checking her out. I mean, I know she has a great body...and..."

"No, wait," Chris said, approaching her. "*You* have a great body."

"Stop it, Chris."

Chris reached for her hips, and Jessi pulled away at first, but a second effort bore fruit. "Have you ever really looked at yourself? I mean *really* looked at yourself? You have a magnificent body, Jess. You don't *have* to flaunt it, and I check you out literally all the time. And…your cousin's an athlete, so of course she looks good. But I don't want an athlete, and I definitely don't want your cousin. I want you."

Jessi peered up at him with expectant puppy-dog eyes. "Are you sure?"

"I've never been so sure about anything in my life."

Jessi smiled slightly and let go of the cornhole bags she was holding. "Fine," she said, surrendering. "Fine, *Romeo*. You've successfully buttered me up yet again. Let's go inside and find them."

Inside the pavilion, bodies moved and cascaded together with every thump and rumble of bass. The closest screaming, pulsating speaker was at least a football field's distance away, but the volume of the music being played was nothing short of earsplitting. Chris found it pointless to even attempt to carry on a conversation. He had tried a couple of times to no avail, and he was even having trouble putting his own thoughts together amidst the drowning commotion surrounding him. The place was a madhouse.

While Chris scanned the crowd in search of Barbie and her tall, rather standoffish jerk of a boyfriend, Jessi followed either alongside or just behind, her body moving and squirming to the tune and beat of the music. She closed her eyes often and had a smile of pure bliss painted on her face, indicating the melody had somehow entranced her. She appeared as though she hadn't a care in the world.

Chris was different, though. He *did* have a care in the world—a number of them, most of which regarded his future. He knew every decision he made influenced that future, and try as he might, he couldn't find any way to just let go and relax. In the past, all it had taken was a beer or two for him to loosen up. He'd seen Jessi partake of several alcoholic drinks from her cooler and even from Barbie's Yeti, but he hadn't so much as touched one tonight.

Chris sometimes felt like he was too much like his father. He'd never been an admirer of large crowds. His father had always been so steadfast with his feelings about how large gatherings of people were potentially dangerous places to be. Not that they weren't fun places to be, but even the most entertaining of places could easily turn bad in the blink of an eye. Adam had told Chris many times before that standing in the middle of a crowd of thousands would be the last place he'd ever want to be if and when something awry happened to pop off.

Chris recalled the biggest concern his father would often lecture about was the immediate human response to an unanticipated occurrence. In the majority of situations, everything goes according to plan, allowing everyone to enjoy themselves and have a good time. No one gets hurt and everyone is able to return home safely. But the moment something goes wrong, it doesn't take long for panic to set in. And when a crowd of people is gathered together and tightly packed into a mall or concert hall, sports arena, stadium, or even a department store on Black Friday, that panic can multiply and become a chain reaction.

Chris had seen it happen before on television and on the news and had seen the look of unease settle on his father's face when they'd visited the Verizon Center to watch a Washington Capitals hockey game. As much as he wanted to have a good time and enjoy himself with Jessi, he just couldn't. Especially now, since they'd become separated from the couple they'd arrived with.

An overhead halogen light glaring at his eyes, Chris sheltered his view with his hand when he thought he might've caught sight of Robbie's head towering over a group gathered around him. Chris lifted himself onto his tiptoes, verifying it was indeed him, then scanned for Barbie, but couldn't see her anywhere.

He pulled Jessi closer, interrupting her mid-dance, and put his mouth to her ear. "I saw Robbie!" he exclaimed.

Jessi jerked away from him, squinting and looking annoyed. "Why are you screaming in my ear?"

Chris could barely hear her, but he could see the irritation building in her eyes as Jessi rubbed her ear.

He realized then, he might have exceeded the necessary volume with regard to his proximity. He spoke again, only not as close as last time. "I see Robbie. He's just over there on the other side of a group of guys. I don't see Barbie anywhere, though."

Jessi shrugged uncaringly and started to dance again. "Okay, whatever! Just go! I'll follow you!"

He latched onto her, then turned and began making his way through the crowd again. Once they got closer, Chris found where Barbie was, realizing he couldn't see her earlier because she was standing in Robbie's shadow. She was actively pulling on him, attempting to uncouple him from an argument that had turned physical with several other young men.

Chris took a second to gauge the look on Robbie's face. He looked intimidating, and the others were either antagonizing him or being antagonized *by* him. Attempting to discern which was which amidst the mind-numbing noise and crowd movement was pointless.

Chris watched as Robbie moved in and shoved one of the younger, shorter boys away from him. His instincts told him to intercede. But when he went to put himself between them and stop what was about to happen, the boy took a swing at Robbie and connected with his chin. The look on Robbie's face forged into sheer anger in a millisecond. Robbie charged at his attacker, tackling him to the ground while taking several innocent bystanders along with them.

As Chris reached in to pull Robbie away, he was yanked away and attacked from behind, a stout punch connecting several times with his left ear. Startled and dazed, he turned to face his attacker, only to have another punch land on his chin. It wasn't hard enough to knock him out cold, but it was enough to further stun him, and Chris fell backward onto his butt.

Confused and defenseless, he held his hands in the air, attempting to prevent being hit again while the music and crowd noise did nothing but add to the overall mayhem. As his vision returned, Chris could see Robbie only several feet away. He was straddled atop someone and was pummeling his face with his fists while his victim pled for the much taller, stronger man to stop. Robbie's melee on the boy was relentless, and the emotionless stare Robbie was giving the boy showed no signs of relinquishing.

Chris tried to get to his feet, but someone kicked him in the back and he felt another strike to the back of his head. In that moment, he began coming to the realization that if he didn't get up and take control of the situation, it wouldn't be long at all before he would be screwed.

In an explosive move fueled by Chris's athleticism, he twisted his body and jutted up to his knees and onto his feet. He arranged his arms before his face as his hands coiled into fists, poising himself to strike at whoever came at him. When no one did, he relaxed a bit, but only for a second, because what he saw next wasn't something he'd ever expected to see.

Barbie had engaged the two remaining combatants and was now fighting them both. With one young man's hair in her grasp, she rocketed her knee into his face, sending him to the ground in a bloody, blubbering heap. When the second joined in, she fought him off with a barrage of solid punches to his face before finishing him with another to his Adam's apple. He fell to the ground alongside his cohort, coughing and gagging, barely able to breathe after the blow.

Chris stood dumbfounded and rubbed his head while he tried willing some of his pain away. "Holy shit!" he said, though no one could hear him.

Barbie didn't even look his way. She moved quickly past and immediately to Robbie, struggling to pull him away from the young boy he was maiming.

Chris moved in to assist, and after a struggle, the two removed Robbie from his victim. Chris disengaged not long after, when Barbie instantly began intensely scolding her boyfriend for his behavior.

Jessi stood close by and remained uninvolved, observing the activity with about half her attention. She was still dancing and singing, still very much consumed by the music and the ambience of the concert. She hadn't even noticed that Chris had gotten involved in the scuffle.

A distressed and highly irritated look on her face, Barbie walked over to Chris and Jessi after her chat with Robbie, shaking her head back and forth in disgust. After rubbing the knuckles on the hand she'd used to knock down one of her adversaries, she motioned with a finger for one or both of them to lend her an ear.

Chris took a quick look Jessi's way and realized it would be up to him. He leaned in and his ear met with Barbie's lips.

"I'm really sorry about all this. Robbie is super drunk!" she said. "I'm going to take him out of here so he can cool down. Do you guys have any water in your cooler?"

Chris nodded his response. "We do…but I think it's better if we all go! It's getting too hectic in here for me, anyway!" He then motioned for the group to follow him.

Jessi remained static at first until receiving an explanation from her cousin. Then, after rolling her eyes, she reached for Chris's hand, allowing him to lead her and the others through the all-singing, all-dancing field of concertgoers.

It took a while to break free from the densest portions of the crowd, but looking just ahead of him, Chris could see a light at the end of the tunnel. An open area in the field lay not far away. He knew it would be best to at least get to that point and then reacquaint himself with their location before continuing. Once there, they could choose a path away from the swarm to get back to the parking lot.

As he trudged on, making it to the edge of the crowd, Jessi's hand went limp and he lost his grip on it. He turned his head to look for it, only glancing down at it for a second before reaching back to intertwine his fingers with hers. At the point of grabbing hold, his fingers slipped away. It felt like her hand had somehow gotten wet. He slowed his pace and reached back again, this time attempting to grasp her entire hand in his. He took a longer glimpse this time around, and that was when Chris noticed Jessi's hand was covered in a liquid, dark red in color, with the consistency of syrup.

An instantaneous need to investigate further hitting him in the gut, Chris stopped walking and turned around. His girlfriend's body, hair, and clothes were now covered in what he could only guess was blood.

Jessi's eyes were wide, and she was no longer danc-ing. Her body was shaking, and she was mouthing something, though Chris couldn't make out the words over the music and crowd noise.

Chris placed both hands on Jessi's head, examining her. "Hey! What the hell happened to you?" He didn't know if she could hear him or not, but it didn't matter. Chris didn't know where the blood had come from. He assumed it was Jessi's, and with that, he began slipping into a panic as adrenaline started to pump its way through his bloodstream. "Jessi? Are you hurt?" He put his mouth to her ear and repeated the question.

Far enough away from the speakers now, Chris could hear her whimpering reply. "I-I don't know. We were walking…and I thought…it felt like someone spilled their drink on me."

"It's not a drink," Chris said, trying his best to keep his composure. "I'm pretty sure it's blood."

Jessi looked at him frantically. "Blood?" Her hands moved to her prized head of hair. "What? It's not mine, is it?"

Chris looked his girlfriend over, his eyes scouring every inch of her head, face, and the rest of her body. He looked for knife wounds or bullet holes or anything else his young mind could think of, having never been placed in a situation even remotely similar before. He couldn't find anything wrong or out of place, other than the fact Jessi had somehow gotten someone's blood all over her. But whose blood? And how?

While he tried rubbing some of the blood away from her face with his hands, Chris looked over Jessi's shoulder, discovering that Barbie and Robbie were no longer directly behind them, as they had been all the way up until a moment ago. His hands fell upon Jessi's shoulders, and his stare went to the ground, where he could now see that Barbie was down on her knees, with one of her hands covering her mouth. His eyes tracked just beyond her. Robbie was there too. He was lying on his back alongside her. And half of his head was missing.

Time seemed to slow at first for Chris. He could only hear his heart beating in his ears, and nothing else in that instant. Then, seconds after, the entire scene unfolded in front of him as if someone had pressed the fast-forward button on the timeline of his life.

While music continued to flood the speakers, the vocalists could no longer be heard singing the lyrics to their songs. Then the sounds of the guitars and drums and other instruments slowly died, followed by the unmistakable high-pitched squealing sound of micro-phones feeding back into speakers.

As the music faded away, Chris's ears perked up upon hearing another rather unmistakable sound, some-thing he'd heard only in one other location before—a gun range. One that his father had taken him to a handful of times to learn how to shoot, unbeknownst to his mother. It was the popping, thundering sound of rapid gunfire, and it came in long bursts, seeming to echo from every direction all around him. The shots were soon followed and accompanied by young voices crying out and screams of terror. The entire setting surrounding them went haywire and completely fell apart.

Chris turned and forcefully dragged Jessi to the

ground with him. With Jessi's body tensing against his, she began sobbing uncontrollably. Chris wrapped his arms around her and held onto her for dear life while the shots rang out around them without pause. He instinctively rolled his head to the side to survey the landscape for incoming danger while young people scattered about in all directions.

Still located amongst the crowd, it wasn't long before Chris realized he had a decision to make. He knew that he, Jessi, and Barbie could not stay where they were much longer.

He looked over at Jessi's cousin, who was kneeling beside the inert body of her nearly decapitated boyfriend. She was bawling and screaming, and what remained of her restraint was on the verge of tumbling out of control. He knew any attempt to move her, or any effort to get her to disengage would be futile and would surely end up in conflict. Chris could almost predict her response. She'd probably just refuse to leave, or if she did decide to go along, she'd only do so if it meant not leaving Robbie behind.

Chris couldn't bear the thought of having to manhandle a half-headless, two-hundred-pound dead body along on their exodus. It was hard enough trying to think of the right words to say to Barbie after she'd probably watched him die only moments ago. He studied Jessi's expression while the multitudes of young people continued to spread out in every direction, nearly colliding with them at times. She had frozen stiff at the point of seeing Robbie's body, and the gunshots were only making matters worse for her. She looked incredulous through her tears, appearing as though she simply couldn't believe any of this was really happening.

Chris considered her and recalled their many conversations regarding the country's issues with gun violence, as well as Jessi's beliefs on the matter. He was well aware of her mortal fear of guns and her overall carefree approach to life. He knew she hadn't a clue what to do. But Chris did.

Though he'd never prepared himself for anything quite like this, Chris had been lectured by his father about similar occurrences and the possibility of someday being present during an active-shooter or localized-terror attack. The country had become increasingly unstable over the years since 9/11, and it was wise to be wary of danger and, as well, ready for it to rear its ugly head even when you least expected it. He'd been to the shooting range with his dad countless times and had gone camping and backpacking, spending hours outdoors, learning skills his dad had been so adamant that he and his siblings learn, citing that those skills bolstered the human will to survive.

But above all, two of the things Chris's father had a habit of saying to him stood out among the rest, one of which regarded communication. It was important never to allow yourself to become cut off from your support group. Always be prepared to find some way of communicating your situation so assistance can be obtained. Chris remembered his dad mentioning the tactical use of telephones, the internet, radios, and even smoke signals and carrier pigeons, even though the latter two were stated in jest. The bottom line was to utilize whatever was available, and to do whatever it took to get the message through.

The second nuance Chris remembered his father homing in on was how important it was not to do what everyone else was doing. Separate yourself from the majority or where most people were congregating, and do so as quickly and as safely as you could. He recollected that in any active-shooter situation, the typical objective was collateral damage: killing as many people as possible before the shooter is put down by a good guy with a gun. Stay away from crowds, but find cover quickly. And try your best to eliminate any risk of being trampled by a fleeing stampede fed by panic.

Chris knew he'd already done this by leading his friends to where they were situated now. Scanning the scene, he palmed his back pocket, remembering in that moment, he'd left his cell phone inside his backpack in Jessi's car after turning it off to prevent hearing from and being reprimanded by his parents for missing his curfew. Jessi's phone was in her pocket, but knowing her as well as he did, it probably had only about fifteen percent battery left. He could make a call or send a few texts, but he needed to remain in contact. And he didn't even want to ask Barbie for hers, especially now. Chris needed to get to his phone.

Chances were, the authorities had already somehow been alerted to this, but he knew it was always better to have more options at his disposal. Chris needed to call home. He needed to get ahold of his dad. His dad knew prepping. He knew survival skills. He knew guns. Hell, the man probably owned more guns than anyone Chris had ever met before. His dad would know what to do.

Instead of trying to get Jessi and Barbie to follow him back to the car, Chris decided it best to have them remain where they were, but he wanted to move them far enough away from the crowd and find a spot for them where they could be shielded from the shooting. He knew he could get to the car faster by going alone. Jessi, in her current state, would only slow him down. He knew Barbie was a sprinter—an athlete, same as he was, but after what she'd most recently experienced, Chris assumed she wasn't in any shape to go on a run with him.

Chris scanned the fence line behind him, soon coming across a large oak tree. He then crawled over to Barbie and put his hands on her shoulders gently, so as not to startle her. "Barbie…I'm going to Jessi's car to get my phone. I need you and Jessi to stay together until I get back." Chris tapped her shoulder and pointed at the oak tree. "Can you guys wait for me over there, near that tree?"

Barbie's movements were hesitant, and she seemed relatively unresponsive at first. She nodded slightly, then froze and turned to regard the tree Chris was pointing at. "Yeah…but what about Robbie? I can't just leave him here."

Chris wanted to tell Barbie how he felt about that. He knew it was pointless to take Robbie along with them, but he didn't know the right words to get his point across. He could feel his heart pulling for her as the tears rolled from both corners of her eyes. "I'll… leave that up to you. I know how much he meant to you…and I'm sorry, Barbie. I'm truly sorry. But I have to go."

Chris rose and went to Jessi, who gave him a 'deer in the headlights' look. "I'm going to the car to get my phone. I need to call my dad. I need the keys."

Jessi didn't say anything at first, her eyes transfixed on Robbie's body. Her eyelashes fluttered, and after a few seconds, she reached into her back pocket and handed Chris her phone.

Chris looked it over, realizing Jessi hadn't a clue what she'd handed him. "Jess, hon…I need your keys."

"Oh…shit. Sorry."

Chris tapped the power button while Jessi dug into another pocket for her keys. Sure enough, it was worse than he'd guessed. The battery icon was blinking red at eight percent.

"Chris? Wait...what's happening?" Her voice rattled as she handed her keys to him.

"Someone's shooting into the crowd," Chris said. "Robbie got hit."

"Hit? You mean he's dead?"

"Jessi, stop it." Chris put his hands on her cheeks. "You can see him...he's right over there. You know what happened." He brushed some of her hair away from her face. "Look—I need you to stay with Barbie. You two stay put and stay together no matter what until I get back to you."

Jessi slowly nodded, and several tears fell from her eyes. She didn't even bother wiping them away.

Chris crawled with Jessi to where Barbie was. He told them both to stay as low as possible and make their way to the fence line and the tree as soon as they could. He wiped some of Robbie's blood from Jessi's forehead with his sleeve, kissed her, and sprinted off in the direction of the parking lot.

NINE

The vibration pattern of Adam's smartphone rattled the nightstand, awakening him in a fluster. The screen alight and shining brightly against the ceiling, he reached for it while he struggled to open his eyes, bringing it to within reading distance after releasing it from an annoyingly short charging cord.

Through indistinct vision, he could see that multiple icons had accumulated at the top of the display. Some indicated application updates, while others were indicative of unread text messages and at least two missed calls. "Great. If that's work with another one of their alleged emergencies…they can have my resignation."

Elisabeth rolled over and put a hand to Adam's shoulder, her fingernails pressing delicately on his skin. "Mmm…what's going on? It's not work, is it?"

"I'm not sure. I hope not."

She moaned and wriggled under the warmth of the blanket. "What time is it?"

Adam yawned with squinted eyes. "Looks like…just after eleven thirty." He sat up a bit and rubbed the corners of his eyes as his vision started to clear. Then he caught sight of something that shocked him as he swiped downward on the smartphone's screen, exposing the full text of his notifications. "Oh, shit," he said, tapping the envelope icon. His voice gained urgency. "Oh, shit!"

"What?"

"It's Chris."

Elisabeth shot up from the bed. "Chris? On your phone? Where is he?"

Adam scrolled through the messages without saying anything.

Elisabeth slid off the bed and away, covering herself in a bathrobe, and jetted out of the bedroom and down the hall. She returned a minute later, pulling the tangled tresses of her hair into a hair tie. "It's almost midnight and he's not in his room. He should've been home hours ago. Where the heck is he, Adam?"

"He's…at a concert. At Jiffy Lube pavilion near Manassas." Adam rose and reached for his pants. He hesitated, wanting to inform his wife of the truth, but not wanting to rile her up. Or frighten her. "There's been a shooting."

Elisabeth's voice dive-bombed into a panic. "What?! Wait a second—what are you talking about?" A rare expletive slipped from her jaws. "What in the *hell* is he doing at a concert?! On a school night?! Argh! I bet he's with that floozy Jessi again. That…girl! I swear before God, I'm going to—"

"Liz, calm down!" Adam held up a hand. "Did you even hear what I said? There's been a *shooting*." He brushed past her, setting his phone down on the way to the closet to get dressed.

"A shooting…" she murmured. "Jesus…another one."

"Yes, another one. And our son is there."

Elisabeth shuddered. Her face turning pale, she wrapped her arms tightly around her bathrobe while she trembled. "Adam—how many casualties? Is Chris okay? He isn't hurt, is he?"

Adam didn't respond immediately. He put on the first T-shirt he could find, grabbed a hoodie and a light jacket, then turned and left the closet.

Elisabeth stopped him with a stiff grip, holding fast to his elbow. "Wait. Just…hold on. Where are you going?"

"Where do you think? I'm going to go get him."

Adam's wife's trembling gained prominence. "No, wait. You can't just leave...you can't just *go* there."

"Yes, Liz. I can. Our son needs help. I *am* going there."

"Oh, God. Adam, no...don't. It's not safe for..." She took a breath and stiffened. "Oh, dear God. Please, just...tell me he's not hurt."

"The last text he sent was twenty minutes ago," said Adam. "So that tells me as of twenty minutes ago, he was fine. Let's pray he stays that way."

"What did the text say?"

"Liz..."

"Please. Adam, just tell me."

Adam sighed. He pulled away and gathered his things, then stopped before leaving the bedroom, glancing at his phone. "It says he can hear screaming, sirens, and gunshots. Police are on the scene, but he thinks there might be multiple active shooters still roving the complex." He paused a moment, struggling to gather his calm. "Apparently, they shot into the crowd at random...when the music was so loud, no one could hear the shots."

"Oh, heavenly Jesus." Elisabeth latched onto him again, this time like a vise.

Adam placed a strong hand onto hers. "Liz, I have to go. The sooner I get there—"

"I know, I know," she said, turning away. She nodded her head while tears began rolling from her eyes and down her cheeks. "Just...please, please be careful."

"I will," Adam said, then kissed her on the forehead. "Listen to me. No matter what happens, and I mean no matter what, keep this house locked down the entire time I'm gone. You protect yourself and our girls above all else, do you understand?"

"Yes, I—"

"Keep the drapes closed, and don't open the doors for anyone. Don't answer your phone unless it's us. Bad things tend to occur in clusters, and I want to rule out any superfluous variables. This night doesn't need to get any worse than it already is." Adam tapped her forearm. "Do you remember how to use the radios?"

Elisabeth hesitated, then nodded. "Yeah—I think so. Why?"

"Keep the handheld I gave you turned on until I get back," he said, moving into the hall as Elisabeth followed closely behind. "Keep it plugged in to the wall charger so you don't drain the batteries down. You'll likely hear some other people talking on it. Don't pay them any mind. It's one of the busiest amateur radio repeaters in Northern Virginia, especially during the morning commute. Listen for my call sign. If you hear me call for you, come back to me and we can change frequencies if we have to."

Liz nodded, but looked confused. "Okay, fine. But...why do we need to use the radios?"

"Because cell phone service could become unusable. There are plenty of dead spots between here and there, but it wouldn't surprise me if the system became overloaded with calls. If I can't get through to you on the phone, we'll need another option. It's one of the reasons I harped on you to get your license for so long."

"Okay."

"Also, you need to keep in mind that texts get through sometimes even when calls don't. So if you call and it doesn't get through, try texting." Adam turned to face her before entering his office. "Are you absorbing this, Liz? You understand what I'm saying to you? I can't stress how important it is that we stay in contact."

She nodded. "Yes. I understand you." Her eyes darted around the room. "I guess I should try to remember what *my* call sign is, now. I haven't used it in over a year."

Adam smiled grimly at her. "That would be a good idea."

Adam's office was where he kept most of his 'man' things. It was where the family's gun safe was located, along with most other items Adam considered his own. It wasn't exactly a man cave, but it had always made Elisabeth feel more comfortable for his stuff to be confined to a single area within the home.

Adam typed a combination into the safe and opened the door, reaching inside for a belt carrying a holstered Glock 19, along with several spare magazines and other pouches on the opposite side. He didn't know if he'd wear it or not, but the belt had everything attached to it he thought he might need tonight.

The rear of the belt sported a Zero Tolerance knife and Adam's homebrew IFAK and trauma kit. He slung the belt over his shoulder, then reached deeper into the depths of the safe, extracting one Kevlar vest followed by another: one for him and one for his son. In an active-shooter situation, he figured it couldn't hurt to have some form of ballistic protection for them both.

Adam locked the gun safe and departed his office while his wife stared at him, the worry evident in her eyes. He kissed her on the cheek and said a few calming words to her, even though he knew it wouldn't do much good for either of them. Then he donned the rest of his everyday carry items and grabbed his go-bag near the front door and departed the house, making certain the deadbolt was secure on his way out.

Several miles down the road amidst a plethora of apprehension and perplexing thoughts, Adam's concentration was interrupted when he heard rustling in the back seat. He slowed the truck and rotated to see the moonlight's glint off a head of purple-tinted hair.

Startled, Adam jumped in his seat. "Jesus! What the hell?!"

"Hey, Dad."

"Fucking hell. You scared the shit out of me, Vi." Adam put a hand to his chest. "What the hell do you think you're doing?"

"What the hell does it look like I'm doing?" Her response was as indignant as it was innocent. "I'm going with you. I can't let you do this all by yourself. What if you…I don't know…die? That wouldn't be good."

"How did you even know what was going on?"

"You know I never sleep."

"Violet, honey, this isn't a good idea," Adam said, now trying to figure out how his daughter had been able to sneak out of the house unbeknownst to him. "It doesn't make any sense, your being here. It's too dangerous."

"Sure it makes sense. You need backup. And that's exactly why I'm going with you—to back you up."

"To back me up?"

"Yeah. Don't get me wrong, you're pretty awesome at a lot of things, Dad. You're even amazing at a few— but you're not Superman. Hell, even Superman gets his ass saved by that dunce Lois Lane all the time." Violet slid herself into the passenger seat, using her father's neck and shoulder for support.

Adam sighed and shook his head. "Christ. Just…put your seatbelt on."

"I am. Give me a second."

"You're something else, kid. I don't know how you do it."

"You don't know how I do what?"

As Adam piloted the Jeep along the interstate, he did his best to keep the vehicle in the lane and maintain some semblance of the speed limit while his mind raced away. His worries of what had already happened tonight, as well as what hadn't yet happened, were ravaging his soul.

Though he'd never been much for praying, he caught himself silently asking God to look out for Chris's welfare. Then it dawned on him to check and see if Chris had tried to make contact again.

Removing a hand from the steering wheel, Adam extracted his cell phone from his hip pocket, taking his eyes off the road a moment to observe the screen.

The screen's illumination flooded the passenger compartment with light, instantly grasping Violet's attention. She whipped her head to the left. "You shouldn't text when driving. Especially at night, Dad."

Adam's eyes bounced between the digital device and the road. "I know that…I'm just trying to see if your brother has sent any updates."

"Are you sure you don't want me to do that for you? So you can…I don't know…concentrate on driving?"

Adam shook his head. "No, I think I can manage."

As the words escaped his mouth, Adam began to veer into the passing lane and into the path of another vehicle, which had moved into his blind spot. The vehicle's driver honked the horn angrily at his misjudgment. "Okay, now that you mention it, it's probably not such a bad idea."

Violet took hold of the phone when Adam handed it to her. She studied the screen. "When's the last time you sent dipshit a message?"

"I haven't sent dipsh…him anything. There hasn't exactly been time."

Violet began tapping both of her thumbs rapidly on the screen. "Then he doesn't even know we're coming. Marvelous…I'll take care of that. Anything else you think I should say to him?"

Adam thought a moment. While Violet had always been open to his teachings over the years, Chris had been somewhat the opposite, especially after he'd begun dating. He was a smart kid, incredibly talented and energetic. He'd just never taken things as seriously as Adam would've liked him to. "There's no telling what's going through his mind right now. And there's no way of knowing if he's doing what he *should* be doing. Hopefully, he's staying low and away from the crowds. I hope he's located a good place to hide—or better yet, found cover…until the authorities can get to him. Or *I* can, whoever's first."

Violet looked away from the screen, peering over at

her father. "You want me to tell him that? Tell him to get his dumb ass some place isolated?"

"That's a good idea—but only if it's safe to move. Truthfully though, I'm hoping your brother already knows that…and doesn't need reminding."

"You shouldn't be so quick to give him credit. Dipshit's probably urinated himself by now."

"What was that?"

"Nothing." Tossing the cell phone into her father's lap, Violet reached forward and popped open the glove box.

"What are you looking for?" Adam asked.

"Really, Dad? I'm looking for a gun. Don't you usually keep a gun in here?"

"No—I mean, I don't anymore. I used to till I thought better of it."

Violet smacked the glove box shut. "What do you mean, 'thought better of it'?"

Adam jerked the truck around another vehicle that had stopped suddenly for no apparent reason. "I read an article in the newspaper about a lady who was accosted by some guys in a van at a stoplight. She had her window down and they told her that her keys were in the door. When she went to look, three of them jumped out and wrestled her from the car."

Violet cocked her head. "Really? Did it happen at night?"

"It happened in broad daylight, actually."

"What a bunch of pricks. And what a stupid woman. The keys were *obvs* in the ignition."

"Agreed," Adam said. "And you're right, they were. The woman had a concealed-carry permit, and she kept her pistol in the glove box. It was too far away to be of any use to her, and even if she could've gotten to it, it would've been too late. She'd already lost the battle in the first place. Her situational awareness was compromised."

"So what happened to her? Did those *randos* beat her up? Or rape her?"

"No, not this time. They just stole the car. But since her gun was in the glovebox, they got that, too. Since then I've changed my ways. It's best to carry on your person, never attached elsewhere—but if it *is* elsewhere, it definitely needs to be within reach." Adam pulled his daughter's hand closer to him, gesturing to the steering column while her eyes followed along. "There, see? Under the steering wheel. That's where I keep it now. Since you're so curious."

Violet reached for the compact Glock pistol. "That's a really strong magnet." She pulled the pistol in close and press-checked it like a professional, exercising textbook trigger discipline just as her father had taught her. "There's been chatter all week long on the dark web about something bad happening at the concert."

Adam glanced at her. "What are you talking about?"

"I'm talking about what goes on behind the scenes,

Dad. You know…intel? Things we aren't supposed to see or supposed to know? Things I make it a *point* to see and know."

Adam frowned. "Vi, I don't want you doing things on the internet that can get you in trouble."

"Dad, please. I'm behind, like, seven proxies," she replied, giggling at the catchphrase familiar only to specific internet subcultures. "I cover my tracks. And I'm just telling you, I saw talk of something like this happening, and it's just ironic 'cause it actually did." Violet looked over at her father, slight concern building in her eyes. "Do you know what you're going to do? Like…do you have a plan for once we get there?"

Adam rubbed his forehead. "No, Vi. I don't." He rubbed his temples, now feeling the full brunt of what he and his daughter were about to face. "I honestly don't have a fucking clue."

A half an hour passed, along with nearly forty road miles, before the two resumed any conversation.

"Dad?"

"Yeah, Vi?"

"I hope you don't care that I'm asking," she muttered, her voice slightly hesitant. "But…are you scared?"

Adam took a long time to reply. "Yeah, Vi. I am."

"Thought so," she said, taking a quick glimpse at him then looking away. "It's probably odd…but I really don't think I am."

Adam nodded slightly. "Yeah, I know."

Violet thought a moment before expounding. "I don't think I've ever been scared of anything before."

"I'm fairly certain you're right about that. I've been your dad your whole life. You've been intrepid ever since you left the womb. Very bold."

"I bet Chris is scared."

"I have no doubt."

"Do you think…Mom is?"

"Of course she is. She's scared for Chris," said Adam. "Both of us are."

"Figures," Violet said, almost with a grin. "And she's not even the one driving head-on into danger."

"Your mother is proficient at dealing with emergencies, Vi," Adam said. "She's a professional. But things change a bit when the emergency involves your own children."

She regarded the Glock handgun in her lap. "Are you guys okay?"

Adam glanced over. "Why are you asking me that?"

Violet shrugged. "I don't know. You guys have been arguing a lot lately. It kind of worries me, but it worries Claire and Lander more. I overheard them talking about it."

"Well, kindly inform your sisters that everything is fine," Adam said. "Husbands and wives argue all the time, Vi. It's a standard form of communication between married couples. Your mom and I may disagree a lot, but we don't fight. We just don't see eye to eye on a lot of things."

"No shit," Violet said through a slight chuckle.

At the point of reaching the exit leading to the concert venue, Adam pulled the truck off the road, stopping it in the emergency lane a safe distance away from speeding cars on the highway. He reached for his cell phone and opened a mapping application, then scrolled through to their location.

"Why are we stopping here?" Violet asked. "Don't you want to drive all the way to the parking lot?"

Adam shook his head. "No, Vi. I don't. In fact, that's the last thing I want to do. God only knows what's going on in that lot right now. I'm guessing there's people trying to get in at the same time others are trying to get the hell out. The entrance to that place is a bottleneck, and even if we managed to get in, we might not be able to get back out. I don't want us to become stranded and lose the only transportation we have to get back home."

Violet tilted her head slightly to the side and nodded a little. "Okay, I get it. That makes sense. So we're just going to hike up this hill and right over into the property, then?"

"No," Adam corrected. "*I'm* going to hike over there. *You're* going to stay here with the truck."

Violet shot her eyes at her father. "Um, what? No

way, Dad. No way am I just going to sit here. I'm going with you."

Adam let out an exasperated sigh. "No, you're not. And I'm not arguing with you about this, either. You're staying behind with the truck. That's final."

"Hmm. Perhaps you don't know me as well as you think you do, father of mine. I'm not *only* your oldest daughter, I'm possibly the most headstrong person you've ever known in your life…at least, that's what you've told me. My brother is in trouble and I will *not* just simply sit here. Besides, I don't want you to go alone—especially with people shooting at each other. What if you need me? You know I can shoot."

"Vi—"

"Come on, Dad. Be logical. Do you honestly think after you leave, I won't just get up and follow you anyway?"

Adam shut the truck off and unbuckled his seatbelt. He rotated in the seat, squaring off with her. Like it or not, he knew what she was saying to be accurate. It didn't enthuse him to know she would defy him, but her loyalty to her family was palpable. And Violet was right about another thing; she was good with a gun. On the off chance he needed her, she would be an asset. "Okay, look. You can go. But you are never to leave my side, do you understand? You are stuck to my hip, right beside me the entire time. Is that clear, Vi? Am I being clear enough for you right now?"

Violet rolled her eyes. "Yes, Dad. You're being very clear. I'm going to be glued to your hip the whole time."

"Thank you." Adam got out of the truck, motioning for Violet to follow him. He opened the rear door and reached for his Kevlar vest, and after removing his jacket, he put the vest on, then zipped the jacket on overtop. He grabbed the second vest he'd pulled from the gun safe earlier and held it in front of Violet. "Here. Put this on."

"Um…you're serious?"

"Yes, Vi. I am. Put it on, now."

"Dad—wait. That's a bulletproof vest."

"I know what it is, Vi. In fact, it's level 3A Kevlar, just like mine. Put it on."

"Dad…hold on. Wait a second. Don't you think, this is just…I don't know…a little weird?"

"No. I don't."

"Well, I do."

"I know you do," Adam said. "It's not a normal act."

"No shit, it's not."

"Are you going to put it on?"

"Yeah…in a minute."

"Violet, I swear to God…"

"No, seriously, Dad. Just wait…don't get mad at me, just think about what we're doing for a second. We're standing on the side of the interstate in the middle of the night. There's cars flying by us at light speed and you're just handing your fifteen-year-old daughter a bulletproof vest, telling her to put it on like you're reminding her to brush her teeth before bed. Don't you think that's even the slightest bit strange?"

"No, I don't. I think it's practical, and I believe it's completely necessary to keep you safe," Adam said. "Look, I know a lot of things I do and say, and things I've done and said over the years, haven't exactly sounded normal...in fact, they've probably made me sound like a lunatic at times. Your mother's told me so, and anyone outside our bubble would no doubt agree with her." He leaned in, locking eyes with her. "But listen...all of those things...every single one of them that doesn't seem to make sense...things you don't necessarily get, just like this, I do for no other reason than to keep you and the rest of us safe, unharmed, and alive." He paused. "Now please just put it on—before I suffer an aneurysm."

Violet shrugged, her legs appearing weak. "Okay, since you put that way." She grudgingly took hold of the vest and examined it. "It's heavier than it looks. Kind of. And it's...hard. And the fabric feels bizarre."

Adam began arranging his gear along his belt, making certain everything would conceal properly. "That bizarre fabric will keep you alive if a stray bullet hits you. Three A can stop everything from a .44

Magnum and down. It provides a damn good amount of protection for the weight of the vest."

Violet began to help herself into the vest with some assistance from her father. "Whoa. It's rigid. This thing is going to totally crush my boobs," she griped.

Adam didn't respond. He merely shook his head at the comment.

"This feels weird," Violet said, examining the fabric with her fingertips. "But I do feel...I don't know...protected."

Adam had been so immersed in worry and preparing his daughter to accompany him, he hadn't noticed she'd been holding the Glock the entire time. After silently admonishing himself, he reached into an open duffel bag in the rear of the Jeep and presented a Kydex inside-the-waistband holster to her. "Vi, would you mind putting that in here, please?" He gestured to the pistol. "I want you to keep that gun hidden from view at all times unless you absolutely have to pull it, okay? The last thing we need is for some rookie cop to turn his gun on you and shoot you for brandishing a weapon."

Violet studied the holster before taking it. "Yeah. Sure."

"I'm not trying to scare you. My guess is these guys are pretty amped up right now, and a lot of what they've learned from training is going to be thrown out the window."

"All the more reason to be wearing this uncomfortable vest thing. Do they even *make* these for women? You know, regarding their stark anatomical differences?"

"I don't know. But I promise you, I'll find out. Tomorrow." Adam handed her two spare magazines for the Glock, fully loaded with hollow-point ammunition. "Stick these in your pockets. Three full magazines should be more than enough for what we might have to do tonight."

Violet nodded and did as she was told, a rare, serious look befalling her. She hesitated a moment, then looked over at him as several gunshots rattled off in the distance. "Dad?"

"Yeah, Vi," Adam said, observing the trees.

She blinked a few times. "I love you."

Adam paused to smile at her. "I love you too, kiddo." He rubbed the top of his daughter's purple-hued head of hair. "Let's go find your brother."

TEN

Adam knew without a single doubt in his mind, he had no business being where he was. The thought occurred to him every time he overheard the occasional pop of a rifle being fired not far from his location. The sound was disturbing, and each time it echoed past, it only reminded him of how foolish he'd been, allowing himself to be coerced into bringing Violet along.

While he surveyed the wooded area around them with his Surefire flashlight, Adam realized the beam could be making him a target while he used it to shy away the darkness. A parking lot of cars lay just ahead of them, and the metal halide lighting atop would soon negate the use of his torch, but he and Violet needed to actually get there before it would be of any use to him.

While keeping the flashlight angled downward and using his fingers to obscure the beam, he continued on and was now able to see where groups of young people had amassed around parked vehicles, some of them with their engines running. Numerous law enforcement cruisers, their red and blue lights flashing and strobing, casted eerie shadows onto other cars and the people standing nearby. Ambulances with emergency personnel had also arrived at the scene, each having their rear doors ajar, though Adam couldn't discern if anyone was inside—emergency medical personnel, patients, or otherwise.

Several SWAT vehicles were parked near the pavilion's entrance, and countless armed law enforcement officers wearing body armor and riot gear were scattered about in numerous locations around the lot. It was at that point Adam realized he had his gun drawn.

Adam had taken multiple firearms-training classes, including tactical civilian- and military-infantry-based courses, but he was far from being an expert and miles away from being a professional in a situation such as this. Walking into a parking lot with a gun in his hand would certainly get him killed on a night like tonight. He made the decision to holster it, and in doing so, his actions caught Violet's watchful eye.

"That's using your head, Dad," said Violet. "The last thing we need is for some rookie cop to turn his gun on you and shoot you for brandishing a weapon."

Adam rolled his eyes, realizing she had just repeated what he'd said to her earlier back to him verbatim. He arranged his jacket to properly conceal his pistol's lower grip, which protruded just above his waistline near the small of his back. "Sounds like good advice...can't remember where I've heard it before, though."

"They might even mistake you for a domestic terrorist," Violet continued. "You *do* fit the description. Male, politically conservative, middle-aged, Caucasian, and heterosexual."

Reaching the edge of the wooded area beside the parking lot, Adam found a tree broad enough to use for cover and dropped to a knee, then motioned for his daughter to move in behind him and do the same.

Violet knelt behind her father and craned her neck to get a better view of the lot. "I just realized something."

"What's that?" Adam asked.

"I haven't heard any guns go off in a while. Do you think that means it's over?"

"I don't know, but that doesn't change anything for us. You keep an eye out for your brother, and both eyes open for threats, Vi...at all times. Let's walk in here... slowly...and do our best to blend in."

"With all due respect, Dad. Of the two of us, *I* won't have any problem with that," Violet said with a giggle, brushing some pine needles from her knees.

"Yeah, I know. I'm not exactly trendy."

The duo continued into the lot and navigated themselves through crowds of people, all of whom were either enraged, terrified, or distraught, many to the point of crying. Many had orange mylar emergency blankets wrapped around their shoulders, having been provided to them by emergency services.

The farther in they walked and the closer they got to the entrance, it seemed as though the threat had indeed been contained. No guns were being fired, no screams had been heard, and a feeling of order seemed to overtake the crowds. This put Adam's heart at ease, but only slightly, having not yet located his son.

"Hey, Vi, did you happen to bring my phone along with you?"

Violet's face contorted. "No, why would I do that? I have my own phone."

"When was the last time you texted Chris?"

"I haven't…not since I did with your phone before we left the Jeep. You've always told me it's dangerous to text while walking. Remember that time I almost fell into that manhole?"

Adam nodded. "Yeah, I remember. Text Chris and find out where the hell he's at. There's so many people here. We could spend all night looking for them and never find them."

Violet pulled out her phone and began tapping the screen rapidly. "You say that, but these people aren't Chris's...brand. We'll find him...he sticks out like a sore thumb—especially with that laughable fuckboy hair of his."

Adam whipped his head around, squinting his eyes at her. "Did you just say 'fuckboy'?"

Violet only nodded, her concentration transfixed on her phone. "I still can't believe he let that *slorch* talk him into it."

"Slorch?" Adam raised a brow.

"Yeah, slut, whore, and bitch all rolled into one," Violet said, her scorn for Jessi evident.

"Jesus. You teens and your urban vocabulary. I need to locate a dictionary for it."

"Google helps," Violet said and, a moment later, held her phone up. "Chris just texted back. He said to look for a red Mustang parked beside a big black truck. He said there's an ambulance parked near them." She pivoted on her heels. "They're in parking lot B, wherever that is."

After taking a moment to acquaint themselves with the layout of the parking lot, they headed off in the direction of lot B, and after several minutes of searching, Violet pointed when she spotted the landmarks her brother had provided as clues of his whereabouts.

When Adam caught sight of Chris, he sprinted to him, overcome with emotion. Though it had sometimes been awkward showing affection for his son, especially in public, Adam embraced him, much to Chris's chagrin.

Chris flailed and recoiled, pulling away from his father while looking around for his peers' prying eyes. "Dad, really? Come on!"

Adam drew back and placed both hands on Chris's shoulders, then looked him over top to bottom. "Are you okay? Are you hurt?"

"I'm fine, Dad. And no, I'm not hurt." Chris turned his head away to check on Jessi, who was seated in the back of the ambulance with an EMT, who was washing the blood away from her hair and skin.

Adam's stare fell to a mass of towelettes and cotton cloths lying in a pile at Jessi's feet, all of which were stained red. "What happened to Jessi?"

"Nothing…she's fine, Dad," Chris said. "She's just getting cleaned up."

While Violet lagged behind, taking in the sights and sounds of the scene, Adam walked closer to the ambulance to get a better look at the soiled pile of fabric. "Is that blood?"

Chris didn't answer him, and Jessi didn't even notice he was standing there.

Adam waited impatiently for an answer. Despite

what he was being told, he could tell something else was going on. "Chris, answer me, please. What happened here? And don't tell me nothing. Is that blood or not?"

Chris sighed and nodded. "Yes. It's blood."

"Okay, so if she's not hurt, why does she have blood on her?"

Chris hesitated. "Because someone else got hurt tonight." A pause. "He...died, actually."

Adam stammered a bit. "Someone you knew?"

"Yeah."

"Who?"

A long pause. "Robbie."

"Who's Robbie?"

Barbie jumped down from the cab of Robbie's truck with a bag full of items, mostly consisting of his personal effects. She brushed by Adam and Chris on her way into the ambulance to seat herself beside Jessi. "Robbie...was my boyfriend," she said, her tone raspy and coated with sorrow.

Adam watched Barbie enter the ambulance, realizing he'd never seen or met her before until this moment. "I-I'm sorry," he said, feeling slightly ashamed of the tone he'd been using and not knowing what else to say to her. After a moment, his attention returned to his son. "I'm sorry, Chris. I'm sorry this happened tonight, and I'm sorry you had to be here to experience it. I'm glad you're okay, and I'm glad the rest of your friends are okay. I know it couldn't have been easy for any of you to deal with."

"Yeah." Chris's response was as impassive as his expression. "Especially Barbie." He reached out for Jessi's tentative hand.

"You do realize, if you hadn't defied us and come here tonight, you wouldn't have been witness to any of this," Adam said. "You could've become a victim tonight. Just as easily as anyone else."

Chris nodded. "Yes, Dad. I know that, and I know you're right. I screwed up…again. I made a bad decision and I know you're going to ground me for it, probably forever." He paused. "But what happened tonight happened because of chance, not decision."

Adam cocked his head. "Now, what exactly does that mean?"

"Jessi was going to go anyway," Chris explained. "She and Barbie and Robbie would have been here even if I hadn't come with them. This whole thing still could've happened…it still could've happened to them."

Barbie stuck her head out of the ambulance while wiping the smeared makeup away from her eyes with a wet towel. "Mr. Young, don't be hard on him. Chris was a hero tonight," she said, sniffling and rubbing her swollen eyes. "We were all scared to death, and I was a blubbering mess…Jessi and I—we didn't know what to do. But Chris did. He told us where to go and what to do, and I'm…I mean, we're glad he was here with us."

Jessi sent a brief cold stare her cousin's way.

Adam nodded and smiled grimly at Barbie, then turned back to Chris. "So. My son's a hero, huh?"

"I'm no hero," Chris said. "But after what happened, I wasn't going to stand there and let them get hurt."

"I'd like to think I taught you better than that."

Chris nodded, pointing to the remnants of blood, which had dried on Jessi's pants. "That's Robbie's blood," he said, making sure both Jessi and Barbie couldn't hear him. "We were all within twenty feet of each other when he got shot, but those two…they were right beside him."

"Did you see it happen?" Adam asked timidly.

"No," Chris said, gesturing to Barbie. "But I'm pretty sure she did."

ELEVEN

FAUQUIER COUNTY, VIRGINIA
FRIDAY, MARCH 28
NIHAYAT AL'AYAM PLUS 2 HOURS, 35 MINUTES

Piloting his Jeep Cherokee westward down the interstate, Adam tried desperately to regain his composure after experiencing several near heart attacks over what had transpired this evening.

His son, Chris, was safe, seated now in the back seat between two teenage girls: his girlfriend, Jessi, to his right and Jessi's cousin Barbie to his left. Adam hadn't met Barbie until this morning and had learned she'd lost her boyfriend when a bullet struck him in the head not long after the shooting had started.

Barbie had been going back and forth through bouts of crying since the time Adam and Violet had made contact with them. She was sniffling and whimpering now, her audibly expressed sorrow being the only sounds filling the interior of Adam's Jeep.

Adam glanced down at the digital clock display on the dashboard. It was nearing three in the morning, far beyond his normal bedtime. A software developer by trade, he spent half his time in the office, the other half working from home. He considered what options he had for going into work in a few hours, knowing he'd probably have to make the call soon and announce his intention to take a personal day. It would put him behind on some key projects, but his lack of sleep was going to drastically affect his productivity.

Adam pressed the power button on the Icom ID-5100A, a mobile amateur radio he'd installed in the Jeep not long after driving it off the lot. The large blue-tinted touchscreen illuminated brightly, and Adam adjusted the volume so it would be loud enough to hear, yet not too loud to startle anyone.

He palmed the microphone and keyed it, then made a call using his wife's amateur radio call sign, followed by his own. When he unkeyed, the amateur radio repeater's familiar courtesy tone signaled, indicating successful contact with the mountaintop station's receiver. Hearing nothing, he waited about fifteen seconds before repeating the call.

A very tired, wispy, familiar female voice came back to him. *"Adam, I've been sitting here worried sick for hours. Please tell me everything is okay. Do you have Chris?"*

Adam waited for the repeater's courtesy tone and the subsequent sound of the carrier dropping before keying up. "That's affirmative. Chris is with me, along with two of his friends. They've had a really rough night, but everybody is okay."

Elisabeth came back to him, this time with distinct perturbation in her voice. *"Am I to assume our oldest daughter is with you, too? Seeing as how she's gone completely AWOL?"*

Adam glanced over at Violet, locking eyes with her for a second. "Also affirmative. She's been with me the entire time, and she's also safe."

Elisabeth keyed up over the repeater's courtesy tone. *"Well, I've been worried sick about her. I looked all over the house literally a dozen times. I even tried calling your cell phone, but you wouldn't answer."*

Violet giggled. "That's because the phone lines were probably overloaded, Mom. Just like Dad more than likely told you."

Adam shook his head at the remark and keyed the mic. "The system probably got overloaded with people calling to check on their family members after hearing about the shooting. Just like I told you, Liz."

The courtesy tone sounded, and the carrier dropped, but Elisabeth didn't reply. Hearing nothing, Adam keyed the mic again. "Listen, I need to run Chris's friends to the other side of town before coming home. It shouldn't take much longer than usual. I'll see you when we get there." Adam signed off using his call sign and then hung up the mic. He waited for Elisabeth to do the same, though she didn't.

Violet took notice of her mother's folly. "Mom didn't go clear. I'm pretty sure she's supposed to articulate her call sign at the end of a conversation—just like you did."

Adam sighed. "That's right, Vi. Every ten minutes during and once at the conclusion. But I'm pretty sure right now FCC Part 97 is the least of your mother's worries."

Each time the headlights from an oncoming vehicle provided enough light for Adam to see, he checked the rearview mirror and got a glimpse of the torment painted on the young peoples' faces in his back seat. Chris looked like he'd been ridden hard and put away wet. His hair was a mess, his clothing was torn, and he had dried blood crusted on his ear, but he was otherwise alive and unharmed. He'd been lucky. As pissed off as Adam was concerning his son's actions, and as much as he wanted nothing more than to tan his hide over them, finding Chris unscathed was all he tried to focus on.

When another set of headlights blew by, Adam took a glance at Barbie, the one he didn't know until tonight, the one who'd lost her boyfriend. She was resting her head on Chris's shoulder now, and she was weeping, though not nearly as heavily as before. He regarded her with compassion, then turned his attention to Jessi, taking notice of her expressionless appearance. She'd been withdrawn and practically catatonic since she'd gotten in the truck, and Adam wasn't sure if it was due to her being traumatized by what she'd seen, or if she was just being herself—too shallow and self-absorbed to allow the evening's events to bother her. Neither would've surprised him.

His contemplations were halted when he felt Violet grab his arm.

"Dad, look." Violet pointed out her window to the north. "The sky over there…it's glowing. What do you think it is?"

Adam took a gander. "I'm not sure, but it looks like it could be coming from Mount Weather. Occasionally they run overnight exercises up there, and they light their portion of the mountain up pretty intensely. If it's foggy out or if the clouds are hanging low, you can see it for miles. We'll be pulling onto 17 in a bit…we should be able to see a little better when we get closer."

Violet seemed unconvinced. "I don't know, that doesn't look like lights to me. It looks like it's pulsating or moving…like it has a life of its own." She whipped her head around. "Do you think it could be a forest fire?"

"After everything else that's happened tonight?" Adam let out a long sigh. "I truly hope not."

Adam merged onto US Route 17 and continued north along the eight-mile, two-lane rural stretch of road. Just before the town of Paris and the intersection with US Route 50, the reflections of flashing red and blue lights became visible up ahead.

Adam slowed his speed and approached what appeared to be a roadblock operated by at least two sheriff's deputies, both of whom were standing in the road outside their cruisers. Both wore reflective vests and had shotguns slung over their shoulders.

"I wonder what the hell all this is about?" Adam said rhetorically, then glanced into the rearview. "Do any of you have any open warrants, by chance?" His attempt at a joke was met with silence and stares from the three teenagers.

Violet tapped Adam on his elbow, then pointed to the orange-glowing sky high above. "See, Dad? It's getting brighter. That's a fire…I knew it couldn't be lights."

Adam shrugged and pressed the button to roll down his window when he neared the roadblock. "I don't know, Vi. But something is definitely up." Seeing a deputy approaching with his hand raised, Adam pulled to a stop, placed the transmission in park, and placed both hands on the steering wheel with his fingers outstretched. "Keep both of your hands near the dash, Violet. Fingers splayed, just like mine."

Violet's face grew sour in an instant. "Why?"

"Just do it," Adam commanded.

"Fine."

The deputies approached, one on either side, each using a flashlight to probe the interior of the Jeep. Neither of them looked friendly or in good spirits.

"Is everything okay, Officer?" Adam asked. "There aren't enough of you for this to be a DUI checkpoint. Did something happen?"

The deputy at his window ignored Adam's question and continued shining his flashlight throughout the Jeep's innards. "What brings you out this way? Where y'all headed this time of night?"

"Home," Adam replied.

"Where's home?"

Adam gestured using only his head. "Just east of Winchester. Why?"

The officer pursed his lips and shone his flashlight's beam on Adam's hands, followed by Violet's. "Any specific reason why the two of you got your hands held up like that?"

Adam tried offering a smile, but he was just too tired, too stressed out, and too spent to muster one. "Because of the handgun mounted to the underside of my steering column. I just assumed it's better for us to keep our hands away from it…and not get shot."

The deputy's expression hardened, and he took two steps backward, shining his flashlight between Adam's lap and the underside of the dashboard. "I see. Are you the registered owner of that weapon?"

"I think so, but then again, I don't have to be."

"Pardon?"

Adam was tired, but he knew he didn't stutter. "In Virginia, private sale is legal, and possession is nine-tenths. Who it's registered to is irrelevant."

"That's correct—so long as the possessor of the weapon is a law-abiding citizen."

"Which I am."

The deputy grumbled to himself and gritted his teeth. "Then I take it you have a valid Virginia concealed-carry permit. Otherwise, we might have ourselves a serious problem, considering the location of that weapon, Mr. law-abiding citizen."

"As a matter of fact, sir, I do," Adam said. "You're welcome to look it up."

"I might just do that."

"Look, Officer…it's been a really long night for us. Can we not go this way or something?"

The deputy glanced at his partner before replying, "A long night, huh? Well, let me tell you, sir, it's been a hell of a long night for all of us." He marched to the front of the Jeep to look at the license plate. "Where exactly are you folks coming from? And do all the juveniles in the vehicle belong to you?"

Adam was taken aback by the officer's spur-of-the-moment line of questioning. "Officer, with all due respect, I haven't committed a moving violation or any other crime for that matter, and I don't have to answer your questions. And I'm quite sure you know that. All of us are extremely tired, and we really would like to get home sooner rather than later. Please…just tell us if we can continue on or not, so we can stop wasting each other's time."

The deputy tilted his head to the side and leered. "Well, check you out, cowboy. You're not one of them 'I know my rights' fellas, are you? Because if you are, let me lend you some helpful advice." He approached, placing a hand on the Jeep's roof. "Don't take that path with me, son. Don't you dare, either. I've been at this job for far too long to put up with any lip from some ham and egger know-it-all at O-dark-stupid in the morning."

Violet whispered into Adam's ear, "Dad—tell him to call his supervisor."

"Violet, shh." Adam blew her off. He readied himself to spout off at the deputy once more, but the deputy's partner moved in to join him and filled in some of the missing pieces.

"The road's closed for the time being," the second deputy said. "There's a pretty bad forest fire on the mountain just a little ways up the road from here, and we don't want anyone driving anywhere near it. Between the heat and the smoke and the weather up there, it could get precarious, and we don't want anybody getting hurt. So I'm afraid you'll have to turn around and find another way home."

Adam thanked the second deputy for his explanation and for his time, and without another word, backed up the Jeep and plotted an alternate course home, knowing the detour would add at least a half hour to his trip.

"Protect and serve. *Robocop* obviously didn't take his Midol today," Violet quipped. "I'll never understand why they feel the need to act like dicks. It's just not necessary."

Adam tapped her on the thigh. "Easy there, kiddo. It's usually better to handle things calmly and not escalate them unless we have to. I agree, he was in a bad mood. But there's no telling *why* he was in a bad mood. That could have very easily turned bad back there."

"Turned bad? You mean, like, police brutality? He could've pulled you and tased you, then beat you into a pulp right in front of us while yelling 'stop resisting, stop resisting' the whole time, like on TV." Violet giggled. "Know why he didn't? Because you had witnesses."

"You think so, huh?"

"I know so. It's always better to have witnesses. And even better than that, to record the whole encounter."

Adam glowered. "Right. Get the whole thing on

video. Then you can upload my trouncing to YouTube for the world to see."

Violet grinned and shrugged innocently. "Of course. It's a surefire way to instant fame, Dad."

Adam took in a deep breath and sighed, attempting to wake himself up a bit. "I don't want fame, Vi. I just want to go home."

At the point they'd finally made it back to town, Chris gave directions to Barbie's house. It was decided between the three, Jessi would be staying with her tonight, both to console her and so Barbie could take her back to the parking lot to retrieve her car later the following morning.

When they got home, Chris strode directly to his room without so much as a word to anyone, and Violet followed not long behind, heading to her bed after telling both her mother and her father goodnight.

Adam gathered his gear from the Jeep and carried it inside, passing Elisabeth on the way to his office. She was standing in the living room with the television on, fully transfixed on the current news broadcast.

After dropping his things off, he returned to the living room and inched his way behind his wife, placing both hands on her waist and a kiss on her neck. It was at that point he noticed she was fully dressed in a set of freshly ironed scrubs.

"It took you a lot longer to get home than what you said," Elisabeth griped. "Where in the heck have you been?"

"We had to make a slight detour. County sheriffs had a roadblock set up at Paris, and they weren't letting any traffic through due to a forest fire on the mountain. We had to drive around Cockrobin's barn and follow interstates back. The rest, I already told you. I had to drop Chris's girlfriend off at her cousin's house before heading this way."

Elisabeth didn't respond. Her attention was absorbed by every word that escaped the news anchor's mouth, only breaking at the point the broadcast switched to commercial.

"Liz?"

"What?"

"Why are you dressed for work? Did you get called in?"

"No, not yet," Elisabeth said, shaking her head nervously. "But I'm expecting to."

Adam didn't comprehend her answer. "I don't understand. And what's on TV that's got you so stupefied right now?"

"I'm not stupefied. I'm worried."

"About what? We're all home now, and Chris is safe."

"I know that, and I'm glad. I'm very glad all of you

are home," Elisabeth said, then paused. "But that forest fire wasn't just a forest fire."

Adam looked confused. "Then what the hell was it?"

"It was a plane crash."

"What?"

Elisabeth elaborated. "A Southwest airliner crashed into the mountain about twenty minutes after midnight. They're saying it hit right next to Mount Weather. It might've even clipped some of their buildings."

Adam studied the television and the reporter's remarks as they came forth. "Damn. How bad is it?"

"No one knows yet. They're still trying to get the fires put down. They won't allow rescue workers on the scene until it's safe…but it doesn't look good."

"That's crazy," Adam said. "You know, a TWA flight crashed up there back in the mid-seventies due to an abnormal approach to Dulles. I wonder what caused this one to crash."

Elisabeth huffed. "Or better yet, what's causing the rest of them to crash."

"What are you talking about?"

Elisabeth began switching channels. On seemingly every news broadcast, there was a breaking news report concerning an airliner that had crashed somewhere in the continental United States. "There's been several other crashes since, and they all started after midnight.

This one at Mount Weather is really bad...I'm just waiting to get the call from work." She turned to him, worry and exhaustion inundating her eyes. "Adam, this is really starting to scare me. You don't think this is a—"

"Liz, honey, I'm too tired to think. I'm too tired to do anything right now, for that matter. It's been entirely too long of a day." Adam stepped forward and pressed the power button on the television, shutting it off. It wasn't that he didn't want to know what was happening, he was just too exhausted to care. At the moment, it wasn't affecting him or his family in their backyard, and he didn't feel inclined to concern himself with it until it did. "Come on. Let's go to bed. Both of us need our sleep. We'll deal with whatever comes when we get up."

TWELVE

Mayflower Hotel, 1127 Connecticut Ave NW,
Washington, DC
Friday, March 28
Nihayat al'ayam plus 10 hours

I awoke in a fog when I heard the alarm clock bellow from the nightstand on Natalia's side of the bed. My nerves were still about half-shot from last night's adventure, and my heart was beating with such vigor it felt like it was trying to break out of my chest.

While taking a moment to catch my breath and gather myself, it was reassuring to see that my instincts were still intact—as evident by the G19 on standby in my clutches. Predispositions aside though, I still felt anxious and out of sorts, and I used my free hand to slap myself a few times just to verify I wasn't dreaming.

I reached over my wife's motionless body to silence the alarm, making several attempts to find the right button. Usually, the snooze bar was the largest and easiest one to locate, but it wasn't my first choice this morning. It had been a long hectic night for us. Even after a few modest hours of shut-eye, I was still dog-tired, and I knew Natalia was recuperating—her experiences having been much more…eventful than that of my own. Her body hadn't moved so much as a millimeter throughout the alarm's squawking tirade, and looking at her now, I didn't believe she'd moved much since tucking her in for the night.

I flipped over onto my back, let out a long breath, and stared up at the ceiling while slowly recalling the roller coaster of events making up the last forty-eight hours. We'd encountered our share of setbacks, but the operation had ultimately been a success. Most of the holdups had been minor, while one of them remained rather significant.

We'd spent the daylight hours yesterday and the day before going over and memorizing the various forms of intel made available to us concerning our target, his fortified security detail, and the compound where we'd ultimately be paying him a visit. We'd studied all the OSINT, or open source intelligence, from maps and satellite images of the compound from various sources to the PHOTINT, or photographic intel, which Jonathon had provided to us. Then we'd performed our surveillance of the compound in the evening hours, by car, by boat, and on foot. I'd even gotten a chance to break in a new pair of Brooks trail running shoes.

Natalia took it upon herself to handle the ground-work portion of the op while I acted as her overwatch. I kept her movements, as well as the actions of anyone within her proximity, aligned with the reticle of the thermal scope mounted to my suppressed Nemesis Arms Vanquish rifle chambered in 6.5 Creedmoor. Natalia had easily infiltrated the outside layers of embassy security without so much as breaking a sweat, and had only encountered resistance twice in the process. The armed sentries had met their demise rather swiftly and hadn't even seen her coming until it was too late for them.

Once she'd gained access to the residence, I'd lost visual of her and only had her voice in my earpiece to go by. While I waited, I watched for her whereabouts through the windows, but never once caught sight of her.

Everything had gone according to plan and had done so in short order. In less than ten minutes upon gaining entry, Natalia had located the target. A minute later, he was confirmed down. She'd sent me the photo-graphic evidence of yet another job well done, and soon after, she'd begun preparing for exfil, dutifully asking for me to clear her avenue of departure.

I'd thought we were home free—that is, until the point of hearing the all-too-real sounds of a struggle through my earpiece. Natalia had fallen prey to an attack by multiple assailants. At first, it had sounded like she was holding her own, all up until I'd heard her screams of anguish through my earpiece. One of them had gotten to her. And that, as the phrase goes, was when all hell broke loose.

It felt like I had translocated—like I had somehow moved outside my own body—by the time I'd departed my roost and tossed what remained of my sanity out the window. Like a bedlamite with nothing to lose, I'd dropped the Vanquish and broke cover, then made a mad dash through the main gate and into the heavily guarded grounds of the Saudi Arabian embassy to retrieve my wife. I don't even remember what opposition I'd encountered along the way. But now, feeling the soreness in my hands and in my joints and the throbbing pain in my forehead and kneecaps, I must've done a number on a few.

I pulled down the sheet, exposing the field dressing that now enveloped most of Natalia's left arm, from her lower bicep to her wrist, while recalling the initial sight of the wound. On her way out of the building, she'd been cornered by two sentries and had engaged them in what she thought would be a short-lived hand-to-hand encounter. But while she was distracted, a gigantic, burly man had attacked her from the shadows with a sword, of all things. If she hadn't sensed his approach and sidestepped right when she had, the blade would've undoubtedly sliced off more than just her skin.

By the time I'd finally gotten to her, Natalia had killed all three men, including the one who'd attacked her from behind. She'd relieved them all of their chosen weapons, but the damage had already been done.

Both the brachial and radial arteries in her arm had been lacerated, and by my panic-laced estimate of vascular fluids puddled on the floor, it looked as though she'd lost roughly two pints of blood. Upon my initial assessment, I'd found her responsive, but very weak. Her skin had been pale and cool to the touch, and her heartbeat was rapid—symptoms of typical vasoconstriction, the body's own built-in survival response to substantial blood loss. I'd surmised that she'd suffered a class two hemorrhage at that point, and any further loss of blood would necessitate a transfusion. Anything worse…hypovolemic shock and possible death.

With no time to lose, I'd ripped off my trauma kit and applied a CAT tourniquet as high up on her arm as I could while simultaneously watching over my shoulder for threats as I cinched it down. I'd used every Israeli battle dressing, gauze patch, and bandage I had to cover her lacerations and stop the bleeding, but they hadn't been enough. I'd ended up ripping off a large section of one of the dead men's shirts to finish the work, and in doing so, couldn't help noticing something awfully fucking peculiar. They were all American, all the way down to their Adidas socks and Timberland boots. In fact, now that I thought about it, every person I'd encountered along the way to retrieve Natalia—dead or alive—within the grounds of the Saudi embassy hadn't been Saudi at all.

Seeing her lying beside me, and watching her body expand and contract when she breathed, was the only thing keeping me from going crazy right now. This was supposed to be our final contract, our last job, and our way out of this meaningless life. And I'd come within inches of losing her.

No job in the world, no paycheck in the known universe could replace Natalia, and her getting wounded only further served as reasoning for a final send-off for us. We'd been living for far too long in a borrowed world, on borrowed time. After this, there was no uncertainty left over in my mind. *We* were through.

The loss of blood would affect her for a couple of days, but I knew she'd recover. Her arm would need to be watched closely for signs of infection and most likely be scarred for life, requiring a skin graft or cosmetic surgery of some type, but nevertheless, she was alive. She was still here with me. Natalia wasn't a cat with nine lives. She was human, blessed with only one. And she was my wife, and there was no way I was going to let something like this happen to us again.

After we made contact with Ammar today and verified our follow-up deposit, I would charter a private jet back to Germany—one way. And there, Natalia and I were going to start planning our retirement and begin our new life.

Despite the fact I felt utterly spent, my thoughts were racing, and with my mind's throttle wide open, I knew I'd never fall back to sleep. So I decided to get up and take a hot shower—the kind where the water was almost unbearably hot while, at the same time, it felt remarkable and filled the entire bathroom with steam. I only hoped the Mayflower Hotel's water heater could keep up with my expectations.

Ironically enough, I soon found that the presidential suite's shower system included an Insta-Hot water heater. I silently thanked Jonathon for being so…considerate.

After one of the most memorable bathing experiences of my life, I threw on a Marriott-logoed bathrobe and stepped into the bedroom while the steam drifted out the door behind me. There, sitting up in bed with the organic cotton sheets wrapped tightly around her, was Natalia. She yawned when she saw me and seemed highly preoccupied with the condition of her arm.

I glided over to her and sat at her side, then went to reach for her, only to have her pull away. Natalia had always dealt with bouts of tactile oversensitivity in the mornings, though today, it was especially noticeable. I gave her enough time to overcome it, and she soon allowed me to run my fingers gently through her matted hair.

After a moment, she pulled together a faint, almost counterfeited smile. "I bet I look like shit," she said matter-of-factly, her voice still raspy from her cries and the environmental variations of the previous evening.

"No, not really…but you could definitely use a shower," I joked.

Natalia nodded and went to rub her nose with her left hand, but did so with her right, sensing her arm's lack of mobility. "Well, I just assumed I looked how I felt…because I definitely *feel* like shit."

"You had a hell of a night; it's to be expected. How are you feeling? Are you in a lot of pain?"

"A little. I'm sore and my arm is throbbing. But nothing excruciating—nothing I can't handle."

"How much do you remember?"

"Everything, almost," she said, wide-eyed. "I remember you carrying me, and I remember hearing suppressed gunfire. We fell—at one point, I think… tumbled down a hill? You must've lost your footing. And I remember the water. It was frigid. That's about it. I must've blacked out after that."

"The river was close, and we didn't have many options," I said.

"It's okay; we got away," Natalia said. "I don't know how, but you got us out of there." A pause. "How bad was I?"

You'd lost a lot of blood and were in and out for a while. You were also borderline hypothermic by the time we made the safe house, and were still symptomatic after we got back here."

Natalia nodded slightly, a thin smile emerging as she glanced under the sheet. "I guess…that explains the nudity."

"I had to warm you back up somehow."

Natalia didn't say anything for a minute while she took turns looking around the room, fiddling with her hair, and poking at her bandages. Then she said, "Q, that op…was a farce. It was fucked from the word go. There weren't any Saudis inside or outside that compound last night."

"I know."

"From what I saw, every one of them was American, with the exception of the target."

I nodded. "I noticed that too. Mostly ex-military types and mercs. Moreover, they all had American-made weapons."

She nodded and rested her forehead in the palm of her hand. "His wife and children weren't even in the house. They're true-to-form Muslims…and live separately in the guesthouse next door. He wasn't using them as shields. And the sentries guarding his room…

were wearing federal IDs. For the love of God, they were Secret Service." Natalia lifted her head and turned to look me in the eyes. "What does that mean? Why the hell would Americans be providing security for an Islamic State imam and his entire syndicate?"

I shrugged. "I have no idea. Maybe they didn't know who they were guarding. Maybe they were just doing their jobs...doing as they were told and getting paid well enough to keep their mouths shut."

"Or maybe Ammar is a fucking liar. And maybe the entire op was a charade."

I nodded my lack of disparity. "That's possible, too. But even so, the contract's been fulfilled on our end. At this point, what difference would it make?"

"None, I suppose," she relented, and went back to being fixated on the damage imposed on her arm. "Shoot me straight, Q. Triage me. How bad?"

I hesitated, but didn't spend much time doing so. She'd see right through me after too long of a pause, and she hated actualities being sugarcoated. "It's not good," I said. "There's a lot of lacerated damage. None of the cuts were clean, and the blade you got hit with was nasty. It's stitched up, and we'll need to monitor it for signs of infection. You're...going to have some scars..."

"Great," Natalia said, not sounding the least bit enthused. "Just in time for retirement. There goes my modeling career."

"It could've been a lot worse."

She nodded and smiled, then reached for my hand, using the hand appended to her good arm. "I know that." She paused. "Thank you."

I squeezed her hand. "You don't have to thank me. I love you, and I only did what any husband would do. And I'd do it again in a heartbeat…if I had to."

That smile again—finally.

"I know you would," Natalia purred. "You've always been my rock. You saved me when we met. And here you are, saving me again."

I hung my head a bit and tried shaking off her praise. I'd never been good at accepting it. "No. I was headed down the road to nowhere before we crossed paths. When we met, if anything, we saved each other."

"Either way, I owe you my life, Quinn," Natalia said, her voice glazed with sincerity. "*Ich liebe dich*…I love you—always know that." She pulled me into an embrace, and I kissed her on the side of the head before we slid away moments after.

Damn. I could feel the heat radiating off her body through the sheets. It was captivating, and I could feel it pulling on me. I wanted her. But here I was, yet again, making excuses to not follow my primal instincts. Maybe it was her injury this time.

"So you want some coffee?" I asked, pushing the errant thoughts from my mind.

Her eyes perked up. "I'd love some coffee."

"Okay. Let me get dressed and I'll head downstairs and get us some."

I went to stand, but she stopped me with a forceful grip on my forearm.

"No," Natalia said. "I want to go with you."

I sent along a gaze of concern. "You sure? You feel up to it?"

She nodded a categorical yes. "We're in the nation's capital. There has to be a Starbucks or Peet's somewhere within walking distance, even for a gimp like me with perilously low blood pressure."

Natalia moved to the bed's edge and stood with the sheets still draped around her. She looked a bit wobbly at first, but she found her equilibrium in short order. Giggling at herself, she sent a grin my way while trifling with her hair and looking herself over in a mirror. She was amazing to me, and she looked incredible, even after all the hell she'd just been through. I'd do anything for her—including giving up my own life just to keep her alive.

THIRTEEN

Peet's Coffee & Tea, 1101 17th St NW, Washington, DC
Friday, March 28
Nihayat al'ayam plus 11 hours, 15 minutes

After the short jaunt to the Peet's Coffee just around the corner from the hotel, Natalia and I entered and found a small high-top table near the entrance, situated in a location allowing us both to sit with our backs against the wall. While she waited, I went to the bar and ordered us two triple iced espressos, a couple of hard-boiled eggs, a ham sandwich, and a tall orange juice, then stood at the pickup line to wait for our order to come up.

I've always made a habit out of people-watching. In fact, it's been one of my preferred hobbies for as long as I can remember. Scanning scenes and studying body language can be vastly informative for the situationally aware, the professionally vigilant, or even the occasionally paranoid.

This morning though, it wasn't what people were doing that was drawing hard on my attention, it was what they were watching on television. And on their tablets. And on their smartphones. In my weariness, it'd only taken a minute or two for me to cue in on the surrounding peculiarities, but something bearing a distinct level of enormity was going on, and it was being broadcast on every news station, on every channel, and on every television in the coffee shop.

The television to my right framed a familiar face from CNN, and on the unmistakably bright red ticker below him scrolled these four words:

AMERICA: NATION UNDER SEIGE.

The words blew by in an instant, then were repeated. A group of patrons who'd previously received their orders and had gathered around the CNN television were also busily tapping on their smartphones and making calls. I peered over some of their shoulders nonchalantly and could see Facebook newsfeeds, Twitter trends, live YouTube streams, and the like, all displaying some form of corroborating visual intel.

I scanned the room again. Fox News was being displayed on the flat screen above the coffee bar, and several baristas were focusing on it, no longer being attentive to their customers. Fox's news ticker read:

BREAKING NEWS: MULTIPLE TERROR ATTACKS CONFIRMED. PRESIDENT TO ADDRESS THE NATION WITHIN THE HOUR.

For my own edification, I decided to take a quick walk outside the coffee shop to gauge the pulse of the city. Along the way here, I must've missed something. I held up a finger to Natalia, which she acknowledged straightaway, and then stepped outside onto the bustling pedestrian-filled east sidewalk of Seventeenth Street.

Literally, the face of every foot traveler, bike rider, and car driver was buried in their smartphone or another internet-connected media device. Normally, I'd think nothing of it, being well aware of how mindlessly addicted society had become to internet connectivity in the advent of social media. But, after judging the frazzled looks on their faces, it came together quickly. Something very bad had happened.

I ambled back inside just in time to hear our order called, and after retrieving our items from the young, very anxious barista, I shuffled over to our table to my now exceedingly pensive German wife.

"Are you seeing what I'm seeing?" Natalia asked, gesturing with a head nod to the television before her.

I acknowledged her and continued surveying the scene while I set our items down and arranged them on the table.

"There have been at least ten attacks so far since early this morning," Natalia said in a low whisper. "A plane crashed near some mountaintop government installation early this morning, and there've been a handful of other crashes reported across the country since then." She shot a discreet finger at the screen across the way. "There are reports of active shooters on two military bases—one at Fort Belvoir, the other at Fort Benning. They're evacuating the Hoover Dam due to a bomb threat, and there's an unconfirmed hostage situation at Johns Hopkins. The ticker on the television in the back said ISIS is expected to admit responsibility. What the hell is going on, Q?"

I shrugged while shifting my attention between every TV screen in the room.

"This all started just after midnight," Natalia continued. "Tell me this isn't somehow coincidental."

I didn't answer. I knew she was being rhetorical, but truth was, I didn't know and genuinely didn't want to know.

Natalia was a notorious problem solver and was busy putting this all together in her mind and, for all I knew at this point, had already found a conclusion. To me, it was just a cluster of terror attacks—something not seldom seen in today's world. It wasn't something to be taken lightly, but equally, it surely had no relation to what we'd done. It just couldn't be.

Natalia and I sat for a moment and managed to get

some much-needed sustenance into our stomachs while we surveyed the parade of passersby, each person seemingly consumed in their own way by the day's events. The more she ate, the better I felt about her overall welfare. There was even a point when I thought we might end up getting away without further incident, until I heard a round of gasps and people crying out.

Natalia's eyes grew as wide as I'd seen them in a while. I followed her stare to the television above the coffee bar, where Fox News had now changed its header to:

BREAKING: UNCONFIRMED MASSIVE EXPLOSION AT MANHATTAN'S MOUNT SINAI HOSPITAL.

The anchor, whose familiar face and occasionally overly dramatized expressions I'd seen countless times before, was in the process of reporting that hundreds were now assumed dead, along with untold numbers injured. Not long into his morbid tirade, the view on the screen changed to a hovering helicopter's camera angle from above.

Through the dust and smoke, which rose stories into the air, the devastation could be seen. It was chaotic, to say the least, and the building was in utter ruin— quickly dredging up memories of the Oklahoma City bombing, the World Trade Center on 9/11, and many of the war-torn cities I'd visited in Afghanistan, Iraq, and Lebanon.

Natalia's face had gone pale again. "We need to get to a computer."

I spoke over the bite of ham sandwich in my mouth. "You want to make contact? Now?"

"Damn right I do."

I nodded. This was about to become an interesting day. Or week. "Okay," I said. "With whom?"

"Let's start with your buddy Jonathon—if he's not already too loaded for a chat. Then we'll move up the asset food chain. Someone has to know what the hell is going on."

Hurriedly, Natalia and I gobbled down our meals and finished our espressos, then exited the building. We made our way through the thick labyrinth of pedestrians and crossed over Seventeenth Street, heading back to the Mayflower Hotel.

Along the way, I noticed her having some trouble keeping up, no doubt due to lowered blood pressure and her body struggling to recover after last night's ordeal. As such, I moved my hip to hers and put my arm around her waist for support. With her eyes locked forward, Natalia gently pushed me away. Either she didn't want the help, or she was trying not to need it, but I could tell she was in the process of steeling herself.

We made a brisk entrance into the concierge lounge and to a laptop computer on a freshly cleaned glass-top desk, where the faint odor of ammonia lingered in the air. I took a seat in the leather chair in front of it while Natalia put her back to me and unconcernedly kept watch for anyone who might decide to pay too much attention to what we were doing.

Jonathon and I had known each other for years. I made his acquaintance at the agency, and he'd been assigned as my case officer when I'd gone non-official cover. During my disreputable stint there, he'd been the sole agent handler who'd ever advocated for me, having done so selflessly on a myriad of occasions while putting his own career on the line. As such, he'd earned my confidence long ago. I didn't have many friends, but I counted Jon as one of them. As far as I knew, he was no longer a company underling, but I was almost certain he still had contacts there and was himself still utilized as an asset.

Jonathon and I had maintained contact and interacted over the years by utilizing a simple dark web message board. It was accessible only by way of a Soft-Ether multiprotocol virtual private network and the portable Tor browser executable, which provided us with both essential anonymity and 256-bit encrypted secure communication. My setup resided on a USB fob and could only be accessed and manipulated using a proprietary standalone Linux-based live operating system.

Jon always carried a technologically advanced mobile device preprogrammed for continuous access via SATCOM, something Natalia and I had never done and would never do. Those gadgets almost always contained chipsets and transponders for the purpose of being located. Anything that permitted us to be tracked was in contradiction of our policy.

After inserting my USB stick, I rebooted the laptop and entered my passphrase to decrypt and mount the persistent storage. I typed the hidden service URL from memory into Tor's address bar and pressed enter. The site took a moment to load, and several seconds after logging on with my credentials, I gained access to our message board. I could feel Natalia glance over her shoulder occasionally while I typed.

AZRAEL: ROCKY4, REQUEST IMMEDIATE SITREP. WHAT THE HELL IS HAPPENING? PLEASE ADVISE. BREAK.

Natalia nudged me with her hip. "Rocky four? Really?"

I shrugged. "It's his favorite movie."

Approximately two minutes later, each going by slowly enough to feel like an hour apiece, I received the terse reply.

ROCKY4: ALL IS WELL. CONFIRMATION OF SATISFIED CONTRACT RECEIVED. TRANSFER CONFIRMED 0800 THIS AM. BREAK.

"What the hell is he talking about?" Natalia probed. "We haven't made contact with Ammar yet."

I nodded, then typed:

AZRAEL: PAID IN FULL? ALREADY? PLEASE
CONFIRM. BREAK.

A minute passed before the reply.

*ROCKY4: AFFIRMATIVE. HUNDO P. YOU ARE
RICH. ENJOY RETIREMENT. BREAK.*

This was uncanny. If we'd gotten paid in full already, it was the first time it had ever happened before confirmation had been provided to the payer.

"Ask him about the goddamn attacks," Natalia hissed.

My first thought was to pacify her in some way, but my interest was starting to pique as well.

AZRAEL: ADVISE INFO ON TERROR ATTACKS.
BREAK.

Several minutes passed, during the final of which, I thought I'd either lost the connection or lost him. Then the reply came.

ROCKY4: UNCERTAIN AT THIS TIME. BREAK.

"Bullshit!" Natalia spat.

I agreed with my wife. That answer was indeed complete bullshit. I made another attempt.

AZRAEL: URGENT. PLEASE ADVISE INFO ON
TERROR ATTACKS. BREAK.

Five full minutes passed. I crossed my arms over my chest and leaned back into the chair. I could hear Natalia tapping her foot behind me while she fidgeted with her wounded arm. Finally, Jon's reply came.

*ROCKY4: EVACUATE ASAP. CITY UNSAFE. REPEAT.
EVAC TO NEAREST KNOWN SAFE LOCATION.
WILL ADVISE FURTHER UPON NEXT CONTACT.
BREAK.*

Natalia let out a lurid sigh. "You tell that drunk bastard to meet us face-to-face somewhere close by and, if he doesn't know anything, to bring someone with him who does, or I'm going to find him and—"

I hushed her with a snap of my fingers and a hand on her hip, then began nervously cracking my knuckles just as a cornucopia of shrieks and loud gasps echoed from around the corner in the lobby.

Natalia didn't hesitate to hurry off and investigate. I turned and hung my arm over the chair while placing my other hand on the laptop, ready to pull the USB drive and terminate the connection at a second's notice if the need arose.

The panicked noises in the lobby reached a crescendo. Some commotion followed and a moment after, Natalia rounded the corner with her head hung low, her eyes sunken, and her expression morose. Something else had happened—something horrible, I suspected.

She glided to stand in place behind me and placed both her hands on the chairback to steady herself as her jaw slackened.

"What is it?" I asked.

She didn't answer immediately. Her eyes narrowed. "A suicide bomber. He just detonated himself…inside an elementary school in Cleveland."

I felt a chill wash over me. It started at the top of my head and slid down my entire body, causing me to shiver involuntarily.

I'd always known I was uncommon to most people in the world. I was someone who'd been born without a conscience—capable of heinous actions against other human beings while feeling no remorse for them, no guilt or shame for what I had done. But hearing those words struck my soul like a phaser set to kill. If these heathens were willing to attack and murder innocent children, there wasn't anything they weren't capable of.

Breaking through my moment of self-reflection, Natalia gestured to the laptop. "Let me talk to him."

I nodded, not knowing anything else to say or do at this point. An elementary school. Children. For Christ's sake.

Natalia slid herself into the chair just as I got to my feet. She placed her hands on the keyboard and typed:

AZRAEL: THIS IS STILETTO. FARRAGUT SQUARE. BRING INTEL. ONE HOUR. OUT.

She then pulled the USB stick from the laptop. The screen went blank and she handed the stick to me with a resolute, sickened look on her face. "Get me the fuck out of here."

FOURTEEN

Adam rose to the feeling of warm sunlight kissing his face. He pried open his eyes, taking note of the brightness in his bedroom, and soon after, the emptiness of his bed. He reached out and patted the sheets beside him, feeling only the plushness of the pillowtop mattress underneath. Elisabeth was no longer stretched out by his side.

Adam rolled over and yawned, then reached for his phone on the nightstand to check the time. "Eleven thirty? Great. The office is probably freaking out now."

He slid out of bed and into the first pair of pants he could find on the floor. The shirt he'd been wearing the previous evening was hanging at the foot of the bed. Adam slipped his arms and head through it, fluffed his hair, yawned again, then stretched as he stood. He then walked out of the bedroom and into the hallway, feeling the soggy bottoms of his feet stick to the hardwood floor with each step.

The first thing Adam could hear was the TV blaring in the living room. He peered left as he walked by and into the kitchen, noticing both Chris and Violet were seated on the couch. He waved to them sluggishly and inched his way to the refrigerator in search of a cold caffeinated drink with which to wet his lips and alleviate the dryness in his mouth.

"Not going to work today?" Violet called from the living room.

"No, I suppose not," Adam replied. "It appears I've overslept. Guess I'll be doing the work-from-home thing. If I still have a job."

"Lucky you," Violet replied snarkily.

Adam uncapped a bottle of iced coffee and took a mediocre sip. "Aside from the television, the house sure is quiet. Any idea where your mother is? She wasn't supposed to go in until two today."

"She got called in…about an hour after you guys went to bed," Violet said.

"She did?"

"Yeah. I'm surprised you didn't know."

"I'm a little surprised, too. Then again, as tired as I was, I must've been sound asleep when she got up."

"Mom was tired too," said Violet. "She wasn't exactly thrilled when she got the call. She did say to have you call her whenever you decided to get up."

Adam nodded. "I suppose I'll do that. Thanks for passing along the message." He turned away, then halted before heading into his office, realizing it was only Friday and, as such, a school day. Because of last night's events, he hadn't expected Chris nor Violet to attend, but the laughing and cackling coming from Claire and Lander's room told him he had a full house. "No school today?"

"Cancelled," murmured Chris.

"Cancelled?"

"Because of the protests downtown."

Adam nodded. "It's probably just the same. I wasn't going to send either of you today. Now…your rambunctious sisters, on the other hand." He paused while gazing around the house. "Vi, did your mom happen to allude as to why she got called in?"

"No. But I'm pretty sure it's because of that plane crash."

Adam rotated on his heels and moved to stand by the couch. In his exhaustion, he'd nearly forgotten.

Violet pointed to the television. "There's been a few other ones too. It's been all over the news."

"Other ones? Near here?"

"No, not near us or anything," Violet said. "Just here and there—it's weird. And there's been a few other attacks."

Adam squinted, taking a large gulp of his coffee. "What sort of attacks?"

Violet rattled off the list of known and purported attacks, and Adam's interest began gaining ground at a rapid pace.

"Chris," Adam said, "let me see that remote."

Chris handed it to him and Adam began flipping through channels, stopping only seconds at each news broadcast, long enough to gather enough information to paint the picture. Each one was reporting a similar headline, that multiple incidents, possibly terror related, had occurred across the country already this morning. Some even included ongoing live feeds of the scenes.

"Jesus Christ."

Violet and Chris both turned to their father. "What is it?" they asked almost concurrently.

Adam turned and darted off in the direction of his office. Once there, he set his drink on his desk, placed his hand on his mouse and clicked from one website to another, attempting to locate as much information as he could on what had happened while he'd been asleep. The more he saw and the more info he gathered, the more his heart sank and the thicker the lump inflated in the back of his throat.

Adam took a long, slow sip of his morning pick-me-up. He set it down and rested the side of his head in his palm as his mouth dropped open. "This can't be happening."

"What can't be happening?" Violet asked, her expression displaying marked concern as she strolled into his office and approached his desk. "Dad…you look nauseated. What's going on?"

Adam's first instinct was to tell her it was nothing. The last thing he wanted to do was start a panic in his own home. But he knew as analytical as Violet was, she would not simply stand for that answer. "I'm not exactly sure. It could be nothing, but then again, it could be something substantial. Something we've never seen before. I haven't felt this way since I saw those planes hit the twin towers." A pause. "We need to keep our eyes open for what could happen next."

Violet's dark eyes grew wide. "Okay. So what should we do first? You want to start calling people? Should we lock down the house?"

Adam started to answer her, but was interrupted by his son entering the room.

"Hey, Dad? I need a favor."

"What sort of favor?" Adam glanced up at him. "This isn't exactly the best time, Chris."

"Yeah…well, I wanted to see if you could run me back to Barbie's house this morning so I can check on Jessi. I'm really worried about her, and I need to see if she's okay."

"I thought they were going to pick up her car today."

"They haven't left yet. Jessi says Barbie hasn't wanted to move around much this morning. Can't say as I blame her much."

Adam nodded ever so slightly. "Okay, yeah. Maybe. I'll think about it."

"Is that a yes or a no?" Chris asked. "Because she's machine-gun texting me about it, and I need to tell her if I'm coming or not. Would it be easier if I just have them come over here and pick me up?"

"Would it be easier? Yes. But will I allow it? No!"

"Whoa, Dad. Seriously?"

"Yes, Chris. Seriously," Adam said. "Are you kidding me? After what you did yesterday? And after what we had to go through to find you? No, I most certainly do *not* want anyone coming here to pick you up."

Chris recoiled at his father's response. "Wow, okay. Forget it! All I wanted to do was check on my girl-friend. But screw it! I'm sorry for even asking." He stormed out of Adam's office and into his room, slamming the door behind him hard enough to knock a picture from the wall.

"Now do you see why I give him so much grief?" Violet asked after a sigh and scrutinizing her brother's response. "He deserves it. He's so infatuated with that *bizznotty*, he can't even see when he treats his own family like crap."

Adam didn't have the mental fortitude in that moment to consider Chris's behavior or Violet's multi-hued commentary. The plane crashes and these uncommon attacks, in combination with what had occurred the previous evening, were really starting to weigh on him. Something was happening here. Something big. Something terrible and beyond compare to anything that had occurred before, and Adam was starting to get a bad feeling in his gut.

"Dad? I can tell you're in think mode. Is there anything you need me to do?" Violet asked. "I'm being serious, by the way. I know it's hard to tell when I am, sometimes."

Adam took in a deep breath and willed himself back to reality. He rotated his head and tried his best to smile at her. "No, sweetie. Not right now. The only thing I want is the only thing I've ever asked you to do for me."

"What's that?"

"Be ready. For anything."

"Oh."

Adam gestured with his head to his computer monitor. "Of course, in light of prevailing events, I don't think it could hurt for us to escalate our preparedness level at home. There's no telling if these attacks are going to fade away or get worse. And I like to err on the side of caution."

Violet cocked her head at him. "I've never seen you act this way before, Dad. What do you think is going to happen?"

Adam sat back in his seat and folded his arms across his chest. "I'm expecting this whole thing to get worse. Way worse. And I think it's judicious that we all prepare ourselves for that very thing."

"No problem. So are we bugging in or bugging out?" she asked.

"In, for the time being."

Violet's eyebrows drew in and a look of urgency crept across her face. She nodded slowly. "Okay. I'm on it. I'll make sure Claire and Lander are occupied; then I'll do a fundamental gear check. And you might want to consider making a run to Costco this morning before everyone else does." She turned away and started out the door. "Oh, yeah…don't forget to call Mom."

Adam smiled at her as she scampered out of the room. "That's my girl."

FIFTEEN

FARRAGUT SQUARE, WASHINGTON, DC
FRIDAY, MARCH 28
NIHAYAT AL'AYAM PLUS 13 HOURS, 30 MINUTES

When I saw Jonathon walking across K Street dressed in full business attire complete with a full-length wool coat, I almost didn't believe my eyes. When I noticed that he'd brought someone with him, I felt like I was hallucinating. I needed to make a mental note of this—the next time we need something from him, allow Natalia to take the helm. Her requests apparently had a much greater effect than did mine.

The man accompanying Jon followed just feet behind him and didn't look particularly happy to be where he was. Actually, he looked just plain nervous and damned near paranoid of being where he was. I assumed him agency by his looks, probably some pencil-pusher or an analyst geek. Someone who didn't get much sunlight. I didn't know who he was, but he was most definitely not an operative. He didn't walk the walk.

While Natalia sat quietly with her back to me on a wooden bench fifty feet away to my twelve o'clock, I leaned against a mature walnut tree, hidden from sight, keeping my eyes in tune with the scene around us. I trusted Jon, but I didn't trust the rest of the world, and meetings like this had always persuaded me to keep my guard up.

I watched as Jon and his partner converged on Natalia, and listened to the ensuing conversation through my earpiece, never once taking my hand from the Glock under my jacket.

"Where's your other half?" Jon asked Natalia, his head on a constant, observant swivel.

Her reply came tranquilly. "Not far. He's never far. Thanks for coming."

Jon sneered. "Like I had a choice in the matter."

"That's right. You didn't." Natalia tilted her head slightly to the side. "Who's your friend?"

The man standing beside Jon took a clumsy step backward and turned his head away bashfully. He said nothing.

Jon pulled a cellular phone from the inside pocket

of his coat. "Someone with information. Someone I trust."

He was lucky. For a split second, I could've sworn he'd pulled a gun on her. It was official—I was seeing things. I really needed to get some quality sleep, and soon.

Jon tapped the screen on his phone a few times and then handed it to Natalia. "Don't worry—it's encrypted. Fully secure."

Natalia looked at the screen for a second and then placed it against her ear, over her earpiece so I could listen in. A few seconds later, I heard a voice carrying an Arabic accent, leaving little doubt who it was.

"Ammar?" Natalia asked.

"*Hello, Mrs. Stiletto. I must say, I am very impressed with your work. You and your husband were well worth the disbursement for your services.*"

"I appreciate the compliment, Ammar," Natalia said. "But would you mind explaining some things— like why the compound was occupied with American sentries? And why we were paid in full before you received confirmation? How did you know the job was complete without hearing from us?"

Ammar paused before responding. He deflected with, "*I am also very glad that I was able to meet you and your husband before—well, before it was too late.*"

"Too late? Too late for what?" Natalia quizzed. "Ammar, I—"

"I am sorry, Mrs. Stiletto, but the time has come for me to move on. My only regret is that I made your acquaintance at such an inopportune moment in history. I do wish to thank you for your assistance, and I bid you and your husband the best. Good luck."

And then the line went dead.

Natalia cursed profusely in German and tossed the phone back to Jon.

Jon caught the phone with both hands, fumbled with it, and slipped it back into his jacket. "I take it he didn't tell you what you wanted to know?"

Natalia bit her lip. "No. But what he didn't say tells me practically everything."

Jon nodded, placed his hands on his hips, and gestured to his companion. "We don't have a lot of time here. Washington, DC, isn't the safest place to be, and it's only going to get worse. We need to get this business over with and evac as soon as we can."

Natalia stood up and moved nearly nose to nose with Jon. "What does that mean, exactly? What do you know that you're not telling us?"

The other man finally spoke up nervously. "We need to leave because every city, especially this one—has become ground zero."

Natalia retreated several steps and turned to the man curiously, then whipped her head over her shoulder to me. The time had come to break concealment and join them.

When Jonathon saw me approach, he smiled faintly and held out his hand. I shook it, but didn't offer him a smile in return. The man with him sent me some questionable microexpressions that I couldn't put my finger on—almost as if he was trying to remember where he'd spotted my face before.

"Is this your intel guy?" I asked Jon.

He nodded.

"Is he first tier? Or some lackey from the farm?"

Natalia backed away, sensing that it was my turn to do some interrogating.

"He's—" Jon's voice sank to a whisper. "He's one of my floaters."

I grinned. I wasn't impressed. "A floater, huh?" I turned to the man, gesturing casually to myself and to Natalia. "Do you know who we are?"

He looked away. After a pause he said, "Officially? No."

I looked him over for a second before continuing. "How about unofficially?"

His eyes found mine. "Admittedly, yes."

"Fantastic," I said, expressing my displeasure. "Thanks a lot, Jon."

Jon threw his hands in the air at his sides. "Quinn, please. Stop pretending you two aren't the real-life underworld incarnates of *Mr. & Mrs. Smith*. You wanted information, he's got information—the information you wanted. And I think you need to hear him out."

"Fine," I said. At this juncture, there wasn't any point in arguing with him. Like it or not, we were involved now for one reason or another and needed to know why. My stare found its way back to Jon's companion. "What do you know about these attacks?"

"More than anyone should," he blurted out.

"Do you know what precipitated them?"

The man cowered behind Jon, pushing his thick plastic-framed glasses higher up on the bridge of his nose. "A signal."

"What? What kind of signal?"

He apprehensively replied, "Specifically…a negative reply. From a transponder chipset."

I turned to Natalia, who, judging by the look on her face, had instantly put it together.

"Are you talking about the microchip we used to trail el-Sattar?" she asked.

The man looked away and then back to us. He started to shuffle step as his eyes darted, indicating fight or flight, but Natalia reached forward, forcibly grabbing his arm. "Don't!"

"Ouch!" the man squealed. "I wasn't going to—"

"Yes, you were. Now, answer my question," she ordered, a sinister edge to her voice.

The man nodded profusely. "The chip used to track him and the one I'm referring to are one and the same."

Natalia let go of the man's arm just as the expression on her face sank. She reached for her injured arm as if she'd suddenly felt a twist of pain from it. "Jesus. This *was* us," she said, almost inaudibly. Then her face turned pale. She looked dizzy—almost faint.

I reached for her and helped her onto the bench behind us while she repeatedly expressed to me that she was okay, her vacant stare telling me otherwise.

"What's wrong with her?" Jonathon asked, a fretful look on his face. "Is she drunk?"

I ignored Jon's witticism and focused my attention on the other man. "So this negative reply...what caused it?"

The man shrugged, his eyebrows raised. "Death," he said colloquially. "Lack of heartbeat or pulse. Nonexistence of brain activity. It was a sum of factors actually, but it's predicated on the demise of the host."

"Who designed this thing?"

The man looked over at Jonathon, who looked away and rolled his eyes.

Upon seeing Jon's expression, I extrapolated the answer. "The agency."

Jon acted as though he'd heard nothing. The man did the same, only to soon change his tune. He looked back at me and nodded his response with a clenched jaw.

I grabbed Jon's arm and pushed my thumb into his inner elbow to get his attention. "And I take it the agency had it implanted? During the dental visit Ammar spoke about?"

"No!" he snapped back instantaneously, shoving away my hand. "That wasn't us! Yes—we designed it. And, yes, it was sold along to various assets for a swarm of reasons. It's how we've been able to track el-Sattar for so long. It's what helped me secure this op for us. But *we* didn't put it there, so please, Quinn. Fucking relax."

It occurred to me that Jon used the objective pronoun *us* and the subjective pronoun *we*. I couldn't tell if it'd been intentional or a Freudian slip, but his use of them allowed me to home in on their shared antecedent. And I took it to mean that Jon was still very much under contract with the agency.

I snarled. "If the CIA didn't put it there, who did?"

The nervous man looked around for a moment, wondering if he should answer. Then he spoke up after a pause. "The Islamic State of Iraq and al-Sham."

I turned to him. "What?"

"It's a new protocol—a procedure that's not exactly customary knowledge. Islamists have been using it to track their leadership and to know when a death occurs. What's happening now, though, is rather unprece-dented. el-Sattar's death wasn't always a trigger mecha-nism, but it somehow manifested into one—due to recent events."

I took in a deep breath. My nerves were nearly shot, and I could feel my patience waning. I warned him. "You'd better start making sense."

"I'm sorry, I'm trying. I'm not the best...talker. I don't get out much," the man said, his voice shaky. "You see, we have it on good authority that el-Sattar came here only to seek asylum."

"Asylum from whom?"

"Islam," he replied flatly. "He was making arrangements...planning to renounce his position as imam and abandon his beliefs."

"Holy shit," Jon said.

"Yes, holy shit," his companion said, gesturing his agreement. "We are of the belief that his supremacy had begun to weigh on him, and he was having, for lack of a better term, second thoughts. By renouncing Islam, he'd become an apostate, which, as everyone knows, is a death sentence. Staying in the Middle East would've been out of the question for him. We know that he was brought here under tight diplomatic security—flown in on a military transport—and had arranged to meet with the president and other leaders for what we believe was to be a systematic decommissioning of jihadist terror cells across the country, and to prevent the declaration of the future caliphate."

"I think I'm going to be sick," Jon said, turning his head away. After a few seconds of studying the area beside and behind him, he reached into his jacket once again, extracting two miniature glass bottles—one Absolut, one Stolichnaya.

"We presume now that ISIS, by some means,

managed to uncover his plan and, in turn, instituted a workaround of sorts to move forward without el-Sattar in play."

"Move forward with what?" I asked.

"Inception. Of *nihayat al'ayam*," he replied cavalierly, as if for some reason he thought I knew what he meant.

"The end of days," Natalia filled in, not having so much as moved from her seated position.

I'd almost forgotten she was moderately fluent in Arabic. The end of days? This was starting to sound more like a vicious nightmare.

The man drew in closer after taking a highly distrustful look around. We were all huddled together now, close enough to become intimate if we elected to. "That's right. And it begins with the crippling of America."

"Keep going," I said.

"It's their final checkmate…a summation of their foreign policies," he whispered. "It's a portion of what Islamic Law refers to as 'offensive jihad'—their violent expansion into non-Muslim-ruled countries. The attacks we've seen so far today are just the beginning. It's going to expand and it's going to escalate. And it's going to get a lot worse, and it's going to stay that way."

I turned to Jon. "Did you know anything about this?"

He shook his head while swallowing down the last droplets from the two mini bottles. "Bits and pieces, Quinn, only bits and pieces. We never saw anything like this coming."

"But you should have," Natalia said, her voice and her empty stare showing her anxiety.

Jon's companion advocated, "These attacks were planned and coordinated over a span of decades and came into being a long time ago. I assure you, the company had nothing directly to do with them. Whether el-Sattar ordered them into being or they ignited on their own, resultant of his death, this event was inevitable."

"Is there any way to stop it?"

The man shook his head and readjusted his glasses. "How much do you know about ISIS?"

I sighed. "Apparently, not enough."

He nodded. "It's okay. Don't feel bad, you're no different than most." A pause. "The general consensus is they're just a bunch of psychos running around blowing themselves up haphazardly, but that's just not the case. ISIS is a religious faction with meticulously considered beliefs. It fundamentally rejects peace, craves genocide, and deems itself the foremost purveyor of the coming apocalypse." He paused and covered his mouth to cough. "Early this morning and today, it was plane crashes, attacks on government buildings, police stations, military bases, hospitals—"

"Schools," Natalia broke in.

The man nodded. "Yes, my apologies. I was about to mention soft targets. It's unfortunate, I know, but before long, it will escalate, I assure you. Oil refineries, bridges and tunnels, hydroelectric dams, power plants, and, eventually, the entire electrical grid will be affected. When the lights go off and gasoline stops flowing, the trucks stop running, and the economy will tank. America falls to its knees. And then they'll go local with an entirely different type of jihad—the 'scare the living shit out of you' kind. They'll forcibly institute sharia law, and we'll see instances of public beheadings, amputations, crucifixions, and the like. ISIS is compelled to not only destroy its enemies, but terrorize them into submission beforehand."

"Jesus. We didn't cut the head off the serpent," I said. "We ignited the fuse to some newfangled holocaust."

"I'm sorry I didn't bring along good news," the man said. "Jon said you needed information, and I'm good with information. For nearly half a decade, I've been the company's foremost expert on Islamic terror."

I looked at him strangely. "That's quite a position to fulfill."

He shrugged casually. "Let's just say no one knows more about it than I do. And I can promise you, there's nothing virtuous or attractive about Islamic apocalypticism."

Natalia stood up and folded her arms over her chest. She looked perplexed, but the color was returning to her skin. "Do you have any idea when this ends?"

The man looked confused. "I'm sorry?"

"How long are these attacks expected to continue?" she asked again. "When does this stop?"

He hesitated, his expression blank. "Um, well…it doesn't."

"It doesn't?" I asked.

"No," he uttered while motioning his head in the negative. "It goes on. Forever. Until nothing remains."

Jon turned his head away and began laughing in his own characteristic fashion. "And you guys wonder why I drink."

SIXTEEN

Mayflower Hotel, 1127 Connecticut Ave NW,
Washington, DC
Friday, March 28
Nihayat al'ayam plus 15 hours, 2 minutes

After our meeting ended, I escorted Natalia back to the hotel so she could get some rest. Considering our most recent discovery, I felt we'd reached a point where we needed to cut bait and get the hell away from here. We needed to liquidate our assets and make arrangements to return to Europe before the situation here worsened and our amnesty elapsed.

I ordered her room service in the form of a grass-fed, twelve-ounce, medium-rare ribeye steak, a side of blanched broccoli and asparagus, and two glasses of freshly squeezed orange juice. I departed only after kindly requesting that she eat and drink everything before my return and try to get some sleep. Natalia's body required the nourishment, and she needed to feel like herself again as quickly as possible before we encountered the taxing predicament we now knew was inbound.

America had become a war theater—a hostile environment—seemingly overnight, and I had a hunch we were about to embark on a precarious journey in the coming days. I needed her to be as close to one hundred percent operational as possible.

I hailed a yellow taxi to transport me to an Enterprise Rent-a-Car five and a half blocks away from the hotel. After a half hour of haggling with a skinny, well-dressed Jamaican man smelling of spearmint gum and marijuana, I threw down a cash deposit, along with Joel Donovan's American Express card, and drove out of the lot in a silver Audi A8. I assumed the wife would approve of my choice, even though the Americanized version of the three-liter turbocharged sedan wasn't exactly made for the autobahn.

As I pulled onto the street amongst the incessant horn-blaring traffic, I made a mental note that it was indeed time to dump Mr. Donovan's identity and assume a new one before day's end if time allowed.

My next stop was at a Nordstrom not far away to purchase two pieces of rolling luggage that I assumed were large enough for the load they were destined to carry. I tossed them into the trunk of the Audi and then made my way through traffic, up Eighteenth Street and back down Connecticut to Brooks Brothers for some specific clothing items I required. My ultimate destination was a rather elite one and, I assumed, would have more of an appreciation for someone wearing business attire, as opposed to the blue jeans, long-sleeve T-shirt, and North Face jacket I had on at present.

With those tasks behind me, I exited the District and drove over the Fourteenth Street Bridge into Arlington, stopping at the Wells Fargo Bank in Crystal City, where Natalia and I had procured a safe deposit box years ago, one of three in the metropolitan area, and one of just under a hundred in the world. We'd chosen this location and others like it because they utilized a retinal scan for identification purposes instead of industry-standard biometrics like most other financial institutions. One effortless insertion of a smart contact lens, and our identities remained as they'd always been—completely surreptitious.

After presenting the proper credentials to a Wells Fargo employee wearing a red cocktail dress and a pair of scuffed four-inch heels, she escorted me to the vault, where I was asked to approach a terminal for the retinal scan. A few seconds later, the screen glowed green and welcomed me, and the clerk handed me my laser-cut key along with a smile and then closed the privacy curtain behind me after I'd stepped inside.

I laid the rolling luggage on the floor and unzipped the top, just underneath the deposit box door, then inserted the key, twisted it, and typed a four-digit pin code into the number pad. It beeped, opened, and revealed a bounty of personal items, along with some professional ones.

Passports, driver's licenses, assorted IDs, credit cards, and one hundred thousand dollars cash, minus the ten grand I stuffed into the front pocket of my new pleated Brooks Brothers wool dress trousers, were amongst the contents I dumped into the case. Several burner iPhones wrapped in mylar bags and an Iridium 9575A military-grade satellite telephone with spare batteries, USB connectivity cabling and a charging kit followed, as did two third-generation PVS-7 night-vision devices.

At the bottom of the container lay a French-made Glauca B1 folding tactical-duty knife, which found its way promptly into my right pocket, two FN Five-seveN high-capacity auto pistols, and finally, a custom Steyr TMP machine pistol with extra thirty-round magazines and matching suppressor. I took a quick glance over my shoulder to verify I was still alone, placed the weapons, ammunition and accessories into a separate zippered area within the case, and took a breath.

My business here concluded, I tossed the key back to the clerk and took my leave of Wells Fargo. I loaded up the Audi and made for Reagan National Airport for the purposes of chartering a private jet that would take Natalia and me back to Germany. I soon found though, my plans to leave the country weren't going to materialize as I'd have preferred, in spite of the coin I'd spent on this faux Cary Grant–look-alike outfit.

The attendant behind the desk at the Charter Flight Group hanger was a balding man in his late forties. When I inquired in earnest about procuring a trans-Atlantic flight, he offered me a confounded look and said, "You do realize Homeland Security raised the threat level to orange, right? There're attacks popping up all over the country now. Word is, they're going to raise it to severe before long. It hasn't been that high since…well, since ever."

"Yes. I'm aware of that."

He looked to his computer monitor, away, and then back to me shyly. "The FAA is considering shutting down American airspace. I take it you were aware of that too?"

I wasn't. But it wasn't surprising to hear of it, either. "But they haven't done so yet, correct?"

"Well, no, but I imagine it's forthcoming. Is that why you want to leave?"

"Does it matter?"

"No, sir. I was just curious," he replied, and then began typing on his keyboard. "I'm guessing by the looks of things, lots of people are trying to flee the country now."

I smiled at him while trying to gauge if he was really this simple or if he was just this stupid. I'd killed men before over less. I figured I'd give him the benefit of the doubt, though. His coffee-stained tie, eyeglasses that had been repaired with scotch tape a few times too many, and pants coated in a thin layer of cat hair made me feel a bit sorry for him. He looked, if anything, lonely. And I didn't exactly know how to charter or fly my own jet. At this juncture, I needed him around. Kind of.

"My wife and I flew in a few days ago, and I wanted to fly her home on a private jet as a surprise."

He adjusted his glasses. "You say you're a pilot?"

"No, I didn't say that at all."

"My mistake. Did you fly in on a private jet?"

I shook my head. "No."

"I see. Is this a special occasion, then? Your anniversary or something?"

"Sure."

"Well, which one? Anniversary or something else?"

I rolled my eyes. "Anniversary."

"That's nice. How many years have you been married?"

Okay. I was certain. He was both simple *and* stupid. I didn't answer him, even after he looked up at me and practically begged me to.

"Okay, well…looks like all we're going to have available for you is our G550. It can depart tomorrow morning at the earliest. Where did you say you were going again?"

"Munich," I said, even though I was certain it had been the first time I'd mentioned it.

He spelled the letters out one by one to himself tediously while typing them. When he finished, his eyes grew wide. He cleared his throat and began to appear very uncomfortable. "Um, sir, we can have that charter ready for you and the bird fueled up by eight o'clock tomorrow. The total's going to be kind of steep, though. You want me to write the estimate down or just give it to you?"

I motioned for him to verbally convey the number.

"Well, for that bird, you're looking at ninety-seven thousand dollars. And sixty-two cents."

My jaw hit the floor. "I'm sorry, but there must be some mistake. I've chartered dozens of flights before, and they've never been that expensive."

The man nodded, his eyebrows raised. "Yes, sir, I understand that. But this charter is for a G550, the largest bird in our fleet. If you'd like to wait a few days for a smaller jet, we might be able to—"

"No. That's fine," I said. "I take it you require all funds up front?"

"If you want to reserve it and lock in the price? Yes, sir. If I'm guessing right, the price of gas is going to shoot the moon in the next couple of days because of the attacks, and jet fuel along with it. The charter might cost darn near a half-million dollars by then. Who knows…"

I hated being sold. But Natalia and I needed to get out of here while we still could. The op was complete. Our mission was over. We'd been paid in full, and the time had come for us to return home.

I unzipped the rolling luggage at my feet and opened it enough to pull out several bundles of American dollars, then stacked them on the desk to the utter astonishment of the attendant. "Do you take cash?"

After leaving the airport, I swiftly concluded that I'd all but exhausted my supply of cash in this most recent venture. Previous experiences, especially those in third-world nations, had taught me that a country under siege wasn't the best place to be without steady access to funds. So, unenthusiastically, I made stops at our two remaining safe deposit locations in the District and liquidated our assets from them, effectively closing our accounts.

My outline of tasks having reached completion, I wove the Audi through the horrendously dense city traffic and back to the Mayflower Hotel. Along the way, I couldn't help but notice that a black late-model Range Rover appeared to be following me. I thought I'd noticed it earlier while on my way into Crystal City, but passed it off since it was a rather prevalent choice of vehicle here. It might as well have been a Toyota Prius.

I made a few evasive turns to the chagrin of the

A8's navigation system, which was deadlocked on the Mayflower's address. While the computerized voice chastised me, I checked the rearview mirror for the behavior of my newly discovered tail. Sure enough, it followed me several cars behind after the first and second turns, but fell away after the third. This wasn't cause to lose vigilance, however. Those proficient at vehicular surveillance would perform this tactic purposefully to prevent exposure.

While keeping a sharp eye on my six, I pulled the car to a stop between two parked SUVs on the right side of H Street and waited. Two minutes passed, and nothing. Five minutes passed, and still nothing. Maybe I was seeing things. It was completely possible, considering how sleep-deprived I was at the moment. Rest was something I desperately needed to find.

Once I arrived at the hotel, I left the Audi with the valet after securing the items in the trunk, made arrangements at the front desk to extend our stay until tomorrow morning, and then headed back up to our suite.

When I walked in and made my way into the bedroom, I saw Natalia sitting with perfect posture and legs crossed on the bed, almost in a meditative lotus position—but she wasn't meditating. Her eyes were fixated on the television screen and the news broadcast it was displaying.

She turned to me and smiled upon my entry. I

smiled back at her, noticing immediately that all the color had returned to her skin. She looked recovered and refreshed, and that in itself took a massive load off my mind.

"You look nice," she said coyly, paying close attention to my rather overindulgent attire. "Looks like you've been shopping."

"Yeah…I wanted to blend in a little better at the bank and at the airport."

"And were you successful? You look like quite the executive."

I shook my head as I pulled off my jacket, folded it neatly and placed it on the bed. "Not really. The Wells Fargo people couldn't've cared less, and I wound up putting down a small fortune to get us a charter, but we're set to go wheels-up at zero eight hundred tomorrow morning."

Natalia half-smiled while turning her head and her attention away from me and back to the television. That was when I noticed the empty plates and juice glasses on the room-service cart.

"Did you get enough to eat?"

She nodded slightly. "Yes, I did. It was delicious, too. The steak was cooked perfectly. Thanks, Q."

"Did you get any rest?"

She shrugged. "A little."

I took a seat on the bed next to her and ran my

fingers through her hair. "You look like you're feeling better. Your skin isn't as pale as it was."

"I do feel better—just a little weak. And my arm is still throbbing like a son of a bitch."

I reached for her arm and she presented it to me, rolling up her sleeve so I could examine the bandages. In doing so, Natalia wouldn't turn her interest away from the television. I tried taking a listen, but she had the volume down so low, I couldn't hear what was being said.

After a moment, I gestured to the screen. "Has anything else happened?"

"You could say that," she said. "There's been sporadic accounts of possible shootings and suicide bombings here and there, but nothing conclusive. People are panicking and calling in everything...journalists can't cover all the reports, so they're sifting. But the FAA just announced about a half hour ago that air traffic controllers have reported two missing airliners. Both 747s."

Jesus. It was 9/11 all over again. American Flight 11, United Flight 175, American 77, and United 93. My mind began to spin with the possibilities. Tomorrow morning couldn't get here soon enough.

Natalia tilted her head slightly to the side and fidgeted with her injured arm after I'd let go. "One flight was en route to LaGuardia out of Chicago Midway. They stopped receiving flight data and the plane went off radar not long after, somewhere near the Great Lakes. The other departed Atlanta several hours ago and was headed here when they lost track of it over North Carolina."

They lost track of it.

I'd heard that phrase uttered a thousand times in my lifetime with regard to aircraft, and it still never ceased to astonish me. There were a host of methods with which domestic flights could be tracked while airborne. Radar, global positioning satellites or GPS, in-flight transponder beacons, and ACARS—the Aircraft Communications Addressing and Reporting System being among them. Most commercial airliners these days had at least two or more of these systems in place and active, some having all of the aforementioned.

Disabling GPS is easy. Find the transponder and remove the power source, or just sever the coax or trash the antenna. The same goes for the beacon and ACARS —a good saboteur would just need to know where to find and how to incapacitate the circuitry.

Evading radar is a completely different animal. Airliners aren't stealth aircraft. A Lockheed F-35 Light-ning II or a Russian Sukhoi T-50 PAK FA or even a Chinese Shenyang J-31 all have the signature of a flock of geese on radar, but an airliner looks like an airliner. Radar sends out light-speed radio waves and waits for the echoes to return, doing so in direct line of sight. If anything gets in the way, whether environmental in nature or otherwise, the signals are prevented from echoing back what's beyond. Evading radar in a jumbo jet necessitates taking control of the aircraft and flying low. Very fucking low.

A lump was beginning to form in my throat and as my thought processes settled, I asked Natalia what the latter flight's destination was.

"Sure you want to know?" she asked.

I nodded affirmation.

"Reagan National." She turned to me, her eyes crowded with concern. "Where *you* just were."

While my mind filled with awful imaginary visions of another plane crashing into the Pentagon or other tall buildings close to our location, she reached for me and rose to her knees, straddling my lap while her arms tied a knot around my neck.

Placing my arms around her waist, I pulled her close to me as a feeling of apprehension loomed beyond that of her warm body converging on mine. "Hey, is everything okay with you?"

I felt the motion of Natalia's head nodding affirmation beside mine as some dense strands of her hair fell over my face. "Other than the world disintegrating around us, as usual? No...no, I'm just glad you're back."

The embrace lasted several minutes before she eased away, kissed me, and returned gracefully to her spot on the bed. She sat silent for a moment, then turned to me. "Q, I know you're exhausted, and I appreciate you making arrangements for us. But there's something I need to say, and I know you're not going to like it. I don't want you mad at me."

That was odd. Natalia hadn't prefaced a conversation with me like that in years. I couldn't even remember the last time I'd heard her say those words—or the last time I'd been mad at her, come to think of it. "You know you can talk to me about anything."

"Yeah. I do know that. But this is marginally different."

"Marginally different or not, it can't be that bad, can it?"

Natalia displayed a very grim yet strangely complacent expression. Her current mindset was difficult to gauge, but there was definitely something of note occupying her mind. She didn't reply or say anything to me for at least a minute. Then, as her eyebrows flattened, she said resolutely, "I...don't want to go home yet."

"What?" I blurted out, though it sounded more like a figurative retort.

She smiled uncomfortably and hung her head for a second. "I knew you wouldn't agree."

"Hold on. Wait a second. I didn't say I didn't agree. I just don't understand fully."

"Q, babe—don't you get it? We *can't* leave now," she said while pointing an index finger to the flat screen mounted to the wall. "Something momentous and life-altering is happening here. Something you and I were accessory to."

"Whoa," I said, holding up a hand. "You and I had no direct influence on this—*end of days* thing. You heard it yourself from Jonathon's pal from the pickle factory—this was inevitable. It would've happened even if we hadn't intervened. Besides, there's no way we could've known there'd be fallout this severe, or consequences at all, for that matter."

Refute. Deny. Disavow.

Natalia huffed and crossed her arms. "Jesus, Quinn. You can't seriously be that coldhearted and apathetic. This is *your* country, and people are *dying*—and you're just dismissing it all effortlessly, as if it didn't matter a single fuck to you."

"It's not that it doesn't matter a single fuck to me, Natalia. It does. It's just that I don't believe what *we* did can in any way be construed as direct involvement."

Elude. Evade. Persevere.

"And because of that, you don't feel the least bit responsible?"

I shook my head. "No. No, I don't."

Natalia rolled her eyes and stared away from me blankly. "Fine. Let's litigate semantics. What about *indirect* involvement? As in, we acted in customary fashion and served as an ancillary catalyst. Would you agree we are at least culpable for what's happening in *that* regard?"

I summed my thoughts for a moment and hesitated. I already knew the remedy to her question. If any operation Natalia and I had ever been involved in resulted in bleak aftereffects or collateral damage, we'd always been an indirect cause or factor. It came with the territory. It'd just never mattered before. We'd complete the task, collect our honorarium, take some time off, and move on to the next. *It never mattered before.*

Natalia was now scowling at me, as if testing me to see if I had any decency or integrity or compassion remaining in my congealed soul. For a moment there, I supposed I was testing myself.

"Yes," I said finally, feeling some of the bulk. "Clearly, we are, in some part, indirectly responsible for this."

She turned away from me and formed a pained expression I couldn't fully read using the mirror across from us. On her face, I saw signs of anxiety, regret, and as well, distinct irritation. But I couldn't tell if the latter was directed at me, the present circumstances, or both.

Natalia sighed heavily and spoke in a mutter. "These animals are targeting and *killing* children, Quinn," she said, her voice low and reserved, as if she were holding back from crying. "Kids. For the love of God, babies. These people…these Islamic State *Arschlöcher* have no soul. They don't vet their targets —they don't care who they kill. They're incapable of deciphering the contrasts in who or what they destroy.

A tactical target or a daycare—it's all the same to them. It's just the latter gets the most attention and delivers a stronger message, making it the more favorable one.

"They don't know pity or remorse or any emotion but hate, and their only desire is to incinerate the world into ashes." She paused for a moment. "I watched Germany transform into a playground for terrorist radicals and fundamentalists...my own people terrified to live their normal lives, powerless to defend themselves after parliament disarmed them a long time ago amidst cheers and praise. And now they've come to America and started an Armageddon they're hell-bent on seeing through to the bitter end. I can't just sit back and watch another civilization be slaughtered. And I can't, in good conscience, go back home now—not yet." She paused and looked at me, her eyes welling up. "We have to stop them, Quinn."

I had no means to argue with her, and I really didn't want to either. Every point she'd made was a valid one. Natalia was the only person in the world who'd managed to show me time and time again what integrity was all about, even though I still felt far from perfecting the concept.

We were killers, it was as simple as that. Both of us, born and bred. One gifted with an innate sense of right and wrong, the other merely devoid of the same.

"Okay," I said with a sigh. "You've made your point. We'll stay. And we'll make some calls and work the system and see what can be done about this. But it's not safe here, Natalia, even for us. We need to formulate some semblance of a plan."

She nodded. "I know that. And I know it won't be easy."

I let Natalia talk through her emotions for a few minutes before I put a stop to it all and did the one thing I knew she appreciated me for more than anything: I suggested a change to our venue. I knew it might take her mind off things, even if only for a short while. It was a strategy that had always worked for me in the past when she'd felt overwhelmed.

We decided to head downstairs and outside to get some fresh air and go for a short walk along Connecticut Avenue. We both agreed it wouldn't be a long one, knowing the city and others like it were on high alert, and a good night's sleep for us both tonight was going to be vital in the days to come. Natalia and I were both exhausted, and I was beyond so, having caught myself already imagining things.

She held my hand tightly while we strolled amongst droves of harried, inattentive pedestrians. After a couple of minutes had gone by, I decided to continue our conversation in a more carefree manner. "You know…this whole situation is a lot to consider. It's bigger than anything we've ever encountered before. It's bigger than both of us."

Natalia smiled. "Nothing's bigger than us, Q. We've

never come across anything we couldn't manage. The two of us have prevailed over extraordinary odds before, a number of times. Both professionally and personally, if you get my meaning."

I nodded my understanding. "So we stay. Sprinkle a little pixy dust and work some magic. And somehow, someway, ultimately take down the caliphate?"

"Sounds crazy...I know."

"Your brainpan is a trifle larger than mine. Do you have any clue just how the hell we're supposed to accomplish that feat?"

"I haven't the faintest idea," Natalia replied, laughing slightly at herself. "I just know that if we leave, nothing stands in the way to stop it. The people here, the law enforcement here...no one is equipped to fight an enemy that hides in the shadows, uses terror as their preferred weapon, and attacks at random. You and I are cut from the same cloth. We have skills that are formidable against enemies like this. We think like they do, and we come from the same neighborhood."

Natalia was speaking allegorically, but I knew what she was saying.

"You mean the bad side."

She nodded. "We aren't exactly good people in the grand scheme of things, Q. All my life, I've only been the best at one thing, and it's in direct violation of the sixth commandment."

"Yeah," I agreed. Natalia was right yet again. We

weren't evil people, but we did do evil things, though it had never felt that way, at least to me. Killing had always served a purpose. It was the solver of all problems. And she and I were the best at it. Neither of us had any doubt in that fact. "I guess retirement gets put on the back burner for a while, huh?"

"What good is retirement if there's no world left to retire in?"

We walked on for several yards in silence while taking turns studying the looks and actions of those around us. A smiling little boy walked past, his mother and father on either side of him, each holding one of his hands while he toyed with them. He looked delighted and carefree, like any other child just happy to be alive, with zero awareness of what was getting ready to happen to his country.

Natalia turned to watch them when they'd passed. "I'm not going to stand idly by and watch them murder children, Quinn," she declared. "I'm going to stop them, or I'm going to die trying."

When we reached the intersection of Connecticut and M Street, something peculiar caught my eye on the other side. While most pedestrians had their faces stuck in their social media applications, one person stood solitaire amongst them, and he was staring a hole through us.

Seeing one, I knew there had to be another, so I skimmed the remainder of the scene. On the adjacent corner, I soon found his counterpart, who represented himself just as shamelessly as the other.

Natalia tuned in to my concentration and mannerisms in seconds. "How many are there?"

"A pair, so far. Charlie one, across the street, my eleven—gray jacket, aviator sunglasses. Charlie two is at three o'clock."

"Black leather?"

I nodded only slightly.

Natalia sighed. "What the fuck? Who else knows we're here?"

"I don't know, it could be anyone." I sighed. "They're not just going to go away. Do we allow them to follow us, or do you want to ask them to dance?"

She shrugged. "Let's split up."

And the game began. I didn't know who these men were or what they wanted, but the situation was about to get very hectic for them.

Natalia disappeared into the crowd, and I went the other direction along M Street, checking behind me periodically using my sunglass lens's reflective interior. Sure enough, my tail engaged and followed me. He was alone though, so I assumed his counterpart had done his due diligence and gone in pursuit of my wife. The poor bastard.

After a couple of minutes of scanning the street for choke points, I found one just around a corner and slid behind a brick wall to lie in wait for my prey. I estimated it would be about forty seconds before I saw his face pass by, but I was wrong. It was thirty-five seconds. And it wasn't his face I saw first, it was the glimmer off the steel muzzle of a pistol he held in his hand.

With one hand, I swiftly disarmed the man while simultaneously putting a reverse knife-hand into his windpipe, causing him to gasp, lurch, and go limp. I took advantage of the strike's effectiveness and pulled the man deeper into the alleyway after applying a chokehold tight enough to stifle his attempts at screaming or calling for help.

After rendering him unconscious, I dropped the dead weight to the concrete, set his weapon aside, and began rifling through his pockets.

Natalia was right, he was foreign. He definitely didn't appear American, but he sure did have a lot of domestic identification on his person—all of it valid. He carried cash, credit cards, and even a Maryland driver's license; but something just didn't make sense.

My mind began shuffling through random images and thoughts until, suddenly, I felt the ground shake beneath my feet like some small earthquake had occurred. Several seconds later, I heard a lengthy and loud *boom*, resembling that of thunder.

"One of the missing airliners, no doubt," I said to myself while speculating over all the possible locations nearby where it could've crashed. I assumed it would be the next breaking news story we'd see on television. All of Washington, DC, was about to go bat-shit crazy, and I assumed other major cities around the country weren't far from doing the same. So much for getting a good night's sleep anytime soon.

I reached to my side and palmed the unconscious man's pistol. It wasn't American made, or even the typical Sig, Glock or Beretta frequently found here. It was an MP-443 Grach, Russian standard military issue. I hadn't seen one since Natalia and I did a job two years ago in Kursk.

I unbuttoned the man's jacket and ripped open his shirt to get a view of the skin that lay beneath. Just as I expected, he was covered in colorful tattoos, some vivid, the lettering all appearing Cyrillic or Slavic.

Now I was really confused. To my knowledge, we hadn't acquired any enemies in Russia, and this man didn't look Bratva to me. He couldn't have been KGB; no skilled spy or agent of intelligence would've stepped into such an obvious trap like the one I'd just set for him.

To hell with this. It was time for us to part ways with this city. I didn't know why this man and his partner were here or why they'd chosen to follow us, but it didn't matter. There wasn't time to fully interrogate him, even if I cared to.

I shoved the Grach pistol into my pants, stood, and went to make my way out of the alley just as a casually dressed stocky man with a buzzed haircut turned the corner and held up a hand for me to stop while pointing to a Glock he had hidden under his oversized fleece jacket. Had I not identified him, he would've been subdued and lying on top of the Russian not one moment later—the second victim of the day for this alleyway. But I knew who it was. Special Agent Dan Prosser, an overachieving, meddling case officer and, from what I remembered, a big-time ass-kisser. After all the bizarre events of today, I was now being paid a visit by the agency.

Dan pulled off his sunglasses one ear at a time in dramatic fashion, like a motorcycle cop preparing to write a reckless-driving ticket. He looked down at the unconscious man lying on the polluted concrete behind me. "Making new friends, Oscar Kilo? Or have you switched career paths and become a thief?"

Oscar Kilo. I hadn't heard that in a while. It'd been my call sign in the Special Operations Group. It stood for and was the two-word phonetic version of *overkill*, one of the many monikers I'd earned as a shooter in the corps.

I turned away for a second and shrugged unsympathetically. "I'm not very good at making friends."

Dan pressed his lips together in a smile and nodded while placing his sunglasses into the breast pocket of his jacket. "That's a nice suit. Brooks Brothers, isn't it? I think I have one of the same style, but in a tad darker shade." He paused, and his tone deepened. "What are you doing in-country, Quinn?"

"I have a better question. How did you know I was here?"

He chuckled slightly. "You know how it is, Oscar Kilo. The company knows everything. No one can hide from us, even you."

"I've never hid from anyone in my life. And you're right, Dan. I do know how it is. What you're saying is bullshit. Someone told you I was here." I wagered a guess, even though I truly didn't believe it accurate. "Was it Jonathon?"

"Jonathon? You mean Rockland, right? Hell no. He's a fucking ghost. As far as Langley knows, he went dark years ago, not long after going deep cover. But you didn't hear that from me."

That was thought-provoking. I was going to file that tidbit away for later.

While Dan fidgeted, I got a good look at a glint in a nearby building's open fourth-story window. It was the sunlight's reflection off what could only be a rifle scope. He'd brought a team along with him that included an overwatch position, leading me to believe this chance rendezvous had been prearranged in advance.

"I don't have a lot of time for chitchat, Dan. It's my understanding the burn notice is a done deal and the feds haven't declared me an enemy, so why the ambush?"

Dan smirked. "It's not an ambush—it's more like a brush pass."

"You haven't been a field agent in years, and that term implies friendliness. Is this a friendly visit?"

"Let's call it professional courtesy."

This back-and-forth was starting to annoy me. "Are you going to tell me what it is you want? Or did you come here to play Scattergories?"

"I didn't come here to play games with you," Dan growled, his eyes narrowing. "But since you asked, I'll tell you what I want. I want your ass out of the goddamn country. That's what I want."

I smirked. "Oh. Is that all?"

"For the moment," he said. "Whenever you're here, everyone I know gets antsy and my phone doesn't stop ringing. They lose their beauty sleep, and then I lose my beauty sleep. And that shit makes me a very unhappy person."

Yeah. I was running on fumes too. I knew the feeling. "You'll get your wish soon enough. I've already made the arrangements. Problem is, US airspace is probably going to be shut down soon. Don't suppose you've heard about the recent terror attacks…"

"If that happens, I suggest you head to the beach. Hope you're a strong swimmer. It's a big damn ocean."

I took a few steps forward. "Dan, I'm still very

much a US citizen. And I'm not a threat to you or the agency…unless you decide to make me one. And if that's how this hand is going to be played, I assure you, old friend, I will bring the hate all the way to your precious doorstep. It just so happens, right now I have more important items requiring my attention. I'd imagine the same for you, considering the current state of affairs."

"More important items, huh? Tell me, Kilo, what brings you and your wife to the US, anyway? For two of the most notorious hired guns in the world to be in town, you must've scored yourselves a monster of a job."

"The company knows everything, Dan, remember? There shouldn't be cause to even pose the question." I moved close enough to him so whoever was listening on the other side of his earpiece could hear me. My proximity to him would also make it nearly impossible for his sniper to get off a clean shot if he'd been so ordered. "When I was excommunicated, I did my part. I signed my final nondisclosure and disavowed all knowledge. The agency doesn't need to worry about me."

Dan smiled and nodded as I backed away. "Okay. Then maybe we should worry about your wife instead."

That will be the day, asshole. Dig your own grave.

"This conversation is over. Goodbye, Dan," I said, and started to walk off.

"Was it the two of you who started all that shit at the Saudi embassy and offed Khaleel el-Sattar last night?"

I stopped walking and turned my head to him, but didn't answer.

"That got your attention," he said. "The reason I'm asking is, that melee started a real political shitstorm. A bunch of federal agents are dead, and now the FBI is involved, and the heat is coming down hard on all of us to find out just what the hell happened there. We're shaking down assets right and left now. Funny thing though, even with all the dead bodies we found, there's no evidence of anyone being there who shouldn't have been. And the few folks left alive, emphasis on few, don't remember seeing a goddamn thing."

"Maybe they should get their eyes checked. What exactly are you insinuating?"

"Nothing, Quinn. Nothing. Just putting out some feelers, that's all. Whoever's responsible got in and got out, and did a damn good job of doing so without being noticed. That type of warrior-of-the-night, shinobi shit just seems right up your bride's alley."

My eyes met his and we had ourselves a bit of a staring contest before he looked away. I wasn't going to give him the pleasure of a direct response—which I presumed was exactly what he was looking for.

"Like I said," he continued, "just putting out some feelers."

"Here's a feeler for you. Want some advice?"

"Well, sure. I love receiving unsolicited intel from former operatives."

"Then you'll adore this. Read my fucking lips— keep your distance. And when you get home tonight, *if* you make it home, pray to whatever god you believe in that we never see each other again."

Dan hesitated. "Oh, don't worry, Oscar Kilo. We won't."

I grazed past him, shoulder checking him to the wall in doing so. As I turned onto the sidewalk on M Street, I looked over my shoulder and said, "Here's some more advice. Tell your faggot shooter in the building across the street to start using an ARD. The sun's glaring off his glass so much it looks like a signal mirror. I can see every time he takes a breath."

Dan turned around, chuckling. "Will do. Oh, and, Quinn? One more thing."

I stopped walking reluctantly, with him still in my peripheral. He tossed me a small transparent plastic bag, which I caught with my left hand. I studied the contents. Individually sealed, recently dated pharmaceuticals, appearing to have originated from a paramedic's kit. It contained several unopened doses of hydrocodone and acetaminophen and cephalexin. Painkillers and antibiotics.

I looked at him curiously. I wanted to offer thanks —maybe he wasn't such a prick after all. But this souvenir wasn't for me, and that meant Dan knew a lot more than what he let on. Typical fucking CIA. Everyone has an angle.

"I'll take care of your friend for you," he said, pointing at my former tail on the ground, who was now starting to come around. "Go take care of the wife and get the hell out of the country double-quick. And take her with you."

Nearly a half hour later, I spotted Natalia walking towards me on the sidewalk about a block and a half away from the Mayflower Hotel. She looked pissed, and her head—which was now missing the white fleece beanie she'd been wearing earlier—was on a constant swivel.

When we'd reached one another, we both said nothing and took a turn into the hotel's heavy brass front entrance doors, heading straight for the elevators. After the elevator doors welcomed us inside, I pressed the button to force the doors closed, and followed it with a press that would take us on an express trip back to the club level and to our room.

"Did you hear the crash?" she asked vacantly.

I nodded. "I felt it. And I heard the explosion not long after." I turned and gave her a quick once-over. "Everything go okay?"

She nodded, her eyes staring a hole through the reflective metal elevator door. "You?"

I shrugged. "Peachy. Would you have any idea why we have Russians tailing us?"

"Ukrainians, you mean," she corrected.

"Ukrainians? How do you know?"

Natalia rolled her lips through her teeth, then smiled weakly. "I just know."

Once we reached our floor, Natalia and I made a beeline for our suite's door. It was obvious to me she now shared the same sentiment about leaving town as I did. I went to open it with my key, but she stopped me —first by grabbing my hand, then by holding up a finger to her lips. She carefully put her ear to the door and held it there for about ten seconds while the look on her face contorted.

Fuck. I should've considered it a possibility after what we'd just experienced, that someone or even a group of someones would be waiting for us when we got back to our room, but the forethought had escaped me. Damn this fatigue.

I knew Natalia was just as tired as I was and had been put through more stress than I had, but at this moment, it was a relief knowing she was still on point. How she was managing to do so was beyond me.

As her eyebrows pulled down and together, Natalia held up a hand and three fingers, then four. She pulled her ear away from the door and backed away, motioning for me to do the same.

Four men waited for us on the other side of the door of our suite, and I had no idea who they were or what they wanted from us, but I could only assume the worst now. Were they Russians? Ukrainians? The KGB? Or were they CIA paramilitary operatives waiting to apprehend and interrogate us for the killing of el-Sattar? I was reaching the point where I was too tired to give a shit. Whoever was behind the door was a threat, and I was a competent, bona fide expert at eliminating that very thing.

Natalia looked to me for what to do next. She rarely deferred to me in these instances, but she knew that between the two of us, I was the most proficient door kicker.

I pulled the MP-443 Grach pistol from my waist and handed it to her. The look on her face gave way to the notion that she knew exactly where it had come from. Without looking at me or giving me a single indication of hesitance, she press-checked the weapon and made ready.

I slipped the Glock from its holster in the small of my back and took a couple of steps away from the door. I was tired and foggy and nowhere near in any shape for another encounter today. But here we were. We were cornered, and I felt about half of the man I normally was, but I knew that even at fifty percent capacity, I could dominate nearly a dozen normal men —or a half-dozen cold, calculating, well-trained ones.

I took several slow, deep breaths to increase my lung capacity and upsurge the amount of oxygen in my blood. Then, while mouthing the words, I counted to three and sent my right foot viciously into the door.

SEVENTEEN

Mayflower Hotel
Friday, March 28
Nihayat al'ayam plus 17 hours, 5 minutes

The hardest part about kicking a door isn't the breaching act itself. In fact, the brute-force portion is purely mechanical, based on physics and largely unsophisticated.

First, attempt to find the weakest portion on the door, typically located near the handle or locking mechanism. Then, drive the foot heel into it with enough forward energy to dislodge it or otherwise shatter it or the surrounding frame. All the while resisting the urge to utilize action movie stunts like the tough-guy shoulder barge or the Bruce Lee–inspired jumping side-kick. If the door opens inwardly away from the kicker and the ensuing strike, you're golden. If it opens outward toward the kick, it's a hair trickier and requires more force. But it is still achievable—especially for the well tenured. The one thing you don't want to do is have to kick a door more than once. You might not get a chance at the second effort, depending on who or what's waiting for you on the other side.

No. By far, the hardest part about kicking in a door is the anticipation—of what lies behind it. I think that holds true for most things, though, with regard to anticipation. I prefer knowing to not knowing, and completing tasks over waiting to find out. The waiting tends to offer far too much time to think.

I've performed this technique damned near a thousand times throughout my career, and discovered anything from a traditional Jewish family quietly reciting a customary *brachah rishonah* before dinner to a full house of teenage bomb-building, Galil rifle-toting, ready and willing to meet Allah jihadists on the other side, each responding dutifully in their own appropriate manner to my spontaneous intrusion.

The double doors leading into our suite opened inwardly and were secured by what appeared to be a formidable brass keypad and lockset in their intermediate. A piece of fucking cake.

After I forced my heel into the door and turned the door jamb leading into the presidential suite into splinters, the scene that surrounded me went into slow motion. I immediately identified four threats in our suite, three of them huddled together at twelve o'clock, approximately eight yards away in the marble-floored living area. One was casually seated with two others standing on either side of him, and both were armed with silenced rifles.

A fourth stood to my left, just inside the hall leading to the walk-in closet space, his silenced pistol aimed at the door, and at me.

Entering the oval-shaped foyer, I immediately went low and left and saw Natalia flash past me to my right. She'd gone even lower than me and dove directly behind the cover of the plaster wall between the foyer and the hall leading into the living area, the Grach pistol leading her way.

As I targeted the man hiding in the closet, it took all of a millisecond to surmise that his weapon was still trained on me while I moved. I dove to the ground, landing on my right side, and snapped the trigger on my Glock 19 twice, placing two shots into his midsection. Crimson blood soaked through his shirt from his torso and blew out of his back in a fine mist. He dropped like a lead balloon. Must've forgotten his body armor. He wouldn't be making that mistake again.

I rolled and allowed my momentum to carry me to the wall adjacent to Natalia, then rose as fast as my body would allow and made eye contact with her. She held up an index finger, and I nodded to her. A split second later, she vaulted out from cover and fired two blazingly fast shots, moving back behind the wall seconds after, her reflexes and agility as fierce and catlike as I'd ever seen them. She was a predator in her element, and her most recent injury wasn't slowing her down in the least.

Natalia and I stepped forward into the hall in parallel and approached the final man, the only remaining threat still alive in our suite. His two fellow sentinels had been armed with modified and suppressed Kalashnikov pistols of some variety, from what I could tell, but he didn't appear to be armed.

Several unsuppressed shots had rung out in this hotel today, and that meant it wouldn't be long before we'd be getting a visit from local law enforcement. With three deceased men in our suite and a fourth most likely getting ready to join them, we needed to make quick work of this and take our leave posthaste.

I stood back and surveyed the scene, making sure to keep a close eye on our foe's hands. I kept constant pressure on the trigger, ready to pull it at a second's notice if he so much as twitched in a threatening manner.

Natalia simply lowered her weapon and daringly approached him. His face offered no emotion, no sentiment with regard to recent events. She began speaking to him in a foreign dialect sounding awfully a lot like

Russian. After a moment, his face softened a bit, and he began conversing openly with her.

The back-and-forth lasted all of about two minutes. Nearing the end, the man had begun to smile and nod and say the word *tak* repeatedly, which I knew to be the Ukrainian word for 'yes'. It was at that point I realized they hadn't been speaking Russian at all, and these men had most certainly been tied to the same crew we'd met on the street earlier.

The conversation ended abruptly when Natalia palmed a thick down pillow from the chair and a half to her right and placed it over the man's face. She shoved the Grach pistol into the pillow and fired two muffled shots, sending a cloud of feathers soaring onto the chair and into the thick layer of blood now covering the back side of it.

With all threats neutralized, my mind spinning, and my body slowly failing from exhaustion, I lowered my weapon and watched his arms fall to his sides and his body go limp.

Natalia dropped the bloody pillow into his lap and casually slipped the Grach inside the rear waistband of her leggings. She concealed it with her jacket, then turned to me. "Q, we...can never come back here again. Okay?"

"The hotel?"

She shook her head. "No, the city. Washington."

I nodded avowal with a bit of hesitation. It wasn't

that I didn't agree with her—I did. I just wanted more of an explanation. I *needed* more of an explanation. But I knew just as much as my wife did, we'd been running on borrowed time for going on far too long. And now it appeared we'd downright run out of it.

"Let's get packed and get out of here, now. Grab only what you need, and don't leave anything behind they can use to track us."

"I know the drill, Q," she said exhaustedly.

"I'll get us a car. We can head to one of the safe houses for the remainder of the night," I said. "I'm sorry...I'd take us farther...but I'm just too tired to go on a long road trip tonight."

"Fine. Tomorrow morning, then. First thing."

"Tomorrow morning, it is."

EIGHTEEN

F AIRFAX C OUNTY, V IRGINIA
S ATURDAY, M ARCH 29
N IHAYAT AL'AYAM PLUS 1 DAY, 6 HOURS, 43 MINUTES

C omfortable silence. It was a foundation I had
grown to both recognize and appreciate whenever Natalia and I were alone with one another. It was a
class of armistice that I had never known to be conceivable until the point I had met her.

Before in my past involvements, no matter how
significant or paltry, I had always distinguished the
opposite. And it didn't matter whom I was with, mere
acquaintance, friend, companion, lover, or otherwise.
Silence, as the idiomatic phrase goes, was indeed deaf-
ening, and oftentimes had a way of making me feel

uncomfortable and somewhat on edge, but never with her. At least, not until today.

Last evening, following our little *Hopak* with a quartet of Ukrainian hatchet men, we had vacated our suite in rapid fashion, taking only the bare necessities along with us for the ride. No less than thirty minutes later, we had arrived at a safe house just outside the capital beltway and had remained there until just before daybreak this morning.

With all the attention we'd been getting, it had become necessary to abandon the Audi, and after a bit of searching, I had found a suitable replacement in the hotel's underground garage. After removing a few sets of keys from the valet's unsecured key box, I chose a pitch-black, late-model GMC Yukon XL Denali, a four-wheel-drive beast of an SUV decked out with leather, a sunroof, and limo-tinted windows. There were so many of these things being sported around town these days by white-collar commuters, politicians, dignitaries, and so on, its presence on DC's streets would be like swimming with the current.

At the point of acquiring it, I considered two distinct drawbacks. Boosting this thing could very easily put us on the radar, but there wasn't enough time to go through another rental process, and we were in a bit of a hurry. The second drawback was the myriad of surveillance provisions that car manufacturers tended to install in them, unbeknownst to their end users.

Modern-day vehicles these days came not only fully equipped with an overabundance of computerized everything, but with a full complement of electronic countermeasures. Along with all the selling-point premium features, such as three-hundred-sixty-degree collision avoidance, moisture-sensing windshield wipers, and high-performance audio and speakers, were an assortment of microphones, exterior and interior cameras, cellular transceivers, and not just one, but several global positioning satellite transponders.

They'll tell you the premise behind all these gadgets is benign, being nothing more than for the purpose of driver and passenger safety. But what they don't tell you, and won't tell you, is that the vehicle is basically one big overpriced spy transmitter. It's capable of listening in to everything you say, watching everything you do, and seeing everywhere you're going, and even tracking you—with astounding accuracy—wherever you are.

If there was one thing I didn't like, it was being spied on, tracked or traced, and Natalia shared the sentiment. So I spent a bit of time disabling the Denali's ability to do so. I decided to target the antenna systems, knowing that after disabling them, any data attempting to transmit couldn't escape the cannister.

During the surgical procedure, I was amazed to find the vehicle even had secondary antenna systems installed as backup. Those options must now come standard in this model…I'm guessing the manufacturer failed to provide that noteworthy data on the factory sticker, though.

Natalia was seated in the passenger seat, staring out the window with her bare feet pressed against the dash. She was becoming fond of the Denali's heated seats, which she had cranked all the way up to the incineration setting. I had mine set about midway, and it was doing a respectable job of melting away some of my aches while leaving the residual stress to remain.

Though the two of us had gotten a decent amount of sleep last night and were both very much awake, it had been silent in the passenger compartment since the point we'd left the safe house this morning. And it was officially the first time I had felt uncomfortable in that silence.

As I weaved the lengthy SUV through the crowded two-lane highway and backed-up intersections, I glanced over at Natalia from the corner of my eye whenever I could, to check if she was still with me. She had her left hand on her knee, taking care not to move her injured arm too often. Her right was taking turns combing through her hair and travelling to her mouth so she could nibble on her fingernails.

Just when I was about to say something to her, Natalia rearranged her seating position and faced me. She crossed her legs, one on top of the other, and tossed her hair over a shoulder. "Q, talk to me. Is everything okay?"

Took the words right out of my mouth. But were we ready to discuss all this? I glanced over. "Yeah. Everything's fine, as far as I can tell."

"Are you sure about that?"

I shrugged. "Tell me why you're asking, and I'll tell you if I'm sure."

She leaned in closer, adjusting her seatbelt for some added give. "I'm asking…because you look preoccupied."

"I do?"

Natalia nodded her head fervently. "Yes, you do. And it's…strange. It's not like you."

"Why?"

"Because you *never* look preoccupied."

I was ready to respond, but the last look she sent me told me she wasn't done yet.

Natalia fidgeted with her hair. "Q, you're a rock. Most days, you're harder than granite. I've seen you turn a building into a human slaughterhouse and strut out the front door covered head to heels in blood, with your shirt hanging over your shoulder, without a care in the world. Normally, you give off the air of a cyborg. What's different about today?"

What was different about today? I couldn't believe she was asking after all we'd discussed and witnessed thus far since our journey to the States had kicked off.

Maybe the time had come to just air it all out. "Oh, I don't know. Maybe it's the fact we somehow got pawned into hitting the big red button that initiated World War Three. And the more I think about it, the more it bothers me. I mean, seriously, why us? I know what Ammar said—the op was meant to be clandestine, no ties leading back to him or his handlers. But if that were one hundred percent true, then why is the damn agency onto us?"

Natalia cocked her head. Her neck craned backward, and her brow furrowed. "Wait. What are you talking about?"

I sighed. I must have failed to mention it, either by accident or on purpose. The evening *had* been moderately eventful. "After we exposed our tails and went split city, I took out my shadow. Then I had a little run-in with an old friend."

"What sort of old friend?" she asked, a slight edge in her voice. "The kind who works for the CIA?"

I nodded.

"Who?"

"An old-school peckerhead case officer. Someone I never got along well with and would've loved to have forgotten a long time ago."

"So the CIA knows we're here?"

"Yeah." I pulled the plastic bag of narcotics and antibiotics Prosser had given me from my pocket and tossed them to her. "But that's not all they know."

Natalia eyeballed the pills a moment, then stared at me, her pupils alight. "And who do we have to thank for that? Your buddy the drunk, I presume?"

I shook my head. "No. Jonathan would never offer up that kind of intel on us, especially to the agency. My guess…is that we were identified by software, by some camera somewhere along the way."

"Facial recognition, you mean."

"We've been moving about undisguised along the busiest streets in one of the busiest metropolitan areas in the land of Big Brother."

"Yeah…but then again, let us not neglect to mention the fucking airport we were flown into." Natalia sighed. "I take it this will only serve to further complicate things."

"It's too soon to tell," I said. "Prosser called it a brush pass—like an agent making brief contact with an asset. But most brush passes don't incorporate sniper overwatch."

"Jesus. He had someone put in place to take you out?"

"Maybe. But I reckon *deterrence* was his primary purpose in being there."

"To keep you from killing Prosser?" Natalia asked.

"Do you blame him?"

"Bearing in mind your track record? No." A pause. "So they know about my arm. Then they know about the raid on el-Sattar…"

"It's safe to assume they know everything, especially now."

"Dammit. No wonder you're preoccupied."

"Yeah, it's bugging me," I said. "Add to it the fact that we're now being tracked by the Ukrainians, for whatever reason. I'm sorry…recent events, tangled with you almost getting killed…I guess my nerves are just a little shot."

Natalia opened the plastic bag and extracted two cephalexin caplets, popped them in her mouth, and swallowed them down short of a chaser. Afterward, she didn't say anything, even though I was hoping she would. I really needed her to explain what had happened back there. For the moment though, I had no other choice than to wait for her and allow the aspects of our encounter with the Ukrainian hit squad to add even more obscurity to our conundrum.

After a few minutes, I decided to break the silence using a sobriquet I'd only ever used to grasp her attention during times when I'd felt forsaken. "Nati?"

A moment passed before her reply came in a velvety purr. "Yeah, Q?"

"Who were they?"

Natalia had been hanging her head, and it took a few seconds for her to acknowledge my question. She looked up at me with tender eyes. "I just knew you were going to ask me that."

"Did you think after all *that* action, I'd forget about it?"

"No. I knew you wouldn't forget, and I knew at some point I needed to brief you." She paused. "And I'm going to. You just have to promise not to freak out on me."

"I'll try not to. But no promises." This wasn't good.

Natalia hesitated a long moment while a distressing smile crept across her lips. "They were sent here by some old colleagues of mine. A particular faction who at one time looked upon me as family. I haven't seen or heard from them in a very long time and, honestly, never thought I would." She paused extensively. "Do you remember our first night in Berchtesgaden? It was a few days before we bought our flat. We got hammered on *Glühwein* and took a really long walk, and somehow ended up going for a swim in *der Königssee*?"

"Of course. I would have frozen my ass off in that lake if I hadn't nearly drowned in it. Lucky for me, I had you as my lifeguard that night."

Natalia chuckled. "Yeah. And that was just the shallow end. I remember a lot of riveting details about that night, but one stands out in particular. It was the first time I told you about Dmitry." A long pause followed. "The men we encountered, all of them…are here because of him. They were sent by Orloff. Dmitry's oldest son."

I glanced over. "Are they looking to retrieve you for a family reunion?"

Natalia gurgled solemnly. "No, not quite. But they *are* here for me."

"For what?"

"For what? Because of what I did. I killed him, Quinn. I put Dmitry in a grave. Orloff's father is dead because of me, and Ukrainians aren't known for taking that sort of thing lightly."

Now my gears were really beginning to churn and grind. "I get that, but you're not the fledgling femme fatale you once were. Does he have any concept of who you are or who you've become? The crew he sent wasn't shit—they weren't even close to being a JV team. I take it he's got better..."

"Oh, trust me, he does," said Natalia. "And, Q? Believe me when I tell you this...our little run-in back there was nothing. This is far from over." She turned away and exhaled gently through her nostrils while staring out her window at the trees and intermittent buildings passing by alongside the road. "You know, I'm really sorry. I've somehow fucked things up again for us. I've added another layer to an already convoluted predicament. But you're in this now just as much as I am. And you need to realize...this changes things a bit."

"I'd contend it changes things *a lot* a bit."

"It does. You know, Q...I still want to find a way to

make this right. I want to put a stop to these attacks somehow. But we might need to go dark for a while before that happens." She glanced over at me. "If Orloff's men are in the country looking for me, they won't stop until they find me. We must go somewhere far away from where they're most likely to look. Somewhere no one knows us."

"Do you think we're capable of stopping them?" I asked.

"Of course we can. But I need to be able to see them coming. I have to get the drop on them, and I can't do that surrounded by city lights."

Though I couldn't see them yet, ahead of us in the distance were the Blue Ridge Mountains, and we were currently travelling west, headed right for them. The more Natalia and I spoke, the more it felt like a magnet was pulling me there. "Then we'll go somewhere that makes sense for us. We'll keep heading west until we find a town rural enough. Someplace we don't see cameras at every intersection."

Natalia exhaled through her nostrils. "Sounds good to me. It's a start, anyway."

Keeping the Denali between the lines on the highway, I looked over at my wife and caught a visual of the concern building in her eyes. I didn't recall ever seeing that look before. She was legitimately worried about this...possibly even afraid for her life, and that was causing my core instincts as her husband and as her protector to flood with a primal emotion.

There was simply no way I would allow anyone, much less these barbarians from the Ukraine, to get anywhere near her. I would spill the blood of a thousand men to keep her safe, without thinking twice about it. Natalia was the only thing that mattered to me. Loving her had become a reflex long ago, and without her, I was as good as dead anyway.

I reached for her hand. "Don't worry about this, okay? I'll put an end to all of it, I promise. One way or another…I swear to you. I will find a way."

She peered over to me and half smiled, taking my hand in hers. Her fingers slid around mine and enclosed them. She squeezed my hand and, for a moment, looked as if she wanted to say something, though nothing escaped her lips, and that was okay with me. Her silence was telling me everything I needed to know. It told me she trusted me and believed in me, and nothing else needed to be said.

While we gradually put distance between ourselves and the city, progressing through and out of the overpopulated suburbs, my level of unease began to evaporate. I still couldn't help but wonder why the hell this all had come to pass in the manner in which it had.

We'd been lying low, keeping our noses clean for so

long; back in business again for one final act—one final op to end all ops. And after today, it felt like we were right back where we'd started from at the beginning. Up to our noses in shit, barely able to breathe.

We were making our way through the last few bustling intersections of Chantilly, Virginia, when Natalia's attention locked onto the instrument cluster. She pointed to the fuel gauge, something that had eluded me until this very second. "What *dummkopf* spends eighty grand US on a monstrosity like this and leaves it parked with a quarter tank of gas?"

After a quick glance at the gauge, I replied casually, "Obviously, the *dummkopf* who procured this monstrosity prior to us."

Natalia placed her elbow next to the window and rested her head on her knuckles. "I suppose we should consider stopping for gas before we get too far away from civilization."

My wife had a point. Our plan was fly-by-night at best, and neither of us knew how far we were headed. It was my intention to keep driving until I saw more foliage than shades of asphalt and concrete, but we wouldn't get far on this little fuel.

With America under attack, population density had become a high-value target, and collateral damage was at the very apex of the Islamists' hit list. Our issues with the Ukrainians notwithstanding, remaining in any city or overpopulated suburbia was practically suicide, and an altogether bad fucking idea.

Natalia rapped her knuckle on the window and pointed, indicating a Shell station just ahead. I acknowledged her and slowed the Yukon, signaled, and pulled into the lot, immediately falling into position in the longest line of cars waiting for gas I had ever seen before.

I slammed on the brakes, just barely missing rear-ending a faded white Oldsmobile piloted by an elderly woman with a globe of bushy white hair. She glanced up at me through the rearview and threw her hands in the air, chastising me for the near miss.

"She looks pissed," Natalia joked.

I nodded. "I see that. Imagine how mad she'd be if I'd actually hit her." I sat up in my seat and leaned over the steering wheel, getting a better view of the chaos in the parking lot. "Look at this shit…it's insane. I take it everyone and their cousin decided to come to this gas station at the same time today? Are they running a sale?"

Natalia started to look nervous. She reached for the Grach pistol under her thigh while cautiously studying our perimeter. "Maybe they're worried about the likelihood of not being able to get gas again for a while."

"It's conceivable. Or maybe they're in hoarding mode—thinking prices are going to skyrocket in a day or two. That's retroactive standard procedure for most people following a terrorist attack."

"Mm-hmm. The human equation and the wisdom of hindsight," Natalia remarked. "But we've seen multiple incidences already, occurring back-to-back, just on day one. Maybe there've been more since then."

I hesitated, glancing up at the Denali's touchscreen audio system, which I was sure included an AM/FM radio. "Speaking of hindsight, there's probably an abundance of news outlets on broadcast radio. But I seem to remember having disabled it last night...for some reason."

Natalia continued her perimeter check with a scrupulous eye while her index finger delicately caressed the Grach's smooth trigger guard. "Look at all these cars. And there's even more pulling in behind us. If we don't get out of here soon, we're going to be boxed in." She looked to me, layering her hair over her ear with a finger. "Maybe we should try the next one."

I nodded and shifted the transmission into drive. "I'm on it," I said, depressing the accelerator and whipping the wheel to the left.

Barely escaping two successive collisions, I powered the Denali back onto US Route 50 and motored west in search of another gas station while my eyes checked the fuel gauge every few seconds, expecting the next green LED to disappear.

It wasn't long before an audible electronic bell

sounded off, bringing both our attentions to the instrument cluster. The heads-up display was now warning us that the truck had only fifty miles' worth of gas left in the tank.

Fantastic. Here we were in the middle of Northern Virginia—the land of plenty—and the one thing we needed, we couldn't have because everyone else needed it and couldn't have it. You sure picked the right car to boost, Mr. Barrett. Better luck next time.

We drove on, navigating around several stalled automobiles and a few inauspiciously located traffic circles before the highway converted from four lanes into two. Crossing over a bridge barely wider than a single lane, we came into the town of Aldie and, after passing a fire station on the left, noticed a small mom-and-pop gas station up ahead.

"There's one right there," Natalia said, pointing. "It's bizarre, though. No long line of cars."

"Maybe word hasn't traveled this far yet."

Natalia giggled slightly. "I'm sure this event has already gone viral. It probably has its own Twitter handle by now."

I slowed the black behemoth again and pulled into the station, right up to the first unleaded gas pump. The store looked far from being abandoned, but there weren't any lights on in the building, and the neon sign indicating whether the store was open or closed wasn't lit. "Think the power is off?"

Natalia peered out her window. "Shit. You might have something there. I don't recall seeing anything lit up for several miles before we pulled into town."

Funny how we tend not to take notice of things that don't occur very often. Typical power outages happened all the time when I was a kid, following a thunderstorm, during heavy snowfall, or whatnot. But a major power outage, something much more long term and widespread, could occur at any given moment while appearing as the same, without providing one iota of how principal of an event it was.

I remembered reading an excerpt on normalcy bias once, not long after leaving boot camp. Sometimes referred to as analysis paralysis, it stated that at one point or another, we may be deployed in a disaster zone or other hostile environment, and find ourselves dealing with people who are wholly affected, yet steadfastly underestimate the hazards. They believe it's temporary and reparable, and completely normal, when it's far from being so. They trust they are safe when they are in danger. It can sometimes lead to cognitive dissonance, where inherent contradictory beliefs clash with their perception of reality.

If this situation continued to escalate, which I was fairly certain it would, after what we had learned, this country would be dealing with the largest case of normalcy bias ever beheld, brought about by an enduring disaster of monumental proportions. Something its people were not only completely unprepared for and not in any way ready to deal with, but also had no means of preventing or stopping. How did you put down an enemy you couldn't see? How did you stop attacks you couldn't predict? What did you do with a ruthless enemy who attacked you at your doorstep, after you'd spent decades pretending and preaching that he never existed and was never a threat to you?

I stepped out of the truck and made my way to a rickety wooden door with several single-paned glass frames, all of which bore stickers with brand names, most of which I recognized. I twisted the brass knob and it didn't give, then I peered inside the glass to see if anyone was milling about inside. The shelves were stocked, but the store was devoid of bodies.

"The place is deserted," I said, motioning to Natalia through the open driver-side door. I got back in the Denali and drove on in search of our next opportunity.

The next town we encountered along the way was the lively and rather ornate village of Middleburg, home to much of rural Northern Virginia's upper class, horse enthusiasts, and a handful of retired sports celebrities. The town was teeming with pedestrians and vehicular traffic, and its one and only gas station had already put signage in place advertising that they'd run out of fuel. We continued without stopping, noticing as we drove that the town's only traffic light wasn't working. This quaint hamlet looked to have been left without power, same as the last one.

Now I was beginning to wonder just how large this outage was. What could have been the cause of it? Had ISIS chosen to attack electrical substations already? Or was this an incident on a much grander scale? Had they taken out a nuclear power plant? There were far too many questions, and we needed to locate some intel.

Ten miles to the west and after passing a handful of ranches and horse farms, we entered the town limits of Upperville. Spotting an Exxon station ahead on the left, I pulled the Denali into the gravel parking lot without thinking twice about it. The truck was running on fumes now, and if we didn't find some gas for it soon, we'd be walking the rest of the way to wherever we were headed.

I got out and took a quick look around, detecting the smell of two odors in the air. The first, the arid smell of wood smoke—the kind that could only be sourced from a nearby forest or brush fire. It was intertwined with humidity, and I couldn't tell if the source was close by or far away from here. The second was the exhaust fumes from an internal combustion engine. Along with the cackling and sputtering of a crude muffler echoing from the rear of the building, it was easy to discern a generator was being operated here. If a genset was running, the lights would be on inside, and with that, the gas pumps might still work. If we were going to have any chance of filling up the Denali's bottomless pit of a gas tank, this was going to be it.

Natalia called to me from her spot in the passenger seat. "Hey, Q?"

"Yeah?"

"I need to don some fresh bandages soon. Care to advise a sitrep?"

I gestured with my head to the building. "This one looks promising. I'm going in. If I'm not back in five, wait another five."

I made my way to the store's entrance, twisted the handle, and pushed the door open to the sound of an assemblage of bells jingling along, indicative of most rural convenience stores I'd visited before. Directly in front of me at the counter stood three men, one behind it and two leaning against it, one on either side. They said nothing to me, no 'howdy, partner' or 'hello, stranger' or mellow greeting of any kind. All they did was stare. And their stares became all the more intrusive the closer I got to them.

All three were middle-aged and had average to semi-muscular builds. They all wore T-shirts and jeans and had farmer's tans evident on their forearms.

The one behind the counter had begun staring me down like I had stolen something from him. I approached the counter, smiled, and placed my hands on it.

"Something I can help you with?" the counter man

asked, reaching for the cash register drawer. It had been sitting open to this point; a pile of small bills, mostly ones and fives, along with several rolls of quarters lay inside.

I tried offering him an innocent look, not exactly my cup of tea. "Yes, sir, I'm hoping you can." I jutted my thumb over my shoulder at the Denali. "The wife and I are in dire need of some gas for that land yacht out there. Guess we forgot to fill her up last evening."

He took a long time to respond. "Is that so?"

I nodded to him. "We're headed west, and everywhere else we've stopped has either been out of gas, out of power, or both."

"Is that so?" he repeated in a grumble.

The man to my right began his interrogation with a look of indignance painted on his crusty countenance. "Headed west?" He let out a grunt. "You and everybody else. Don't suppose you've noticed, stranger, but the whole goddamn world is falling apart today."

I glanced at him and nodded. "Oh, I've noticed. A plane crashed not far away from where we were staying yesterday."

"They've been crashing all over. One crash-landed on the mountain just up the road from here last evening," the counter man said. "Killed quite a lot of people, from what I heard."

"I'm sorry to hear that," I said. "Look, I'm fairly certain, in lieu of our current predicament, the price of gas has gone up, and I don't have a problem paying you whatever you ask for it. In fact, I'd be willing to make it worth your while. I have cash. Just name your price."

"Name my price?" He chuckled, then leaned over the counter, placing his face a little too close to mine. "Suppose I decided to charge you five hundred dollars a gallon? What say you then, stranger? How's that for a price?"

The counter man's breath smelled like the sulphur of overcooked hard-boiled eggs, chewing tobacco, and homemade rye whiskey. I expected the bouquet to be accompanied with eau de rotten teeth, but it hadn't. His fangs had either rotted out long ago or been knocked out by someone. On any normal day, that someone could have very easily been me. "I'd say that makes you a businessman. I'm a businessman myself. I understand the law of supply and demand. We all must do what we feel necessary to survive, especially during a crisis. Now, my truck out there has a twenty-six-gallon tank. At your price, that makes it, what, about thirteen grand to fill me up?"

The man chuckled again and sucked on his gums. "Sounds about right."

"Cash all right with you? I'm all out of personal checks."

The counter man guffawed. "You a high roller, stranger? It's kind of dangerous to be toting around a bankroll that size, don't you think?"

"I'm not anything. Just somebody who needs some gas," I said. "Someone who's offering you money for the gas you have. Now, do we have a deal, or do I need to take my business elsewhere?"

The man on the left, who had yet to make his presence known, took a wide step away from the counter. "I think you're forgetting a few things," he growled. "There's a few other options available to us worth mentioning."

"Such as?" I asked.

"Such as, we forget about the deal altogether."

I sighed. "There is that."

"Yep. We say screw your deal and we just take your truck, keep our gas, and kindly relieve you of all your fucking money." He lifted his shirt to present a chrome-plated 1911 .45-caliber pistol in an appendix-carry holster. He tapped his fingers on the handle while he eyeballed me, like a gunfighter challenging me to a duel. "Then we tie your ass inside that eyesore truck of yours and bury you alive in it somewhere."

I couldn't tell which of these three hillbillies was the drunkest. The trio had apparently decided to get together for some stress relief upon learning of the attacks. Perhaps it had escalated a bit for them when the power went off. Little did they know that at the point of presenting and threatening me with a loaded weapon, it was nearing the point of escalating for them yet again.

If Appendix drew on me, I wouldn't go for my

Glock. I would go for Appendix, disarming him and fracturing both his arms in multiple locations, leaving them to dangle by his sides like a couple of wind-chimes. When the other two joined in, it'd be a toss-up, but I'd most likely shoot them with Appendix's 1911— if the damn thing was even loaded.

I shrugged, indicating my indifference, and sent a searing look Appendix's way. "You sure you want to take that route with me?"

"I might," he said. "Think you're faster than a speeding bullet?"

In less than two seconds, he was going to find out.

"Holy shit!" the man to my right exclaimed, jerking his head around. "Would you look at the set of tits on that!"

The other two followed their partner's gaze through the storefront windows to the Denali, where Natalia was now standing. Either my initial five minutes had elapsed, or she had grown tired of waiting. She was perched with one hand on her hip and the other at her side balling into a fist, her expression obscured only by the designer sunglasses she was wearing.

While the three yokels unleashed lewd and lasciv-ious comments about my bride and parts of her body, referencing things they'd like to see her do to them and what they'd levy upon her to even the score, I impro-vised my next move. I realized she wouldn't be fond of it, especially regarding her injury, but I also knew

Natalia would have no difficulty whatsoever handling this inopportune state of affairs with one arm literally tied behind her back.

"Look, I didn't come here to argue or fight…or get buried alive, either. That being said, maybe money isn't the proper form of…legal tender for this transaction."

One by one, each man turned his eyes back to me while displaying difficulty in doing so, each not wishing to remove his attention from Natalia's form.

"You got a proposition for us there, buddy?" the man behind the counter asked.

"I might. Depends on the outcome. I'd like to see us all get what we want."

Appendix spoke up again as he unholstered. "Oh, believe me. We are going to get what *we* want," he said, licking his lips. "A whole damn lot of it."

"I do believe you," I said. "But you're not going to need that."

He gave me a bewildered look.

The gun, stupid. I'm referring to the gun in your hand. I used my eyes and tilted my head, gesturing to it.

He glanced down at it, then squinted, finally picking up on my signal. "Oh? And why is that? It's worked pretty good so far."

I shrugged. "Because, she's…well, she's…" I tried to sound unsure of what I was saying.

"She's *what*?"

"She's…into it."

Counter man grumbled. "Into it? Into what?"

I turned to him. "It."

All three men stared blankly at me, either in fear, disbelief, or feeblemindedness. Or perhaps a mixture of the three.

After checking Natalia out through the window once more, the man to my right said, "Come on. You ain't serious."

"Serious as a heart attack. My wife loves that kind of stuff. In fact, she might prefer more than just one of you at the same time, if you catch my drift."

"What the hell? She some sort of freak or something?" the man holding the 1911 asked.

"That's something you might want to propose directly to her, or maybe find out yourself by doing. I can guarantee all of you, she's ready, willing, and highly capable of making all your dreams come true." I chuckled to myself. "She even has this...I don't know...motto of sorts."

"What motto?" counter man asked.

I scoffed at myself. "For the life of me, I can't recall it word for word. But it's something along the lines of '*come hungry, leave happy*'."

Only a few seconds went by before the two men with teeth made their way to the door. They stood there a moment, waiting for their compatriot behind the counter to join them.

Mr. Toothless eyeballed them as they beckoned. He

turned to me just before leaving the counter. "Don't bother nothing while we're gone," he said. "I'll turn the pump on for you once we get back."

I gave him an odd look. I was still in utter disbelief that not one of these men had been aware I'd just sold them with a slogan used by the International House of Pancakes. "So you actually have gas?"

He nodded. "Tanker truck showed up two days ago, right before the attacks. As of this moment, all my underground tanks are filled to the brim. And that shit is pure gold."

"I see. Well, I won't keep you. Get your time in while the getting's good."

"We'll just be a few minutes. You sit tight and make yourself good and comfortable while we get comfortable with your old lady."

I sent a wave their way as the trio exited to the sound of jingling bells. "Pleasure meeting you, boys. Y'all take care, now."

NINETEEN

I ncluded in the stunted list of positive traits bestowed upon me by my maker, I was fortunate to have been born a partial autodidact. That is, a person who's able to learn things simply by teaching himself. I couldn't do it with everything under the sun, but I'd been able to teach myself certain ideals, strategies, subjects, etcetera, over the years, though unnecessarily, overcomplicated proprietary software had not been among them.

It was taking me a while to figure out how to activate the gas pump, but with my new friends having found a pastime of sorts, I knew I had plenty of time to learn my way through the system. Natalia's near-flaw-less form had ever so graciously afforded me that time. From the muffled hollers, grunts, screams, thuds, and thumps I was detecting from outside the store, I presumed she was giving each of her newfound shifty escorts a proper tuning-up.

After activating the pump, I wandered through the store, helping myself to a road atlas, a cold Coke, and a few candy bars. Then I went back to the counter and dropped a few hundred bucks on it, feeling obligated to, for some mysterious reason.

As I began questioning myself while wondering just why the hell I had bothered to do so, my eyes caught sight of a thin gloss-blue Dell netbook with a few greasy fingerprints on the cover. Thinking it might prove useful to us should we decide to make contact, I snatched it up just before making my exit and strolling back to the Denali.

The bodies of the three men with whom I'd recently made acquaintance were face-down on the gravel near my wife's feet when I got there. Their clothes were torn, and they were all lying completely motionless—so much so, I couldn't tell if they were dead or merely unconscious.

Natalia was busily examining her hands. She looked up at me briefly upon hearing the sound of the gas cover release and pop out.

After tossing my newly acquired items into the back

seat, I reached for the fuel nozzle and pretended to tip a hat on my head that wasn't there. "Top of the morning to you, ma'am," I said, using my best hillbilly drawl. "I'd like to welcome you to Bubba and Cooter's country store. Pump one is now on for the black *yuppiemobile*."

Natalia looked away and shook her head at me. She said nothing, only toyed with her fingers.

I faltered at the initial aroma of unleaded gas fumes. "Everything turn out okay?"

Natalia replied without looking my way. "Sure. Fine. Perfect. Why do you ask?"

I shrugged. "No reason."

She sent me an aggravated look, still fiddling with the fingers on her right hand.

"They didn't hurt you, did they?" I asked, gesturing to the bodies. I was starting to feel a little guilty.

"No, they didn't hurt me."

"What about your arm? You didn't hurt it, did you?"

"My arm is fine."

"Okay…what's wrong with your hand, then?"

"Nothing's wrong with my hand, either." She paused extensively—really extensively, then said, "I… broke a fucking fingernail."

I wanted to laugh at the remark, but there was no way I was going to.

Natalia motioned to the pile of men she'd just taken out. "Am I to assume this was your idea?"

I shrugged again. "Maybe."

She sighed. "Of course it was. Jesus. Of all the crazy notions, Quinn," she spat. "And even the not-so-crazy ones. Would you mind explaining to me why you chose this particular scenario over...hell, I don't know, a hundred other more sensible ones?"

Another shrug. "You were distracting them," I said, peering over at her. "And I needed a distraction."

Natalia added a smirk overtop a mutual look of interest and disdain. "They came out here staring at me and saying some really awful things, none of which I found the least bit flattering."

"I can only imagine."

"I'm sure you can. What...exactly did you say to them?"

"Nothing, really."

"Q, don't." She pointed her finger at me. "Don't do that."

"Don't do what?"

"Stop it! What did you tell them?"

I hesitated. "I told them...you weren't from around here. And you were very, I don't know...friendly and were looking to make some new...friends."

"Friends?"

"Yeah."

"I see. I guess that *could* explain why they were being so presumptuous and tactless."

The tone of her voice told me she wasn't buying it.

"Okay, maybe friends isn't the right term. It was more like…participants."

"Participants…" She drew the word out as if trying to discern the rest without bothering to ask another question. "Okay, I give. Participants for what?"

I didn't offer a direct response.

"Quinn?"

"Yeah?"

"Answer me," Natalia said sternly. "What was I allegedly in need of participants for?"

I sighed. This answer necessitated caution. If I answered too quickly, it would appear as though I'd rehearsed this, which I hadn't. If I took too long, it would look like I was searching for an answer, which I more or less was. Either way, my only preference was for my wife not to become more agitated after the injury to her digit. "It was for a…ménage à trois. Kind of."

Natalia scowled, though surprisingly enough, she didn't appear angry with me. "You've *got* to be kidding me," she said. "Quinn, you and I aren't swingers. And for the record, ménage à trois is French for 'household of three'. It infers an aggregate of *three* people. There were three of them *and* me, for a sum of four."

"Right," I said. "My fault. I guess the term I should've used, you know, for the record, should've been gangba—"

"Don't you *dare* even utter the word," Natalia said,

interrupting me with a snap of her fingers, almost in a laugh. "I know what you meant. You're referring to a-a...*karusel*."

"A what?"

"It's Russian slang. It means...well, the same thing. Only it doesn't sound nearly so uncouth." Natalia took a few steps closer. "Curious. What did you need the distraction for?"

"Threat mitigation."

"Threat mitigation?"

"When I inquired about purchasing gas, I opted for the affable Dudley Do-Right approach, but that only made them want to fight me. In fact, one of them even drew his gun on me. Go figure."

Natalia nodded, then underhanded Appendix's chrome 1911 my way. It was all I could do to catch it before it smacked the Denali's unblemished rear quarter panel.

"Thanks," I said, dropping the magazine out of the magwell and extracting the loaded round from the chamber. "Suppose I'll keep this as a souvenir."

"Why didn't you just fight them?" she asked. "The presentation of a firearm never stopped you before."

"I was actually getting ready to. But when they caught sight of you, they quite literally fell in love. So I just went with it."

"You *went* with it..."

I nodded, trying to maintain a look of innocence. "I

knew it would get them away from the counter and out of the store. And I needed those things to happen so I could figure out how to get the pump running."

Natalia shook her head in disgust. She turned, knelt, and began scouring through her victims' pockets, pulling out sets of keys along with their wallets.

I watched her rifle through their things, careful not to use her middle finger. "I'm sorry about your nail."

"Yeah, me too. Just...do me a favor the next time you resolve to pull one of those wild hairs from your ass."

"Sure. Name it."

She sent me a cantankerous look accompanied with a grin. "Either make me aware of what you may or may not propose beforehand, or handle the belligerent, drunk, oversexed townies yourself. And leave me and my poor nails out of it."

I attempted an offer in compromise. "Tell you what. If we find a nail salon open on our way, I'll stop and get you a manicure."

"Thanks. That's sweet of you." Natalia rose and craned her neck to peer around the building. "So, while you were inside making friends, did you happen to see a ladies' room?"

I offered her a negative response, then pointed. "It's probably around back, but I highly doubt you'll want to use it. Most places like this don't prioritize the cleanliness of their lavatories."

"I'm afraid my body isn't giving me a choice in the matter."

I snickered. "Need help?"

"No, you've provided enough assistance for me today," she said with a coy smile. "I'll manage."

I told her where to look for the keys behind the counter. Natalia went inside to get them, then strolled behind the building to locate the restroom.

While perusing the atlas I'd taken from the store, I steered my eyes along the red and blue colored road-ways to our west, using my index finger as a guide. I broke open one of the candy bars and took a big bite out of it, then chased it with a swig of Coke, feeling the near-instantaneous effects of a much-needed sugar fix.

A few minutes later, I saw Natalia on the approach after she'd finished 'powdering her nose'. She cocked her head at me and strutted up to the Denali, placing both her hands on the hood, one of which was holding a rather large iron ring. There was a length of chain and two keys dangling from it, which I assumed to be for the bathrooms. The ring was damn near six inches in diameter and had a small yet very heavy-looking cannonball attached to it. The cannonball even had the letter L stenciled on it in white paint.

"I'll never understand why gas stations in this cursed country feel the need to keep their bathroom doors under lock and key," Natalia griped. "Seriously… what do they suppose you're going to do? Pilfer the sink or the toilet? Or perhaps it's the slime green pumice soap they're worried about."

"That's a pretty impressive key ring."

She held it aloft and studied it. "Yeah. I thought so, too. Guess they didn't want anyone stealing the keys to the bathroom, either. This cannonball thing has to weigh at least twenty pounds. And where the hell did they manage to procure a cannonball?"

I snickered at the remark. I grew up in an area not far away from the West Virginia border, where most gas stations handed out bathroom key rings that blew this one away. "This is Virginia…we're smack-dab in the middle of Civil War history hell. Believe me, it isn't hard."

She nodded indifferently, taking a quick look around the parking lot. "So, not to add more weight to those big shoulders of yours, but do you have any idea where the hell we are? Or where we might be headed? I'd try the navigation system in our getaway vehicle, but *someone* disabled it."

"I'm working on it," I replied. "Actually, we're only about a half an hour or so from where I grew up."

Natalia tilted her head. "You're kidding."

"Nope." I motioned for her to come closer and arranged the map so she could get a better view, then pointed to the area just west of our location on the other side of the mountain. "That's Clarke County, and that's Frederick County, and this is the entire Shenandoah

Valley…my old stomping grounds. We should be able to find a place out this way to hole up for a while."

Natalia studied the map, paying close attention to the shades indicating population density. "It looks nice, but it's nowhere near any of our caches in the States. What do we do about supplies?"

"We have a decent arsenal in-hand already, plus IDs, credit cards and plenty of cash. We'll make do," I said. "The national forest is just west of the valley. It's mostly vacant this time of year, from what I remember. We're talking thousands of acres of forest land…it stretches along the state line with West Virginia for a hundred miles."

"I take it you're familiar with the area within?"

"Yeah, but it's been a while. If our goal is to remain unseen and set up a base of operations for the interim, it's a good location to make it happen."

Natalia reached for my arm and wrapped hers around it, pulling herself close enough to me that I could feel the warmth of her body on my own. "So we're moving to the woods?"

"Do you object to those plans?"

"No. I love the woods," she cooed. "And I trust you. Wherever you go, I'll follow, you know that. You've done a pretty good job so far of keeping us both alive."

I nodded. "Thanks. But I have to say, I'm not used to hiding, Nati. I've always preferred the opposite—

hitting my enemy head-on and eliminating the threat. This is different for me."

"As in bad different?"

"Not necessarily. I just see a lot of changes on the horizon for the two of us."

Natalia squeezed me. "We're together. We'll be fine. I know it."

"I hope so."

"Stop hoping and start knowing," she said, then paused. "I do have a question for you. Something caught my eye while I was inside the store...something that seemed rather odd to me."

"Like what?"

"I saw a small pile of money on the counter," Natalia said. "All hundreds. Did you put it there?"

"I might have."

"Okay. Why?"

I shrugged. "To pay for the gas we needed. And also for the map and snacks and the laptop I took."

Her eyes narrowed. "Laptop?"

"For making contact at some point."

"You realize, of course, you didn't have to pay for any of those things."

"I know I didn't."

"Yet you did anyway," she said.

"Yeah."

"Why?"

I thought a moment. "I guess I wanted to. I shoot people for a living, but I'm no common thief."

Natalia's face slowly lit up and a smile crept across it. "Well, Quinn Barrett. My hard-as-nails, unwavering, no-remorse, contract-killer husband. Could it be true? Has a miracle occurred unbeknownst to us? Could you somehow be developing a conscience?"

Within the hour, and with a full tank of gas in the guzzler, we crested the Blue Ridge Mountains and I pulled into a small commuter parking lot alongside Route 50 at Ashby Gap to take in the view.

With Natalia napping, I decided it would be a good time to gather some last-minute intel. I stepped out and closed the door as quietly as possible, then made my way to the rear of the truck to gather the devices needed to make contact. My nose caught the arid aroma of wood smoke lingering in the air, while the memories of my youth started to scroll across my mind's eye. I soon realized that my recollections of the life I'd once known in the valley below hadn't gone anywhere, despite my efforts to suppress them and purge them from memory.

Gunnery Sergeant Blaylock had told us at the onset of boot camp that at the point of coming under his command, we were no longer the people we once were. We had therefore ceased to be the owners of the names printed on our birth certificates, social security cards, and driver's licenses. The lives we had once lived had ended, and we were thereby commanded to be born again. From that point forward, we had all begun new lives as Marines.

I'd put my full belief in what he said, consecrated it, and used buckets of willpower to vehemently push away my previous life. There wasn't much about it worth remembering, anyway. My past hadn't exactly been a colorful one. In seeing the view below and to my west, I recognized now, I hadn't done a good enough job of interring the old me. Gunny wouldn't be pleased.

I connected the Iridium satellite telephone to my newly acquired Dell, surprised to see it still had about three-quarters of its battery life remaining. After inserting my USB fob and rebooting it, I snapped a battery onto the sat phone and dialed into the internet. Once the connection was verified by means of the tether, I performed the final steps to secure the connection, connected to the message board via Tor, and began typing.

AZRAEL: ROCKY4, REQUEST SITREP. ARE YOU OPERATIONAL? BREAK.

I wasn't sure if Jonathon would even bother being connected, with everything that was happening now. He surprised me yet again when his reply came about a minute later.

ROCKY4: OSCAR KILO? FANCY MEETING YOU HERE. WHERE THE HELL ARE YOU? THE CITY IS CRAZY, BRO. THESE ATTACKS ARE CRAZY! IT'S NUCKIN' FUTS! HAVE YOU AND YOUR COMPANION ARRANGED FOR EXFIL? BREAK.

Our normal comms protocol was being cast by the wayside. Either he was drunk or didn't give a shit, or both.

AZRAEL: AFFIRMATIVE. MYSELF AND COMPANION HAVE ACHIEVED EXFIL. MADE ARRANGEMENTS WITH EFG ZüRICH. HAVE YOU RECEIVED YOUR HONORARIUM? WAS SUM ADEQUATE? PLEASE ADVISE. BREAK.

ROCKY4: AFFIRMATIVE. THANK YOU. AND THANK YOU AGAIN. SUM WAS VERY FUCKING ADEQUATE. TEN PERCENT OF TWENTY MIL? IF ONLY YOU COULD SEE THIS FACE.

I could only envision the smile. Admittedly, I felt warm at the thought of his happiness. I only hoped he could remain that way.

A moment went by before he resumed typing, and I allowed it to pass, having not yet seen him key in a break.

ROCKY4: GLAD YOU AND COMPANION ARE SAFE.
PLEASE DO WHATEVER YOU CAN TO REMAIN
THAT WAY. CAN YOU ADVISE LOCATION AND
DESTINATION? BREAK.

My reply was immediate.

AZRAEL: NEGATIVE. BREAK.

I shuddered at the thought of anyone besides Natalia and me knowing our whereabouts, especially now. Especially with so many already being aware we were here, and countless affiliates of the nefarious underworld wanting us dead.

Even as much as I trusted Jon, there wasn't any way I would come clean with that info. This wasn't the time to start developing bad habits and breaking protocol.

ROCKY4: THIS CHANNEL IS SECURE, QUINN.
COULD YOU AT LEAST ADVISE GENERAL
LOCATION OR GRID COORDINATES? I MIGHT
WANT TO FIND YOU SOMEDAY. BREAK.

AZRAEL: NEGATIVE. SECURE OR NOT, THERE
ARE EYES AND EARS EVERYWHERE. HAVE
YOU OBTAINED ANY NEW INTEL ON ATTACKS?
BREAK.

Jonathon didn't respond immediately. I took that to mean he was either satisfied with my answer or utterly dissatisfied with it.

ROCKY4: AFFIRMATIVE. ENOUGH INTEL TO KEEP ME BUSY FOR TWO CONSECUTIVE BENDERS. WILL ADVISE AT NEXT F2F. I'LL LEAN ON YOU TO MAKE THAT HAPPEN. BE SAFE. CLEAR ON YOUR FINAL TX. BREAK.

After bidding him farewell, I extricated the USB fob, and the laptop shut down instantly. I used the Glauca B1 to break apart the laptop into two pieces and separate it from its power source to render it inoperable, not having found any other method to remove its battery.

I glanced over the hood of the Denali and down into the valley where we were headed, and started to contemplate a moment just before hearing a commotion behind me. I turned to see what it was just as an old, rusty, beat-up pickup truck crested the top of the mountain with its driver and passengers singing loudly to the country music blaring from the truck's speakers. Even at the truck's high rate of speed, it was easy to see that the passenger with his arm hanging out the window had a bottle of liquor in his grasp. In fact, I could almost surmise what brand it was by the shape of the bottle and color of its label.

"Fantastic," I said. "Welcome back, Quinn. Home sweet home."

I got back in the truck and took a quick glance at Natalia, who was doing her best to remain asleep, recalling the unsure look in her eyes I'd seen earlier, and wondering if I was wearing a look to match. Though our intentions had been the opposite, we were once again preparing to tread into unfamiliar territory.

Our futures had always been arbitrary. To date, we'd lived our lives spur of the moment, and tomorrow would be no different. What we were about to face was truly unprecedented, and despite Natalia's unwavering trust in me, I had to admit I was having a hard time trusting myself. I wasn't sure which move was the right one to make…the one that would keep us both safe and secure. I didn't even know if that move existed, and I hadn't the slightest clue what tomorrow would bring for us.

I could see the outline of Great North Mountain directly ahead, across the valley to our west. It acted as a backdrop for the town and the county where I'd once lived, up until my early teenage years. Familiar landmarks were calling to me, almost as if they knew where I was headed. It was a strange feeling being here again. This place hadn't been home to me in years, but it still felt like it, in a way. Hopefully, we would indeed find temporary refuge here.

I placed my hand on Natalia's forearm, noticing her

skin felt warmer to the touch than it had earlier. The back of my hand transferred to her forehead, and I could sense a similar heat radiating there as well. She was a warm sleeper and I wanted to believe it was just that, but there was no way of knowing for sure. If Natalia was developing an infection from her wounds, it was going to seriously compound our problems. The antibiotics provided so graciously by my agency contact would help, but if the infection worsened, it would require a distinct augmentation to our plans.

I'd never been a worrier by nature, but what was happening here was really getting to me. Would this series of attacks, with supposedly no end in sight, spell the end of times for the United States? With regard to the country itself, its politicians and the government, I couldn't care less. But the people living here were different.

Natalia was right about them, at least the majority of them. They didn't deserve what was coming to them. War was one thing, democide another, but this was an outright extermination of a species. It was a primordial ideology, prone and well adapted to violence, choosing to unleash Armageddon on a society that, on the whole, had done nothing to deserve it.

And then there were the children to consider. Who targeted and attacked schools full of young kids? Such heinously cruel acts of violence shouldn't be tolerated, much less permitted to exist on this planet. Something had to be done about it. Natalia had been right about that, too.

Then it dawned on me. Could I, in fact, be developing a conscience? I considered it a moment, especially after what Natalia had pointed out concerning my negligible act of charity at the store, then contemplated the long list of ramifications. I thought I'd postpone answering the question until the next chapter in our lives began. At this point in our story, with so many other ambiguities to consider, I felt it was only best.

TWENTY

Elisabeth Young felt beat after working what had turned out to be a very prolonged and arduous shift, both inside and even outside the emergency room.

The airliner crash on the Blue Ridge east of town had effectuated hundreds of casualties, most of whom, it turned out, hadn't been passengers on board the aircraft. Rather, they had been homeowners, tenants, and their families living within and along the damage path. The number of residential casualties had been abetted by scores of government employees, all of whom had been working in their aboveground offices at

Mount Weather Emergency Operations Center when the plane had gone down.

In December 1974, Trans World Airlines Flight 514, a Boeing 727 with eighty-five passengers and seven crew members on board had been the first ever to crash into the mountain. And up until a short time ago, it had also been the only one.

The Southwest 737 in transit to BWI Airport yesterday, along with its full complement of passengers and crew, hadn't bisected the eighteen-hundred-foot mountain like its predecessor had. Instead, its flight path had been unique, appearing to have been purposefully aligned in parallel with the summit. It had dropped from the sky and swooped down directly on top of it, as if the pilot had been using the heavily forested ridgeline as a runway.

Estimated to have been moving at near cruising velocity, the plane had sliced through and collided with several federal office buildings before skimming through a parking lot littered with cars, bounding over a tree line, and exploding into a neighborhood of occupied homes just north of the FEMA facility. All told, it had left behind a corridor of fiery devastation stretching nearly a mile long.

After her normal shift had concluded, and without regard for how tired she had been, Elisabeth had done something she ordinarily wasn't compelled to do. With concern for the area's well-known and often discounted deficiency of emergency first responders, she had volunteered to ride along with an already overworked and overextended ambulance crew.

Elisabeth was a registered trauma nurse, but had already completed her one hundred hours of didactic education, clinical competencies, and field internship, as required by the Virginia Nurse to Paramedic Bridge Program. As such, she had been able to fill in as an interim EMS team leader.

The crew had taken Elisabeth along with them to the grizzly scene of the crash. There, they had treated and stabilized patients and transported them to either Inova Hospital's Trauma Unit in Loudoun County or the renowned Level II Trauma Center at Winchester Medical Center, where Elisabeth worked.

On their final voyage back to WMC to reunite Elisabeth with her vehicle so she could return home, they'd stumbled upon an MVA, or motor vehicle accident, at the base of the mountain, just past the bridge over the Shenandoah River. It appeared an older-model pickup truck had pulled out in front of a sizeable modern sport utility vehicle. The driver of the truck either hadn't been paying attention or hadn't seen the much larger vehicle coming. The SUV looked to have collided with the truck broadside, entangling the vehicles and sending them both off-road and into the trees and brush.

Upon spotting the skid marks on the road and the wreckage up ahead, Brad DeHaven, a veteran paramedic and ambulance driver, had flipped on the lights and sirens and called the incident in over the radio. When he pulled off the road beside the smoking, steaming heap of gnarled vehicles, Elisabeth had leapt from the rear of the ambulance with two junior EMTs in tow. They'd dashed to the scene, medical kits in hand, all expecting to witness yet another episode of unpleasantness.

On their approach, they encountered a couple, one male and one female, appearing to have been the previous occupants of the black SUV. They were standing outside and behind the wreckage, and with the exception of some minor scratches and torn portions of clothing, seemed to be uninjured. The resultant preliminary analysis for the driver and two passengers in the other vehicle did not seem nearly as promising.

Elisabeth ordered the other EMTs over to the truck while reminding them to watch their distance and be ready in the event it suddenly caught fire. "Environmental hazards first, you two. Remember your safe operating area. If you smell gas fumes, it's already too late." She turned her attention to the couple after making certain Brad was moving in to follow up with his junior techs. "My name's Elisabeth. I'm a registered trauma nurse and a paramedic." She set her kit on the ground and slid on a pair of blue nitrile gloves, then studied the couple with a keen stare and knowledgeable eyes, notwithstanding her exhaustion. "Were the two of you in the black truck?"

The man nodded a casual response while peering over at the mangled automobile.

"Okay…how many were in the vehicle with you when you crashed?" she asked. While awaiting their reply, Elisabeth considered the two victims spared by the accident. Both possessed a set of striking features, and there was a certain presence about them that seemed very much out of the ordinary. It was giving her a strange sensation, though she couldn't figure out why.

The man was handsome, tall, and muscular, and he had short, well-groomed hair and grayish-blue eyes, which seemed capable of staring straight through her. He carried himself confidently, in a manner seeming almost arrogant, though Elisabeth could only surmise it as such by his unflustered and nonchalant expression. She couldn't help but feel slightly intimidated by him.

His female counterpart, though about a half-foot shorter, was also muscular and had a very feminine, athletic build. She appeared in good shape, and she had glowing olive-hued skin and shiny light brown hair, and her smile, while not nearly so confident as her partner's, seemed almost tranquillizing.

The pair was well-dressed and appeared just as relaxed and comfortable in their situation as they were unharmed and uninjured, though they did look a little misplaced. And for a second, Elisabeth could've sworn they looked familiar, like she had seen their faces some-where before.

"It was just the wife and myself," the man said. "No one else."

Elisabeth squinted at the wreckage, spotting a few bags and some luggage she assumed had been removed from the vehicle following the crash. "Is there anything dangerous inside your vehicle we should know about? Any flammable liquids or gases? Or anything that could catch fire or explode?"

The man didn't hesitate to shake his head. "No, not hardly. I'm confident we've removed all the hazardous and unsafe items." He grinned irreverently, attempting to make light of her question.

Elisabeth didn't get the joke. "Are either of you hurt or injured in any way?"

The pair shook their heads in unison after looking one another over.

"Okay. How are you feeling? Any pain or difficulty breathing?"

The man put a hand on the woman's shoulder and shrugged. "In light of what happened, I don't feel half bad," he said, gesturing to the wreck. "I guess it's safe to say those guys in that truck over there don't feel the same." He paused. "We were lucky."

Elisabeth glanced at him for a second while trying not to make eye contact. She turned to regard the calming facial features of the much more approachable brunette. "Ma'am? How about you?"

"I'm fine, thank you," the woman said with a luminous smile. "Twenty or so airbags exploded out at the point of impact. I suppose my husband and I have them to thank for our lack of injuries."

Elisabeth inched closer to them. "Would you like for us to assess you anyway? A lot of times, injuries, such as those incurred in automobile accidents, don't manifest until hours or even days after. It's completely up to you, of course. But if you refuse treatment, I'll need you to sign a refusal form. It protects us…and well, keeps the lawyers happy."

The well-developed man shrugged. "Just show us where to sign. No sense in your team wasting time on us. I'm sure in light of recent events, you've all had your hands full."

"Isn't that the truth," Elisabeth replied with a sigh. "I've been at this going on thirty hours now. We were on our way home when we came upon you." She turned away when one of her fellow EMTs called out to her. "All three DOA? Damn." A pause. "Neither of my patients are reporting injuries. Brad? You want to relay that in so dispatch can relegate the first responders to code two?"

About an hour had passed. Several fire apparatuses, including a tanker and crash trucks from multiple companies, arrived on the scene, some with extricating equipment. State and local law enforcement also responded to investigate the crash, write reports, and file the necessary paperwork for the deceased. After the vehicles had been separated, two rollbacks winched each wreckage onto their beds and were preparing to leave.

Elisabeth, who had reached the point of falling asleep while standing up a few times during the wait, approached the two survivors of the crash on her way back to the ambulance to hitch a ride home. "I couldn't help but notice the two of you don't have a ride yet. Couldn't get a hold of anyone?"

"This might sound…peculiar," the woman began, "but my husband and I don't carry cell phones."

Elisabeth looked surprised at first. "I see. Well, you're welcome to use mine if you like. Or I could call someone for you. It wouldn't be a problem."

The man and the woman traded near-expressionless glances.

"We appreciate the offer, as well as your generosity, thank you. But we'll manage," the tall man said.

Elisabeth gave them both looks of disbelief. "Are the two of you local?"

No response.

Elisabeth smiled awkwardly. "I'm sorry…I'm just wondering if you're familiar with the area. Reason being, it's a really long walk from here to anywhere."

After a slight hesitation, the man shook his head in the negative. "No. Neither of us are from around here."

"Where were you headed before this happened?" Elisabeth asked. "I'm sorry...I know the question makes me sound nosey. I'm really not trying to pry."

The man squinted and pointed to the west, offering Elisabeth a more reassuring smile. "It's quite all right. We were headed towards Winchester. My wife and I are here visiting family. They live just west of there."

Elisabeth nodded and grinned with recognition. "Oh, I see. Well, the squad is taking me back to the hospital, which is on that side of town anyway. You want to hitch a ride with us? We could at least get you that far. It sure beats walking there."

After a bit of deliberation, the couple boarded the ambulance with Elisabeth through the rear door. The ambulance soon left the scene and headed west on US Route 50 toward the town of Winchester.

About ten miles into the trip the radio burped, and a loud sequence of piercing tones blasted over the speaker. Following the tones, the fire and rescue dispatcher announced an emergency call.

Brad, the driver of the squad, reached for the microphone. "Squad three one responding with three."

Elisabeth whipped her head to the front of the vehicle. "What do you mean three? There are four of us."

"Nope. There's three," he replied. "I was watching

you back there, Liz. You need to get some rest. You're fading fast."

"I'm tired...but I'm not *that* tired, Brad."

"Yes, you are. And you are because I say you are," Brad said. "You don't do this day in and day out like we do, Liz."

"Sure, point that out," she said. "Why not just insult me and tell me I'm too old or something."

"That's not it at all, and you know it. Look, we appreciate all the help and the time you put in. But right now, you need to get some rest. If the hospital calls you back in, you're going to wish you had it. You're no good to anyone in the shape you're in."

"Did you recently graduate med school without me knowing, *doctor* DeHaven?"

"Liz..."

Elisabeth huffed. "Fine, fine. Whatever. I guess just take me back to my car, then."

"Not going to happen," Brad said, reaching for the lights and sirens. "I'm sorry...we're on a call now and this train isn't going that far. You know how that works."

Elisabeth shook her head in disgust and looked to the husband and wife. "I'm really sorry about this. I'll get you where you need to be, I promise."

"It's no problem. Don't let us be a burden to you," the woman said, in the most charming way imaginable.

"Brad, can you at least run me by the house? I'll get

Adam to take me to my car, and we can give these two a ride wherever they need to go." She turned back to the couple. "Oh gosh…I am so sorry, I feel like an idiot. I just realized—I don't even know your names."

The man glanced at his wife and smiled at her, then both of them traded kind stares with Elisabeth. "No need to apologize; we don't offend easily," he said, holding out a hand for Elisabeth to shake. "I'm Joel, and this is my wife, Kate."

"Forgive my husband. It's Kathrine," the woman said, then paused and presented her hand. "We're the Donovans."

ACKNOWLEDGMENTS

First and foremost, my wife and kids. Your support for this hobby turned dream turned part-time writing career has been untiring, and your loyalty means the world to me. I love you.

Thanks to my editor, Sabrina, and my proofreader, Pauline, for working me into your busy schedules and helping make a veritable masterpiece out of my mess. Also, thanks and a shout-out to Felicia Sullivan for cleaning up my blurb for me. I'm indebted to you. I hate writing those things.

Thanks to Kim, Milo, Darja, Tanja and the crew at Deranged Doctor Design once again for their expertise and captivating cover designs. See you guys in Europe!

Thanks to Kevin Pierce, for giving my words meaning and my characters personality. You, sir, are indeed *the man*. I owe you a hug or two. Or maybe just a beer.

And it goes without saying, I thank you, the reader, for your continued support. I'd call this writer/author gig work, but I enjoy it too much to insult it.

ABOUT THE AUTHOR

C. A. Rudolph is a self-published "indie" novelist who lives and writes within the pastoral boundaries of Virginia's northern Shenandoah Valley.

His first book, What's Left of My World, published in December 2016, became an Amazon post-apocalyptic and dystopian best seller.

Readers and fans can find Mr. Rudolph online on social media (using the links below) or via his website at

http://www.carudolph.com